In a
Perfect
World

Also by Laura Kasischke

In a
Perfect
World

A NOVEL

Laura Kasischke

HARPER ● PERENNIAL

NEW YORK ● LONDON ● TORONTO ● SYDNEY ● NEW DELHI ● AUCKLAND

HARPER ● PERENNIAL

P.S.™ is a trademark of HarperCollins Publishers.

FIRST EDITION

Designed by Joy O'Meara

Library of Congress Cataloging-in-Publication Data
Kasischke, Laura.
In a perfect world : a novel / Laura Kasischke.—1st ed.
p. cm.
ISBN 978-0-06-176611-4
1. Married women—Psychology—Fiction. 2. Stepmothers—Psychology—Fiction. 3. Marriage—Fiction. 4. Plague—Fiction. 5. Psychological fiction. I. Title.
PS3561.A6993I6 2009
813'.54—dc22
                                                    2008049378

09 10 11 12 13 OV/RRD 10 9 8 7 6 5 4 3 2 1

for Bill
with love to Jack & Lucy Abernethy
and with vast eternities of gratitude to Lisa Bankoff

But I must go back again to the Beginning of this Surprizing Time . . .

DANIEL DEFOE, *A Journal of the Plague Year*

. . . and the branches, full of blossoms, closed over them . . .

HANS CHRISTIAN ANDERSEN

Contents

Part
One

CHAPTER ONE

If you are READING THIS you are going to DIE!

J iselle put the diary back on the couch where she found it and went outside with the watering can. It was already eighty-five degrees, but a morning breeze was blowing out of the west, sifting fragrantly through the ravine. She breathed it in, knelt down, and peered beneath the stones that separated the garden from the lawn.

She had been married, and a stepmother, for a month.

In a bit of shade there, a tangled circle of violets was hidden—pale blue and purple. Small, tender, silky, blinking. If they had voices, she thought, they would be giggling.

She'd first noticed them a few days earlier, while raking dead vegetation out of the garden. That splash of color among the washed-out fallen leaves and other summer debris had caught her eye, and she knelt down and counted them (*twenty-three, twenty-four, twenty-five*) before covering them up again.

Somehow those violets had managed to stay perfectly alive through the scorching summer weather and all through the drought. The hottest, driest summer in a century. Maybe *ever*. They deserved special consideration, didn't they? If God wasn't going to give it to them, she would have to.

Now, every day, Jiselle took the watering can outside, and was always surprised to find those violets alive and tucked away in their shady crack.

Still, she knew they couldn't last much longer—even hotter, drier weather had been predicted—so that morning, after watering them, she plucked just one. She covered the others up and brought the plucked one into the house, set it in a little souvenir shot glass from Las Vegas, with some cold water, placed it on the kitchen counter, and stepped back to admire it, deciding that she liked the little feminine gesture it made in the kitchen (Mark would be home in a day, and he would appreciate such a thing, as if she were settling in, getting comfortable, starting to decorate the place as if it were her own), until she turned her back on it, headed out of the kitchen to the bedroom to make the bed, and heard it *scream*.

A high, piercing, horrible, girlish scream that made all the little hairs on Jiselle's arms rise and a cool film of sweat break out on the back of her neck. She whipped around, heart pounding, and hurried back into the kitchen, a hand covering her own mouth, to see.

Of course the violet hadn't screamed. It rested quietly where she had placed it, drooping over the side of the shot glass. If anything, it looked more defeated than it had a few seconds before—head bowed in acceptance over the shot glass, as if waiting patiently for the ax.

It would never have been capable of screaming.

That had been Sara, howling at the news that Britney Spears was dead.

～⚬～

No one had said the word *epidemic* yet, or the word *pandemic*. No one was calling it a *plague*.

The first outbreak had swept through a nursing home in Phoenix, Arizona, over a year ago, leaving the elderly miraculously untouched but killing seven nurses and aides. Some people fled Phoenix after that—taking their vacations early, boarding up their houses, staying in cabins in the mountains, visiting relatives—but they did not evacuate in droves. The Phoenix flu seemed contained, explainable. The new carpeting in the nursing home was blamed, and then the contaminated air ducts, in which a dead bat had been found.

It was mummified. It was ashes. The biohazard men came in their orange jumpsuits and took what was left of it away in a plastic bag.

Then, a few celebrities nowhere near Phoenix died of what seemed to be the Phoenix flu—a soap opera star, Shane McDermott, Gena Lee Nolan, and the daughter of an actress who'd had a small role on *The Sopranos* years before—and although the non-celebrity deaths weren't made public, it was said that the nation's florists could not keep up with the demand for flowers. FTD changed its one-day delivery service to "Only two full days for most arrangements!" and it was reported that people were buying antibiotics and Tamiflu in bulk off the Internet, which resulted in shortages. But only the hysterical pulled their children out of school or left the country.

When a passenger fell ill after flying in a plane in which the body of a flu victim was being transported in cargo, a law was passed requiring airline passengers to be informed when human remains were aboard their planes. But, with the war on, this was such a common occurrence that it had no noticeable effect on travel habits. Flight attendants were encouraged to time their safety instructions to serve as a distraction while baggage-handlers loaded caskets, but on that side of the plane, the passengers, who had never been interested in safety instructions anyway, watched the procedures solemnly from their seats, sometimes pressing their faces to the windows for a closer look.

No one had, to Jiselle's knowledge, ever demanded to be booked on another flight because of a corpse in cargo, and, in general, there was very little talk, public or private, about the Phoenix flu, although there was endless excited talk about what a strange year it had been.

Full of curious weather, meteor showers, and the discovery in rain forests and oceans of species thought to be extinct, it was the kind of year you might associate with an apocalypse if you were prone to making those kinds of associations, which more and more people seemed to be.

Sunspots. Earthquakes. Hurricanes. Tornadoes.

More than a year before, in what would come to seem to her to have been another life, lived by a different woman—Jiselle had been in a bar in a hotel in Atlanta, watching a Weather Channel meteorologist (bleached blonde, hot-pink suit) on the television. The meteorologist held a spinning Earth in the palm of her hand and predicted more crazy weather everywhere.

All across the globe!

It was March, which had come in that year, they were saying, like a lion being chased by a lamb.

When Captain Dorn spoke to her, Jiselle turned from the television to him, holding a glass of wine in her hand—sipping from it, stem dangling between her fingers, the way the blond meteorologist held the world.

"Can I buy you another glass of wine?" the pilot asked.

Jiselle was in her uniform—the pressed blue pencil skirt, silk hose, light-blue blouse—and the little brass wings were spread over her heart, as if her heart might have the gift of flight. She was wearing, too, a pair of beautiful shoes she'd bought weeks earlier in Madrid, at an old-fashioned shoe store in the heart of the city. A salesman with a thin black mustache and goatee had said, watching her walk across the wooden floorboards wearing them, *Perfecto!*

Sitting on the barstool, she had one long leg crossed over the other and was swinging the crossed leg slowly, trying to calm herself down after that terrible evening spent stuck on the runway in a driving rainstorm only to be turned back at

7

the gate. It was nearly midnight. As Captain Dorn waited on the barstool beside her for an answer from her, one of the beautiful shoes, the one dangling from the swinging foot, slid right off her foot, and onto the floor.

In less than a second, he was on his knees below Jiselle, holding up the shoe as if considering it in the bar's dim light, and then he slid it with a swift whisper back onto her foot, while a group of businessmen at a table nearby laughed and clapped, and she blushed, and Captain Dorn stood, smoothing down his pants, and gave her a courtly little bow before he sat back down.

That night, Jiselle was thirty-two years old.

She'd been a bridesmaid six times.

It was always a surprise to her, being asked to be a bridesmaid. In truth, she'd had only a few close friends in her life, and none of them was one of these six brides. But flight attendants made acquaintances quickly, and friendships became intense easily—a long layover, a blizzard, a terrible landing—and ended just as quickly and easily.

"You just look good in an ugly dress," one of her boyfriends had suggested when Jiselle wondered aloud about her popularity for the position.

And maybe she did.

She had a bridesmaid's shapely legs, wasp waist, blond hair that fell around her shoulders. The photographers at these weddings always seemed particularly interested in her, waving her over to stand by the cake, calling on her to kneel beside the bride and hold up the lacy train.

She'd worn green satin, and yellow chiffon, and something pink and stiff. She'd worn ribbons in her hair, or pinned to the top of her head, or down around her shoulders. One bride asked her bridesmaids to wear rhinestone tiaras, and although the last time Jiselle had been near a tiara was during a dance recital in second grade, *The Nutcracker*, she did—just as she obediently leaped to catch each bouquet as it sailed over her upturned face while the cameras flashed.

She'd been felt up by the drunken uncles of brides and been crushed on dance floors by their burly brothers. She'd been taken aside by a bride's mother and asked, "Jiselle, darling, when in the world will we be attending *your* wedding?" and had simply smiled, blinking.

"Always a bridesmaid," her mother had said on a couple of these occasions, "never a bride."

"Mom, I—"

"You don't have to explain to *me*," her mother said. "Do you think if I had a choice about whether or not to get married again, I would?"

"No," Jiselle said, clumsily, as if it had actually been a question. There *was* no question. After she'd kicked Jiselle's father out of the house, along with Bingo, the little dog he'd just brought home, Jiselle's mother had taken their wedding photos out into the backyard and lit them on fire one by one while Jiselle watched from the window over the kitchen sink. They shriveled up into black bats, and then into ashes, before her mother let them go.

Jiselle herself had fallen in love, too early, with two distracted boys—hockey and basketball, respectively. And then a few years escaped from her along with a married man. There'd been a British Royal Marine between scenes, and then a kleptomaniac. A drummer. A baggage-handler with a drinking problem. Then a few years passed during which she thought she'd given up men for good.

Already she'd buried the friend who would have been her maid of honor, and the father who would have walked her down the aisle. When people asked if she'd like to meet their cousin the doctor, their husband's shy best friend, Jiselle politely declined. She kept busy, pretending to herself and to everyone else that she wasn't waiting.

When she wasn't working, she started crochet projects or bought journals she made plans to write in. She needed only a few plates, a couple of cups, in her rented house, while her acquaintances' lives grew unfathomably cluttered, took on meaning, accumulated in detail. A few of the brides got divorced, and Jiselle bought them margaritas when the paperwork was complete. She attended a few second weddings in courthouses, casinos. She watched their children while they worked out custody disputes with their exes. One night she stayed up late with another flight attendant whose teenage son had disappeared.

"Never have children," Angela had said, holding her cup of tea so fiercely that all the tiny bones and muscles in her hand glowed in the light of the television, as if lit from within. Down the block, Jiselle could hear a dog bark, sounding terrified and angry at the same time. "Just be glad you have no one, Jiselle," Angela said, and then looked embarrassed to have said it, but also too distraught to take it back. They both knew what she meant.

When the son came home a few days later with a pierced lip and a tattoo, Angela called Jiselle and said, "When I was done kissing him, I told him I was going to kill him."

Jiselle felt relieved and heartbroken at the same time, to think she might never know what it was like to love a child like that.

Once, in Florence, on a bus back to the airport, she had glimpsed a love like that. She was sitting behind a beautiful young girl with a glossy black braid down her back. Outside the bus window, a woman stood and watched. Clearly, she was the girl's mother. The two of them had the same eyes, the same cheekbones. The girl put her hand to the bus window, and the mother put her own hand to her heart, and as the bus slid away, Jiselle couldn't help but put her own hand to the glass as the mother's love poured off of her toward them—as rolling fire, great sheets and waves of love, whole cathedrals filled with flickering candles, hurricanes, tornadoes, vast human migrations of love. Jiselle had wanted to keep watching but couldn't help closing her eyes.

11

❧

Like Angela's son, the years ran off. But, unlike that son, they never came back, changed or otherwise.

"You're only twenty-nine . . . thirty . . . thirty-one . . . thirty-two," the six brides said. "I hardly think it's time to give up."

But Jiselle saw less and less of those brides as the years went by. They were so busy. *So* busy! After a while there was almost nothing to talk with them about on the phone, even if they'd had the time to return her calls, even if there wasn't usually a child screaming in the background or waiting somewhere to be picked up, either in their arms or in their SUVs.

Also, Jiselle traveled for a living. She never met anyone in her own neighborhood because she was usually there for only a night or two before she left again. All the things people said to do to make friends, meet men—take a class, join a gym, attend a church—were impossible for her to do. She worked out in hotel gyms. She ate in hotel restaurants. She slept in hotel beds, where, occasionally late at night, she paged through the Gideon's Bible in the hotel nightstand.

Once, in a Holiday Inn in Pittsburgh, she came upon a Gideon's that had been bookmarked and highlighted for her:

Then I heard a voice from the sanctuary calling to the seven angels, "Go and empty the seven bowls of God's anger over the earth." And HEY PLEASE ARE YOU PAYING ATTENTION? was written in small red, block letters in the margin.

Jiselle slid the Bible back into the nightstand and closed the drawer, feeling as if she'd disappointed someone (Gideon? God?), but also too tired to offer the kind of attention that reading the Bible would require.

<figure>12</figure>

There were hundreds of takeoffs and landings, and, occasionally, vomit in the aisles. Sometimes it was Jiselle's turn to sprinkle coffee grounds on the vomit while the other flight attendants stood around in the galley holding their noses and rolling their eyes.

There were hundreds of layovers and delays, and then, that one windy March evening in Atlanta, seven hours were spent on a runway while the plane was slapped around boorishly in the dark, rain whipping sideways across the windows, only to have the plane turned back to the gate when the flight was canceled.

It had been a full flight, too—the proverbial sardines— with a large number of elderly passengers. There'd been a woman with a black eye sitting in silence beside a man with clenched fists. There'd also been a frat boy with a cat in a pink plastic cage beneath his seat. The cat yowled pitifully, and the frat boy, even more pitifully, kept looking under the seat with a worried expression on his face, saying, "It's okay, Binky. Zacky's here."

That night Jiselle's job was to rush up the aisle and tell anyone who tried to take off his seat belt and make a break for the bathroom to sit back down.

"Why?" they wanted to know.

"Getting out of your seat is prohibited," she said, "on the runway."

"But we're not going anywhere. The plane's not moving."

This was true enough.

Outside, surrounding the plane, was the sense of weather growing vindictive—an accumulating energy with its own agenda. The weather didn't care that they had connections to make, medication that needed to be taken, appointments that would be missed, vacations that were ruined before they'd even begun.

A baby began to shriek, and then a little girl with a crusty nose, wearing a purple tutu, took up the shriek. Her mother leaned over her, holding the child in her arms. As she passed their seats and looked down, it appeared to Jiselle as if that mother were trying to smother the child or wrestle with her—but, as with the frat boy and his cat, silly endearments were being whispered as she did it.

In the seat in front of the mother and child, a middle-aged man slid his toupee off his head in exasperation and set it on his lap. He stroked it with his right hand while running his left hand nervously over his hairless head.

Then, as if someone were spraying the aircraft with a high-powered hose, rain began to splash against the side of the plane. Wind rocked them harder. There was the sound of heavy breathing coming from the passengers—deep sighs, stifled sobs. Jiselle had the impulse to announce to the cabin that it wasn't her fault. *It's the weather. It's the airline. There are strict rules and procedures. I didn't invent them.* But she knew there would have been a reprimand for such an announcement:

> *Dear Ms. McKnight, It has been brought to our attention etc. etc. etc. on the evening in question etc. etc.—and in conclusion may we remind you that your job is not only to be liked by the passengers but to maintain safety, order, and a professional outward appearance of calm . . .*

But it was nearly unbearable, passing down the aisle, having to endure the glares directed at her. It had happened before, of course, but how could anyone get used to that?

When Captain Dorn's voice finally came over the intercom and he said they'd been directed back to the terminal,
something like a cry of despair and an exhalation of relief
rose from the passengers at once, the kind of sound Jiselle
imagined a crowd gathered at a mining disaster might make
upon receiving news that one of the fifty miners had been
found alive. She tried to smile as she passed back down the
aisle this time, but the only passengers who would look at her
did not smile back—and then an elderly woman reached up
and grabbed her wrist.

Jiselle stopped, looking down at her own wrist in this
woman's bony hand, and then into the face of the old
woman, who said nothing but who fixed Jiselle with an expression of such bitter rage and contempt that, until all the
passengers were off the plane, Jiselle could not stop shaking.

15

"What did the hag say to you?" Jeremy asked. He was
wearing so much ChapStick that his lips shone from the
overhead lights. Earlier, she'd watched him applying it, over
and over, from the corner of her eyes as they sat strapped beside one another in the bulkhead during the turnaround.

"Nothing," Jiselle said.

And it was true.

But the old woman's eyes had been ice blue. Her hair,
pure white. She'd hated Jiselle. The expression on her face
said it so clearly that the old woman hadn't needed to speak.
Her hatred had been projected so powerfully that Jiselle felt
she could read the old woman's mind, hear the old woman's
voice inside her head, saying:

You think you can pass through this life pretending, and

smiling, and acting as if nothing of this has to do with you, don't you?

But you can't.

A curse.

A spell.

Later, at the hotel bar, when Captain Dorn glanced down at her legs crossed on the barstool a few inches away from his, Jiselle took a sip of her wine and tried to will that old woman and her evil eye away.

"What a life," he said, raising his glass to hers.

She raised hers to his, and they touched the glasses together just lightly enough to make the faintest of sounds—the muffled sound of a very tiny glass bell ringing on the collar of a cat, which might have been rolling in some lush green grass under a warm sun in a country far away.

16

CHAPTER TWO

The afternoon Jiselle announced her engagement to Captain Dorn, she saw them for the first time: The white balloons.

She was driving on the Red Arrow Highway, which meandered along the Lake Michigan shoreline, back to Illinois from the small Michigan town in which her mother lived.

She gasped when she glimpsed them.

The balloons must have originated in Chicago. Now they floated in her direction over the lake, which rippled under them in bright brain waves. At least fifty balloons, their strings trailing silver tails behind them.

Jiselle had heard of the groups of volunteers and activists who gathered every Sunday in cities all over the United States to set them loose—a white balloon for every victim of the Phoenix flu—but as yet she'd seen them only on television.

They were controversial. There had been objections. Some

said that the balloons served no purpose other than to scare people, that they were really about inciting panic. Not the compassionate expression they pretended to be, but an implicit criticism of the present administration, a political maneuver rather than a commemoration of the dead. Others said they were simply, purely beautiful.

And, seeing them for herself that afternoon as she drove away from her hometown, Jiselle had to agree. The silent, swift, traveling emptiness of those balloons, their strings glistening loosely on the air as they lifted higher in a steady stream toward the sky. They seemed to be lifted in unison by a gust of wind, trembling a little against the backdrop of blue.

Intellectually, Jiselle knew what they stood for, but like so many other things at the beginning of this surprising time, they appeared to her more as a wonder than a sign.

She had never been so happy.

Could she ever be happier?

Even after the sharp words with her mother, and the dead man in his coffin, Jiselle could not help but feel light-hearted.

Jiselle's mother had asked her, "What kind of a woman agrees to marry a man she's known for three months? A man with three children? A man whose three children she hasn't met?"

If Jiselle had been a different kind of daughter, or woman,

she might have said, "The kind of woman *I* am, Mother," but even as an adolescent, when her best friend was regularly screaming "I hate you, you bitch!" at her own mother, Jiselle was apologizing to hers for forgetting to say *please* when asking for a second helping of salad.

She said, instead, "Mom, I *love* him."

Her mother snorted.

Of course, it was more than that, more than love, or why *marriage*, why the rush? But how could Jiselle have explained to anyone what a strange wild mystery this was to her? When it came to imagining herself a bride, she'd given up! And then—Captain Dorn! The handsomest man in the land!

He was a pilot with eyes the color of the grass in spring. When he stood in the threshold of the control cabin after landing a plane, men, exiting, would nod solemnly to him, offering their thanks. Women, smitten, made expressions of surprise, sheepish appreciation, when they saw him there. Leaning on the doorjamb of the cockpit, wearing his uniform, his jacket unbuttoned and all those dials and knobs behind him, Captain Dorn sometimes caused those female passengers to freeze in their places, open their mouths as if to speak, nothing coming out—love at first sight. Annette would elbow Jiselle and whisper, "Another one bites the dust."

A few always tried to come back to the plane, to see him again. ("Did I leave a book called *The Single Woman's Guide to Rome* in my seat pocket by any chance?") Sometimes they stalled near the gate of their arrival, waiting to catch another

19

glimpse of him. He'd tip his cap. Flash his smile. Walk crisply past—those long strides, pressed black slacks, shining shoes. Sometimes a fluttering suit coat, sometimes a pilot's black leather jacket. Women looked up from their magazines and their cell phones, from the pacifiers they were struggling to place in their squirming toddlers' mouths, to watch him pass. If there was a female flight attendant in the country who did not know who Captain Mark Dorn was, Jiselle hadn't met her.

He looks like a movie star. Those eyes!

And his wife . . . I don't know.

Something tragic.

Brain tumor.

Suicide.

Car accident.

He never talks about it.

That he was a widower made him even more mysterious and romantic.

The other flight attendants were ebulliently envious. "You hit the jackpot," one said, "you fucking bitch." Another said, when Jiselle announced her engagement, "I'm so jealous, I want to kill you. I could kill you. We all wanted to marry him."

If there was a single woman—and a single woman in her thirties!—who would have said no if Captain Dorn had asked her to marry him, Jiselle hadn't met her, and couldn't imagine her.

Even the children. The romance of the handsome devoted single father, reliant on nannies and fast food, calling before takeoff to find out who'd won the soccer game, how the math test had gone. He carried their photographs in his wallet, although he apologized that each one was outdated. The children had grown older more quickly than he'd remembered to exchange each year's school photo for the next.

Camilla, in her picture, was a ninth-grader. A cascade of blond hair. Her perfect teeth, gritted. Sara was in middle school, wearing a black beaded headband and a low-cut T-shirt. Looking at the photographs of these beautiful, provocative girls, the flight attendants would joke, "You're going to have your hands full there, Dad! I hope you're ready for that!"

And his son, Sam. In the photograph Mark carried in his wallet, Sam was only six, with a big gap in the front of his smile—but smiling nonetheless, as if he were perfectly happy with this life, as if the whole idea of life itself pleased him beyond all reason. He had masses of curly, shining, strawberry-blond hair—the kind of hair Jiselle suspected women had been touching, longingly, since he was a baby, saying things like, "Why are the beautiful curls always wasted on the boys?"

Those children were frozen at the ages they'd been on some past Picture Day. The school photographer's absurdly blue sky behind them swirled with the implication of summer clouds.

"You're not marrying the man," her mother said. She was wearing a black skirt, black blouse, a string of black pearls,

21

and had her hands on her hips. Jiselle took a step backward, shook her head, and looked toward the coffin, as if for help.

The dead man in it was a great-step-uncle. He'd been ninety-two years old when his heart finally stopped. Even the people gathered around the corpse, laid out in a tuxedo, were laughing, patting one another on the back, punching each other in the arm. Jiselle, her mother, and the dead man were the only ones in the room not smiling, the only ones wearing black, which Jiselle had worn only because she knew her mother would say something about it if she didn't. Even in his coffin, Uncle Ernie looked comfortable with the idea that he was dead—hands folded over his ruffled chest, chin set, eyebrows raised above his closed eyes. He might as well have been twiddling his thumbs. It had been a decade since Jiselle had seen him alive, but she could tell he hadn't changed. Really, she'd come to the funeral to tell her mother, in person, in a public place, about her engagement.

"No," Jiselle said. "I *am* marrying him, Mom."

Her mother shook her head, looking around the room as if for a silver lining, and then she said, "Well, you're not going to live with him."

She was serious, Jiselle realized. It wasn't a question. It was a command—like, *Clean your room.* Or, *Clear the table.*

"Mom, I'm—"

Her mother raised a hand, pointed a finger at her daughter, and said, "You're not going to move in with a man with three children—"

"Mom—"

"—a man who's out of the country half the month and

out of town most of the month. Have you *thought* about *why* he's in such a big hurry to marry *you*?"

Her mother was not, of course, the first one to suggest to Jiselle that perhaps this dashing pilot pursuing her with flowers, and jewelry, and strolls along the Seine, and proposals of marriage, might be looking for someone to take care of his three children. One older flight attendant, who'd known Mark since his first flight, said, when Jiselle told her they were going to be married, "So, I guess his latest nanny didn't work out?"

Jiselle flushed, and the woman hurriedly insisted that she was only joking, but Jiselle knew exactly what the woman meant, and she was right about the latest nanny, who'd given twelve weeks' notice because she was going to marry a geologist and move to Wyoming. All the flight attendants knew the trouble Mark had with nannies, and childcare, and children. Before Jiselle started seeing him, she'd heard members of the flight crew advise him, "Captain Dorn, you need to get married again. That's the only answer to your problems."

"No," he'd say, "I can move my mother up from Florida if I have to. Believe me, there's nothing she'd like better than to raise my kids. If I get married again, it will be because I'm in love."

When he said this, all the flight attendants tilted their chins, lifted their eyebrows. Some even sighed.

Jiselle's therapist also asked Jiselle if she might be "at all concerned about his motives."

Jiselle put her hands on the leather armrests of the chair in his office and said, "He doesn't need me to take care of the children, if that's what you mean. They have a grandmother."

Dr. Smitty Smith looked down at his fingernails and asked, "Did I say I thought he was marrying you to take care of the children?"

Jiselle knew exactly where this was supposed to go. Instead of answering, she lifted one shoulder, and let it drop.

"I just don't want—" Dr. Smith stopped himself in midsentence. He almost never gave advice, although he occasionally stammered out the beginning of it. "I'm concerned, as I'm sure you are, that there not be any *fuzzy logic*."

Fuzzy logic.

Like *sins of the father*, it was a catchphrase between them, left over from Jiselle's first session, when she'd made an appointment through the University Health Services—right after she'd dropped out of college but before they'd canceled her student benefits. Her father and Ellen had been dead for a few months, and Jiselle was flunking out, when she'd gotten a paper returned to her from her Western Civilization course.

On the bottom of it, scrawled in red pen, was "F—Fuzzy Logic."

Nothing else.

As if no further explanation could be given or would be needed.

Jiselle no longer had any actual memory of the paper it-self. Of writing it, of stapling its pages together, of her thesis and argument and support, of handing it in, but the words had stayed with her over the years. They were the words that had brought her to Smitty Smith, in whose office she had wept on that last winter day of her college career, and in which she was smiling helplessly now after announcing her engagement to Captain Mark Dorn.

Dr. Smith said nothing more until a few minutes had passed in silence, and then he said, "Well, we'll have to finish talking about this next time," and then, wearily, like a man with a low-grade fever, "Congratulations, Jiselle."

"Thank you," she said.

He nodded and said, "But just, you know, think hard about this. Think clearly."

25

But there were others—plenty of them—who urged Jiselle not to think too hard, to act quickly.

"Find me a man like that, Jiselle," another flight attendant said, "and I'd stay home with his brats, I'd iron his shirts, I'd wax his floors."

A chorus of flight attendants gathered around her at the gate and agreed.

When Jiselle herself uttered reservations ("You know, I haven't even met his children yet . . ."), this chorus sang out in unison, "Who cares? They'll be awful! All children are awful, whether they're yours or someone else's! But you'll be married to Captain Dorn!"

• • •

In Jiselle's fantasy, the children were not awful. When she imagined herself with Mark's children, they were always sitting in a circle around her in a forest. In this fantasy, a soft bed of fallen pine needles was spread out beneath them, and Jiselle had her gilt-edged collection of Hans Christian Andersen tales open on her lap—the book from which her father used to read to her—and she was about to start a story.

It didn't matter, for this particular fantasy, that Mark's daughters were certainly too old to be read to, or that once, when Jiselle visited his house while the children were in Madison with their nanny, she'd picked up the diary of one of the girls and read the most recent entry:

If he marries that fucking bitch, I'm going to make her life a living hell.

The diary was black and leather-bound and had been left on the kitchen counter, where, surely, the new girlfriend of her father visiting the house that weekend was supposed to find it.

Jiselle had put it down and stepped away from it slowly. Her heart had been thrumming like a bird trapped in a box.

But, in Jiselle's fantasy, Sara would come to realize how much she had in common with her new stepmother, and how much she had missed not having a mother all these years. She would confide in Jiselle and grow to love her.

In her fantasy, Jiselle and the three children in the forest were all wearing white, and although they were sitting on the ground, their clothes did not get dirty.

The afternoon he asked Jiselle to marry him they were in Kyoto, in bed in a hotel room full of cherry blossoms, and they'd left the curtains open while they made love.

Afterward, they went to the window and looked down.

The roads were thronged. It was the day of the Lantern Parade, which was one of the city's most important festivals, or so Jiselle had been told by her taxi driver, in perfect English.

Conceived during a plague in the ninth century as a ritual to purify the land and to appease the rampaging deity Gozu, the first parade had ended the plague, and so had been held every year since by the citizens of Kyoto, who even managed, the driver told her, to keep the Americans from dropping an atomic bomb on their city with their religious devotion and their beautiful parade.

27

Ten stories below them, a float made entirely of pink blossoms moved along slowly, trailing long silk flags through the streets. From a throne at the center of it, a little boy in Shintu robes was swinging a pale yellow lantern. When the boy looked up, Jiselle yanked the curtain around her naked body as quickly as she could, although he couldn't have seen her so far above him—a woman in one of a hundred tiny windows in a tower, looking down.

"I'm not a perfect man, Jiselle," Mark said. "I've got some baggage. But I'm in love with you. And I need you." He turned from the window to her. "They need you, too," he added. "We'll be a family."

An automatic family.

Was it such a crazy thing to want?

At the checkout lines at every airport gift shop were women's magazines and tabloids announcing HOW TO KEEP YOUR FAMILY SAFE IN TROUBLED TIMES, beneath the stunning, smiling, face of Angelina Jolie, as full of inner peace as any medieval Madonna, her brood of twelve children gathered around her.

"Why wait?" Annette said when Jiselle expressed surprise that Annette was already pregnant only a month after marrying her pediatrician, Dr. Williams, thirty years her senior, the very doctor who'd administered Annette's first vaccinations, treated her strep throat and sprained ankle.

Why wait? had, in fact, become a kind of mantra. Advertising campaigns repeated it over and over, as did religious leaders. Waiting to buy a thing or to repent of your sins could be equally foolish. The recent increase in the number of marriages was swiftly followed by a skyrocketing number of pregnancies. At the top of the bestseller list was *What to Expect When You're Expecting*, followed by *The Prophecies of Nostradamus*.

It was said that college students across the country had formed groups devoted to the study of Nostradamus. Why wait to see what the future will hold if we can find out from the past?

The media connected the war, the fears of the flu, the beautiful and alarming weather, to the behavior of teenagers and adults alike. Bars were crowded in the middle of the day. Workplace affairs were ubiquitous. Unplanned pregnancies and planned ones. There was a pregnant woman on every street corner, it seemed, and a baby being pushed in a stroller on every street. The boys who didn't go into the military after high school dropped out to become poets. It was said that in Las Vegas it had become so common for gamblers to sit at their slot machines until they collapsed that ambulances were kept idling behind casinos. The twenty-four-hour wedding chapels were busy twenty-four hours a day. So much champagne was being demanded that liquor stores across the country had instituted a one-bottle-per-customer rule to avoid the violent outbursts of customers who came in and found the shelves empty.

Jiselle, however, wasn't thinking about the news when she told Mark that, yes, she would marry him.

She was thinking that she'd waited a long time for this.

She was thinking that she'd waited long enough.   29

⤙〰⤚

In Montreal, Jiselle found the perfect dress. Off-white linen and lace. Just above the ankle. A low neckline sewn with seed pearls.

"Four hundred dollars Canadian," the salesgirl said, "and we can tailor it for you."

But it didn't need to be tailored. It fit Jiselle perfectly, as if it had been made for her. And in her hair she would wear a band of lace from her grandmother's wedding dress—which had arrived in America in tatters in a moth-filled trunk on a Danish ship. Her mother had kept the scraps of that in her attic all these years.

"Let me see," Mark said at the Budget Roadway Inn.

"No," Jiselle said. "You're not supposed to see the bride in her dress until the wedding day. It's bad luck."

"To hell with that," Mark said. "Life is short. Let me see."

"Mark."

"What if I die before I see it?" he said. "I'm in a dangerous profession! You'd have to live another sixty years knowing you'd denied me the greatest pleasure of my life."

Jiselle laughed, and then went into the bathroom and took the dress out of the tissue in which it was wrapped. A few minutes later she stepped out wearing it.

"Here," she said, offering herself in the dress.

Mark stood up from the edge of the bed. His mouth was open, but he didn't say a word. As he stepped toward her, Jiselle was astonished to see that there were tears in his eyes.

Outside their window, a truck roared by, rattling the windowpane with its speed. They were staying in a dirty, noisy motel near the airport. As Mark had warned her she might, the owner of L'Amourette Inn, the lovely B-and-B Jiselle had found for them on the Internet, had refused to check Jiselle into their reserved suite when she was unable to convince the woman that, despite the plates on her rental car, she was Canadian

The border patrol guard between New Hampshire and Quebec had warned her, too.

"Nobody's renting rooms to Americans, Madame."

"I'm staying with relatives," she'd lied.

He returned her passport and nodded disapprovingly.

Jiselle had followed her MapQuest directions up a long

winding road to L'Amourette Inn, glimpsing it through the pines from a mile or two away—a Victorian mansion with a wraparound porch. Rocking chairs on the porch. Shutters on the windows. A cupola. A red weathervane and a wishing well. She parked her rental car in a litter of aspen leaves in front of the inn and walked up the stairs to the porch, carrying her cell phone, her purse, her overnight bag.

"Hello?" she called, raising a hand to her forehead to peer through the screen.

A large woman in a white apron whirled around then, at the foot of a long oak staircase, and sputtered in her lovely French accent, "Oh my, you scared me. I'm sorry. I'm sorry. Come in. Come in," and bustled to the door, opened it—but before Jiselle could step in, the woman's smile faded. She said, "You're not Canadian."

"Yes," Jiselle said. "I am. I—"

The woman shook her head. "No. No U.S. citizens. I can't risk it."

Jiselle told the woman that she was from Toronto and hadn't been to the States except to drive through New Hampshire after visiting relatives in Boston. She would have happily produced her passport, she said, but she'd left it behind with her fiancé. He'd be arriving soon. He'd bring it with him.

"I don't believe you," the woman said. "You can't cross the border without your passport. There will be no one from the States staying at my inn. You're all going to catch this and kill the rest of us. It's just a matter of time."

She shut the door so hard that the little diamond-shaped

31

panes of glass rattled in their frames, and Jiselle, whose heart seemed to echo the rattling glass in her chest, went back to the car and called Mark's voice mail, letting him know she'd call back when she found them another place—which she was unable to do until the Budget Roadway, which had a Vacancy sign posted beside a small, hand-drawn picture of the U.S. flag.

In that hotel room, Mark came to her, standing before him in her dress. He knelt down, took her hands in his, brought them to his face, kissed them slowly. After a long time, he stood up and said, "Now take it off."

She did. As he watched, Jiselle stepped out of her wedding dress, and then he took it from her and placed it carefully over the back of a chair, and picked her up in his arms, and placed her on the bed.

CHAPTER THREE

It was lovely summer weather in the country, and the golden corn, the green oats, and the haystacks piled up in the meadows looked beautiful. The stork walking about on his long red legs chattered in the Egyptian language, which he had learnt from his mother. The cornfields and the meadows were—

G oddamnit!"

The cornfields and meadows were surrounded by a large forest, in the midst of which—

"Where are you? Where the hell is my *black dress*?"

In the midst of which were deep pools. Indeed, it was delightful to walk—

"Didn't you *hear* me? What the hell happened to my black dress? It was on the *fucking hook* on the back of my *closet door.*"

Jiselle kept the book open on her knees but looked up from its pages.

Sam shifted nervously beside her.

Sara was wearing only a black bra and panties, standing at the threshold of the bedroom. Jiselle recognized the panties as a pair of her own. Jiselle had bought herself those panties—mesh and lace—for almost fifty euros in Paris. She'd stood at the edge of a large four-poster bed covered with blue pillows at a hotel in Edinburgh as Mark slid those panties slowly down her thighs, to her ankles, where she'd kicked them away with the toe of her Spanish shoes. Sara had been taking things out of her dresser again.

Well, she had been stealing Sara's things, too.

Jiselle looked back down at the book and said, "I didn't do anything with your dress."

"The hell you didn't," Sara said as she stomped back out. "My collar's gone, too. Stay out of my closet!" She slammed the new bedroom door behind her as hard as she could. The air pressure in the room changed with the force of it. The lace curtains fluttered in the windows, and Mark's uniforms shifted in his closet.

Jiselle looked over at Sam. His eyes were wide but also amused. He said, "Keep reading?"

Jiselle inhaled. She swallowed. Deep in the back of her closet, her stepdaughter's black dress—the one that covered, maybe, three inches of her thighs at most, the one with the

34

rip in the spandex lace just over her right breast—lay on the floor like a call girl's shadow—along with the spiked black leather dog collar Sara liked to wear with the dress. Her fishnet stockings were there, as well, and those black combat boots that, it seemed, Sara had not yet noticed were also missing. Jiselle turned the page.

It was, indeed, delightful to walk about in the country. In a sunny spot stood a pleasant old farmhouse close by a deep river. And from the house down to the waterside grew great burdock leaves, so high that under the tallest of them a little girl could stand upright.

❧

35

Jiselle had begun reading the book to Sam a few weeks earlier, when one night before dinner, she found him under his bed.

"What are you doing under there?"

There was no answer.

What could she do? Mark had been gone four out of every five days since the beginning of the month. If she didn't get Sam out from under the bed herself, he might stay under there until Mark came home again. A child's skeleton in jeans and a T-shirt. Strawberry-blond curls and dust.

"Sam?"

He didn't answer, so she sat down on the bed.

"Sam?"

Jiselle heard him sniffle under there and felt her own

implication of tears then, just behind the bridge of her nose, somewhere around her sinuses. She bit her lip to stop the tears. It would do Sam no good if she started crying, too— although, she supposed, the girls would love it. ("Are you *blubbering* again?" Sara would ask. "Gee," Camilla would say, as if simply stating an interesting fact, "our mother never cried. Our mother always said, 'Be strong, girls. Nobody likes a crybaby.'") Jiselle pinched the place between her eyebrows and lay on her back on Sam's bed, her feet still on the floor. She swallowed, and then counted to ten before saying it again.

"Sam?"

A muffled sob.

"Please?" she said to the ceiling. "Come out?" And then, trying to control the little quiver in her own voice, the anxiety that she imagined would sound to him like impatience, she said, "Sam? I can't let you just stay under the bed. Can I?"

Even to her, it sounded weak, the question childlike, as if she really were expecting an answer to that question from the ten-year-old under the bed.

Sam went completely silent again. Not even a sniffle. Jiselle knelt down beside the bed and tried to look under it, but all she could see was darkness and the white rubber sole of one shoe.

"Okay, Sam," she said. "Tell me what's wrong. Can you please tell me?" She waited.

This time she counted to fifty.

Finally, she reached under the bed, fishing around until she'd gotten a grip on what she was fairly sure was a tennis shoe, and then a second one, and pulled Sam out by his feet as gently as she could.

He didn't struggle. He emerged with a long strand of dust attached to his head, and his face a mess of tears and snot, wrinkled and blotched from crying.

"What's *wrong*?" Jiselle asked, leading him to the edge of the bed by his wrist and sitting him down beside her.

"I miss my dad," Sam sobbed.

"Oh, Sam," she said, and she couldn't help it then. A few tears ran from the corners of her eyes into the little valley between her lips and her nose. She wiped them away and said, "I'm so sorry. I miss him, too."

So, they decided together that they needed to keep themselves busier. They wouldn't miss Mark so much if they had more to do. Especially in the evenings, after dinner, and just before bed. Jiselle would, they decided, read aloud to Sam in the evenings. He agreed that the Hans Christian Andersen looked good. She'd taken the book down from the shelf and held it out for him to see. "My father," she told him, "read this whole book to me one summer."

She placed it on his lap.

The heft of it was satisfying. The gilt-edged pages glowed. Opened, it smelled of pine trees and the past.

❧

It was a hundred and two degrees that evening in the center of the city. For heat that summer, every record that could be broken had been. From the sewer grates rose a smell so sweet and terrible that people held tissues and pieces of clothing to their mouths and noses. A few wore surgical masks. The latest thing was surgical masks with noses and mouths printed on them.

Bozo noses.

Smiles with front teeth missing.

An elderly woman had tied a little scrap of pink chiffon scarf loosely around the muzzle of her poodle, which trotted beside her, looking about shyly, as if it were embarrassed about the scarf.

Some said it was the heat that was causing the Phoenix flu—which health experts were no longer referring to as the Phoenix flu but as hemorrhagic zoonosis, because it was not an influenza, they said, but an antibiotic/vaccine-resistant strain of *Yersinia pestis*.

Phoenix flu, they believed, was not only an inaccurate term; it was an incendiary one. People diagnosed with it were shunned, isolated in corners of emergency rooms, refused small-town hospital beds, driven out of apartment complexes, expelled from institutions of all kinds. It was hoped that calling it something scientific might lessen the public's fear of it.

The public continued to call it the Phoenix flu.

It was not caused or spread by the heat, experts said, despite the ill effects the heat had on those who were already sick.

And birds, too, had been ruled out as infection-carriers.

If anything, it was said, *humans* were infecting *birds*.

Still, biohazard teams were sent out in yellow suits whenever a dead bird was found on the sidewalk or in a backyard—to take it away, dispose of it. The days of birdbaths and birdhouses and birdfeeders seemed over.

Then, after an outbreak at a daycare center, outraged citizens demanded a ban on imported toys—although no connection to the toys and the disease was ever confirmed. The Chinese government retaliated by banning flights from the United States to China if they held even the cremated remains of American dead, devastating Chinese Americans whose loved ones had requested to be returned to their homeland after their deaths.

But the Chinese government compared the scattering of American ashes in China to the medieval practice of catapulting plague-dead corpses over fortress walls to infect enemies.

There was nothing the U.S. government could do about the ban, except make threats.

Quarantining oneself, experts agreed, was futile. The virus could be in the water, in the dirt, in the air. Who knew? It could take years to discover the source of the infection, and more years to find a cure. Most people quit trying to guess where it might be, and how to avoid it, and simply went on with their daily lives. A poll asking, "How concerned are you about the Phoenix flu?" reported that 61 percent of Americans were *Not very concerned*. Another 10 percent were *Not concerned at all*.

As well as being the day of Britney Spears's death, it was Jiselle's birthday, and they were meeting her mother for dinner at Duke's Palace Inn. It wasn't the first time they'd eaten together since Jiselle's wedding. There had already been a disastrous dinner at the house that had ended with Sara leaving the table without touching the food on her plate, and Sam running to the bathroom to throw up the liter of root beer he hadn't mentioned having guzzled before sitting down to chicken and dumplings. ("For God's sake, Jiselle, why do you let that boy drink soda?") Fearing something even worse this time, and in public, Jiselle had almost canceled the birthday dinner, but she knew what her mother would think about that—about her new marriage, about her stepchildren, about her whole life, and all of her decisions— if she did. She would say, "How sad for you, alone on your birthday. Mark simply couldn't take one day off to spend with you?"

They were still a block away from the restaurant when a bus rolled by, and the exhalation of diesel fumes came as a nearly pleasant relief in the stifling heat. A woman ran past with a baby tucked into her blouse. From under the damp white silk dangled little porcelain feet.

When they reached Duke's Palace Inn, the front window was dark, but Jiselle could see the ghostly flickering of candles on the other side.

⊸⊘⊶

The year before, to celebrate her birthday, Mark and Jiselle had met in Copenhagen at the Tivoli Gardens, where they strolled among the flowers. The Danes said there had never been a summer like it—so much color, and the swarms of strange, stingerless bees hovering over everything in a shining, golden hum.

Together, Mark and Jiselle watched the changing of the guard outside the palace, and then took a boat ride along the canals, got a glimpse in the distance of the Little Mermaid shining against a gleaming sea—a provocative naked fish-girl, head bowed, as if she were self-conscious or a little sad, or both.

It was like seeing a character from a dream, in life. On the fireplace mantel in the house in which Jiselle grew up, her mother kept a figurine of the Little Mermaid—green, like the statue itself, but ceramic, and about the size of a lap dog.

Once, and only once, despite her mother's many warnings not to, Jiselle had taken it down. She was twelve or thirteen, and holding it in her hands that day for the first time, she realized that it was hollow—and also heavy, especially for something hollow. When her mother walked in and saw her holding the Little Mermaid, she shouted, "Put that back. Your grandfather gave that to me."

Jiselle had turned hurriedly to put the figurine back on the mantel, stammering something about just blowing off the dust, but her mother rushed at her, grabbed it out of her

41

hands. "I'll take care of that. You keep your hands off of it," she said as she straightened the mermaid on the mantel, and then turned back to Jiselle with a look that was both threatening and beseeching. "Please."

It was the first time Jiselle had considered the possibility that her mother might have loved her own father as much as Jiselle loved hers. It was the first time she'd ever even imagined her mother as a little girl—a girl sitting in a father's lap, being patted on the head by his rough hand, maybe while he sang the Danish folksong Jiselle's own father had sung to her:

Min Tankes Tanke ene Du er vorden, Du er mit Hjertes første Kjærlighed . . .

"You alone have become the thought of my thoughts. You are my heart's first love . . ."

Her own father used to call Jiselle "my Danish princess," and had told her, in fact, that her name in Danish meant "little princess." Throughout her childhood, Jiselle had taken his word for it, until, in college, she looked it up.

By then it was already old news—old news of the most sordid nature—that her father was involved with Ellen, who had been Jiselle's best friend since second grade. She'd thought by then, when it came to things having to do with her father, that nothing would surprise her. How many girlfriends had he had since her mother had thrown him out of the house, and how many of those girlfriends had been young enough to be his daughter, even if they weren't his daughter's age?

And still somehow it had surprised Jiselle to find, in that reference book, that the meaning of the name Jiselle was not "princess."

It was "hostage."

When she told her father this during one of their strained weekly phone calls, he snorted and said, "I wouldn't know about that. Your mother was the one with the European pretensions. She certainly never asked me what I thought of the name." But when, at Thanksgiving that year, Jiselle asked her mother how she'd come to give her the name Jiselle, her mother rolled her eyes and said, "Your father picked that one out." And then, "How is your dear father?" she asked. "And your darling stepmother?"

"He's not *marrying* Ellen," Jiselle had said, trying not to sound defensive—but even to her it sounded protective and aggressive at the same time.

"God, Jiselle," her mother had said, "I can't imagine what kind of denial you're in, to stand up for *him*."

And, in truth, how many such denials had Jiselle managed to flimsily construct over the last few years?

He's not *dating* Ellen.

He's not *in love* with Ellen.

He's not *sleeping* with Ellen.

All the time, apparently, he was.

But even before he'd been thrown out, and long before he'd started up with Ellen, it had seemed to offend and amaze her mother that Jiselle loved her father so much. When he came home from work and Jiselle ran screaming through the house

43

to greet him, her mother would say, "Lord, Jiselle, he was just at the pharmacy, not the Crusades."

So, the day she took down the Little Mermaid figurine, it was a revelation that her mother might have once loved her own father. He'd died many years before Jiselle was born, and her mother had always spoken disparagingly of the farm on which she'd grown up, her father's endless labor. The manure, the pigs. The uncles in a perpetual war against the weather. Their hands under the hood of some machine all day. Her own mother's exhausted death from heart failure at the age of fifty-three.

Standing with her back to the mantel and the Little Mermaid, her arms crossed, her mother had said to her, "It's the only thing I have."

44

In Copenhagen, Mark and Jiselle had taken a limousine together to the airport, although they had different flights back to the States. Mark was piloting a jet from Paris to Atlanta. Jiselle was headed to London, to LaGuardia, and from there to Detroit.

Their limousine driver was a young blond man, no older than twenty, who only nodded to the two of them after putting their luggage in the trunk. Between the front and back seats was a Plexiglas partition, and behind it, Mark kept Jiselle wrapped in his arms as the limousine moved smoothly through the flowers and towers and spires of Copenhagen on a Sunday morning. Church bells rang and echoed, rang and echoed, both monotonously and wildly, as if they had never really started and would never stop. Mark's uniform smelled pleasantly stiff, like dry-cleaning chemicals, and like Mark. When the limousine stopped at an intersection, hundreds of bicyclists sped past, bikes flashing in the sunlight, sounding like the stingerless bees hovering over the yellow tulips in the Tivoli Gardens.

Some of the bicyclists were wearing the now-familiar American flag with a heavy black *X* through it.

Jiselle had glimpsed these all over the world.

Everyone hated the United States now, it seemed. For decades they'd been ruining the environment with their big cars and their big wars, and now they wanted to spread their disease to the rest of the world, too.

Yankee go home.

U.S. not welcome.

But, even as it got harder to travel—more bureaucracy, more hostility—during the glorious early months of their courtship, Jiselle and Mark met in exotic cities all over the world, spent their time in hotel beds, DO NOT DISTURB dangling in several languages from doorknobs.

They ate chocolates, drank champagne.

They took baths together, Mark's knees up around Jiselle's shoulders, Jiselle's soapy feet sliding around his crotch, gingerly.

They ordered room service, ice cubes between her breasts, between his teeth, traced down her torso.

Afterward, they'd laugh about the sheets, which were damp, tangled.

As soon as they got into a room, they'd pull the curtains.

They ignored the fire alarm. *Let's just burn.*
Together.
Oh. God.
In Brussels, Mark bought Jiselle something pink and battery-operated with long waving fronds. He had only to touch her with it to bring her to panting, helpless orgasms. When she opened her eyes afterward, he was looking down at her, smiling.

On the Italian Riviera, they went to a topless beach, where Mark rubbed suntan oil on Jiselle's breasts in full view of the teenage boys smoking cigarettes under an umbrella beside them. When she looked over, one of the boys was rubbing his erection happily, unabashedly, through his cutoffs, looking at her.

When Jiselle rang the bell on the door of Duke's Palace Inn, a man in a white apron unlocked it to let them in. Most of the more expensive restaurants in Chicago and on the outskirts had a locked-door policy now, and required reservations—ostensibly because, with the economy the way it was and the fears of the flu having changed the dining-out habits of the whole nation, chefs and restaurant owners had no way of estimating, any longer, the amount of food that would be needed on any given day or night.

But there had also been talk that this was just an excuse, really, to impart a false sense of safety to customers, who, it was presumed, would feel better about going to a restaurant to eat if they didn't need to worry about unexpected people wandering in off the street—sick people, homeless people, strangers, the whole potentially infected population of those who would not think ahead far enough to make reservations at a nice restaurant.

The doorman locked the door behind them after they stepped inside.

At the hostess lectern, Jiselle stood blinking in the candle-light, scanning the dining room until she saw, at a round table in the center, her mother, who did not look up from her menu until Jiselle was standing beside her, touching her shoulder, looking down onto the top of her head with its ice-blond hair. She looked up then, and her gaze fell on Jiselle, Sam, Camilla, and Sara in turn. "Hello."

Camilla smiled wanly and nodded at Jiselle's mother. Sara stared at a vague place in the corner of the restaurant. Sam, bobbing on his toes, said, "Hi!" so loudly that a couple dining in a far corner of the restaurant looked over.

Jiselle sat down, trying not to look at her mother looking at Sara. Earlier, she'd given Sara her own black dress to wear when Sara couldn't find hers, and had lent her, too, the beautiful black shoes she'd bought in Madrid.

It was a conservative, funeral parlor outfit, nothing like the one Sara had wanted to wear, and still, somehow, Sara managed to make it look provocative, managed to look like a girl whose job it was to deliver pornographic birth-day greetings to corporate businessmen. Jiselle might have managed to hide the dress, but she hadn't been able to keep Sara from wearing black fingernail polish, black lipstick, all that black eyeliner, the ring piercing her lower lip. She was pretty sure the black eyeliner was her own—the Chanel ebony pencil missing from her dresser drawer for a week—but God knew she was never going to say anything. She'd already resigned herself to the petty thefts. On the couple of occasions when it was something she couldn't live without or couldn't replace—the onyx ring Mark had bought for her from a street vendor on Isla Mujeres—Jiselle went into Sara's room while she was out and searched around until she found it.

Then Sara waited until Jiselle was out, and went into Jiselle's drawers and stole it back.

After that, Jiselle had no choice but to snatch it again and then to wear it day and night.

48

Her mother inhaled, looking from Sara to Jiselle. "Nice to see you," she said. "Happy birthday, Jiselle."

"Thank you," Jiselle said. She sat between her mother and Sara, and across from Sam, who tucked his linen napkin into the collar of his shirt and kept it there until Jiselle managed to catch his eye, shake her head. Then he spread it theatrically onto his lap, smiling.

They ordered drinks when the waiter came over—sodas for the kids ("Just one tonight, Sam, okay?") and champagne for Jiselle and her mother, along with an appetizer. Snails. Jiselle's favorite dish at Duke's. Bread was passed around in a basket so light it was hard to hold on to, as if they had been served emptiness in a basket made of air.

After the sodas and champagne arrived, Jiselle's mother

raised her glass and said, dispassionately, "Many happy returns."

Jiselle and the children raised their glasses, too.

Jiselle was surprised, when she did, to see that her own hand, holding up the sparkling glass, was shaking.

"Let's try to have a nice meal, shall we?" her mother said, looking around at the children.

"Yes," Jiselle said, as if her mother had been talking to her.

They'd taken only a few, silent sips of their drinks before the snails were brought out on a little silver plate and set in the middle of the table. Sam leaned toward the plate, curious, but the girls recoiled. Sara put her napkin to her mouth as if to stifle a scream, as the smell of garlic rose from the small, curled, dark gray flesh. Camilla looked away, grimacing. Jiselle pierced one on the end of her small silver fork, brought it to her mouth, placed it on her tongue, and ate it slowly.

49

It was delicious—the soft, luxurious density of something delivered divinely from the sea, liberated from its shell by nymphs, relaxed into death by butter. That snail seemed nothing at all like the kind of creature Jiselle used to find clinging to rocks in her grandmother's garden—its whole body a small, hopeless, damp tongue, bearing all that weight from one place to the next, seeming to think its shell might save it.

As she chewed, Jiselle kept her eyes on her plate, except to look up one time when her mother said to Camilla, "Aren't you going to eat?"

Camilla didn't answer. She was staring at the candle in the center of the table. It flickered, surged, contracted in a blue-and-orange dance, trying, Jiselle knew, to eat up all the oxygen in the room.

"Camilla?" Jiselle said. Camilla looked up then. Her eyes were so red and swollen they were painful to look at, and Jiselle looked away.

For hours after the news, Camilla lay on her bed with her face in her pillow, weeping, while Sara stomped around the house with her cell phone, spreading the bad news, sharing the grief. Jiselle hadn't known they even *liked* Britney Spears. Wasn't Camilla, at least, too old to be a Britney Spears fan? Wasn't Sara too punk for a Barbie doll like Britney? Wasn't Britney Spears, by then, old news anyway?

50 Apparently not.

Apparently Camilla and Sara had thought of Britney Spears as a kind of immortal sister. They were inconsolable. No, they did not want breakfast. Or lunch. Or to talk. Finally, after the second hour of weeping, Jiselle went to Camilla's room, stood in the threshold, and said, "I'm sad, too, Camilla, but we can't let it—"

"Let it *what*?" Camilla asked. Her tone, hysterical and angry at the same time, sounded vaguely threatening, and it was at that moment that Jiselle realized she'd had no earthly idea what she was about to say, anyway. In truth, was she even so sure she fully believed that it was inappropriate to grieve so deeply for Britney Spears? And if it was, *why* was it? They'd prefaced the special news bulletin with a few bars from "I'm Not a Girl, Not Yet a Woman," and the tears had pricked Jiselle's eyes before she'd even had a chance to blink.

Britney Spears, back then, with all that flaxen hair, still a child, half-naked, the wind blowing some wheat around behind her a long decade or more ago. The kind of girl who might own a winged horse—dead? Of the flu? Of hemorrhagic zoonosis? All that self-destructive energy, that combustion, just to die of the same infection that might kill the odd, unlucky nurse's aide or mallard duck?

Anyway, she knew that even if she had managed to say something coherent to Camilla about how, maybe, it was inappropriate to grieve for a pop star the way you would grieve for a member of your own family, Camilla would have nodded politely through her tears, wiped her nose with a piece of tissue, and agreed—to Jiselle's face. To her face, Jiselle was always right. Only later would Jiselle overhear Camilla muttering to her sister, "That bitch is so cold."

Sara would simply have stomped out, saying something like, "Spare us your philosophy, *Mommy*."

(In the previous week, Sara had taken to calling Jiselle—ironically, in italics—*Mommy*, while Camilla had still never called Jiselle by any name at all. Jiselle had no idea what, if Camilla were forced to get her attention in a crowd, she might have been able to bring herself to call out: *Jiselle*, or *Stepmother*, or *Second wife of my father*?)

What had Jiselle, standing at the threshold of Camilla's room, thought she might say?

That was the problem with being a stepmother, Jiselle was beginning to realize, or with being a mother, for all she knew: you went around trying to convince children of things you weren't that sure of yourself. That it was inappropriate to cry yourself sick over the death of a pop star. That it was better to read with the television off. That eating cookies before dinner was inherently wrong.

Sam was only ten, and he'd already figured out that a room looked just as clean if you kicked the laundry under the bed as it did if you spent the hours it would take to sort and fold and put the clothes in closets and drawers.

Wasn't that what Jiselle herself had done for years?

Hypocrisy had somehow not been one of the "cons" she'd considered when thinking about resignation from her job to stay home with Mark's children. When he'd first proposed the possibility, there had been so many things to think about that hypocrisy could never have fit on the "con" list.

Loss of seniority, pension, and job security; financial dependence after so many years of being on her own—*these* things had occurred to her.

52

⌖

When Jiselle's mother asked her again if she planned to eat anything, Camilla finally said, in a quavering voice, "I'm not very hungry."

Sam chased a snail around his plate with his fork, caught it, put it in his mouth, chewed, and said, "I don't get why it's such a big deal."

Instantly, Jiselle recognized it as the worst possible thing he could have said, but by then it was too late. Sara whipped around to glare at her brother with her mouth open. Jiselle's mother looked over. Jiselle cleared her throat nervously. "Sam," she said. "Let's not talk about that, okay?"

Obediently, Sam gave a world-weary shrug, and then he reached across the table for another slice of bread, dragging his elbow through the butter dish as he did. He wiped the butter off his elbow onto his pants leg, smiled pleasantly up at Jiselle's mother, and continued to eat.

"What are we talking about?" Jiselle's mother asked, looking around the table.

Jiselle cleared her throat, and then, under her breath, leaning toward her mother, answered, "Britney Spears. She died."

Her mother blinked noncommittally. Camilla drew a ragged breath. Sara choked out, "Excuse me," and stood up, heading for the women's room. When she did, her linen napkin slid off her lap and onto the floor. They all glanced down at it, but no one made a move to pick it up.

"Britney Spears?" Jiselle's mother asked, raising her eyebrows.

"Yes," Jiselle said, scrambling to think of a way to change the subject. "The singer."

"I know who Britney Spears is," her mother said. "I just don't know why we'd—"

Jiselle raised a desperate hand in the air over her mother's head and began waving at their waiter. Her mother turned to look at him, too, and in one second he was beside the table. "Yes, ma'am?" he said to Jiselle, who opened her mouth with no idea what she should ask him for. Thinking frantically,

53

she was surprised to hear herself say, as if she'd intended all along to say it, "It's my birthday. Do you think we might have a cake after dinner?"

"*Certainly.*" The waiter smiled and bowed.

When he was gone, Jiselle's mother said, shaking her head, "We haven't even gotten our main course yet."

"Oh," Jiselle said. "I know. It's just—you know. My birthday! I'm excited."

Sam beamed. "Tell him to make it chocolate," he said.

Part
Two

CHAPTER FOUR

F ar more people are *not* going to die of the Phoenix
flu than die of it!" one television doctor said on a special news report. "We'd better keep attending school, paying
our bills, and floating the economy. Otherwise, when the
hysteria dies down, we'll have something to be hysterical
about."

Healthy people, it was said, could withstand this rather
minor infection. Drug users could not, of course. Nor the
children of drug users. It was true that medical profession-
als and the depressed were at special risk. People who did
not have the right attitude often succumbed, and that was
why the Wholeness books and tapes, which could easily be
bought off the Internet, were so helpful. Even if you weren't
sick, ordering and listening to the tapes, reading the books
about how to strengthen your character, alleviate stress, clean
yourself of unhealthy thought patterns could ward off the
disease.

Jiselle was given one such book by the mother of Camilla's boyfriend, Bobby Temple.

"Honestly," Tara Temple said, "it changed my life."

Jiselle had almost never spoken to the woman before that evening, although she had met Bobby's father, Paul Temple, once or twice when he came by to pick Bobby up for some sort of lesson or sporting event.

Paul Temple was a tall man with the same sand-colored hair as his son. He taught history at the local high school, and Jiselle thought he looked knowledgeable and sheepish about being knowledgeable. When the subject of current events came up on the front steps as he waited for his son, Paul Temple referred to the thirteenth century as if it had been last week—but then looked embarrassed to have slipped it into the conversation, like the smart boys Jiselle had known in high school, who would rather have walked straight into walls than worn glasses.

His wife, Tara, seemed his opposite. Whatever she had, she had on display. That day, her hair was dyed a metallic blond, and she was wearing large silver-and-turquoise earrings and a sheer blue blouse. She said she was just stopping by to drop off Bobby's track shoes, and Jiselle was surprised that she would think to give her anything at all—and especially surprised by the bright, lightweight book Tara Temple handed over.

Its cover was slick, shiny. A whiteness at the center of more whiteness. CURE YOUR SELF! was written in gold letters across it. It was no longer than fifty or sixty pages, and holding it in her hands, Jiselle had the feeling that if she didn't hold on to it tightly, it might float away.

"Thank you," she said, "but are you sure? I could get my own copy."

"I *want* you to have it," Tara Temple said.

Only later, turning the book over at the kitchen table, did Jiselle understand. On the back was written, *Buy a copy of this book for everyone you know! Give this book away! It will increase your good fortune, and CURE YOUR SELF!* This book—it was a kind of chain letter, spread from one person to another to another, mystically, like a virus.

"What we need are better vaccines and antibiotics, not *good fortune*," Mark said, picking up the book and tossing it back down on his way out the door.

"It's not my book," Jiselle said to his back.

"Well, that's reassuring," he said.

"It's Tara Temple's."

"Oh *God*," he said. "*That* woman."

"Mark," Jiselle asked, "Do you think this is going to be a big thing?"

"The Phoenix flu?" he asked, and then shrugged. "That depends on what you mean by 'big thing,' I guess. But aren't you glad you're not flying?"

⤜∾⤏

The media connected the fears of the flu, the war, global warming, and the end of the world to the number of women who were dropping out of the workforce.

What was the point of two incomes if your money

59

couldn't buy you the luxuries you worked for? If you couldn't even afford to put gas in two cars, let alone install a hot tub, why not have someone at home watching the children, folding the laundry, making nice dinners during the day?

A stay-at-home mother was even one of Dr. Springwell's secrets—number five or six on the famous list of "Immune Boosters" promoted by the portly physician whose popular show was devoted entirely to advice on avoiding an illness, which he never called the Phoenix flu but which was, of course, the Phoenix flu.

Jiselle had watched the show only once, in a hotel room in Minneapolis. "We are like fish in a small bowl," Dr. Springwell was saying. He had two goldfish in a glass bowl on a table in front of him. Behind him was a painted sky, heavenly blue, in which a few cottony clouds sat motionless and serene. The doctor wore a white shirt unbuttoned at the neck. His bald head gleamed. "The slightest shift changes everything."

Dr. Springwell tipped the bowl a little to the left then, and the camera closed in on the two bright fish, who had been floating in it peacefully, seemingly asleep, but who were now trying frantically to swim, with their tiny, fluttering fins, against the current. Those fins looked as if they were made of the thinnest tissue. Useless.

"See?" Dr. Springwell said. "This is the *barely perceptible change* in our climate, but it *alters everything*. The fish have to learn to swim all over again in this new world. Like us! What we experience in *our* fishbowl is the gradual shift in our resources, our economy, our way of life, and, most important, our *immune systems*."

Here, the words *Dr. Springwell's Secret* and the cover of his bestselling book began to flash against the blue sky behind him. Dr. Springwell righted the bowl, and the fish, disoriented, began to swim in what appeared to be hopeless, exhausted circles.

"*Do* it," Annette had said. "Quit. Stay home. Just think, no more puke. No more pretzels. I *love* being home."

Annette was four months pregnant by then, and there were complications, but luckily she was married to a doctor. She watched television all day. She made phone calls. She kept a bucket beside the bed and threw up in it every half hour. She jokingly called her husband Dr. Williams and said that Dr. Williams said not to be concerned. Many women had morning sickness all three trimesters, and she must just be one of the lucky ones.

"I don't know," Jiselle said. "Sara, the younger daughter— I think she hates me."

"So what? Does she hate you more than those old ladies who can't get their bags stuffed into the overhead compartment hate you? Does she hate you more than *terrorists* hate you?"

"But," Jiselle asked Annette on the phone, "won't I feel like I'm trying to—?"

"Take their mother's place? *Forget* about her!" Annette said. "She's dead! I mean, it's not like *you* were never with any other men."

61

True.

But Jiselle had never been married. She'd never had a child with a man. She'd never been widowed.

His first wife's name had been Joy, and it was amazing how many times a day one heard that name or saw it in the form of the word. On a card, followed by an exclamation point. On the lips of the president nodding over a lectern on television: *It is with great joy that I am announcing today that seven thousand troops will be returning to the United States next month.* On the lips of the president's opponents when it didn't happen: *What happened to all that "joy"?*

The Joy of Cooking.

The Joy of Sex.

Joy to the world . . .

No Joy in Mudville.

Cultivating a sense of inner joy in troubled times . . .

Mark had told Jiselle the basics of their meeting (college), and their courtship (two years), and their decision to marry, to move to Wisconsin, to have three children, and then he ended with "and then she was hit by a school bus. In front of our house. In front of our *children.* What else can I say?"

"That's horrible," Jiselle said to him, holding her head with one hand and covering her mouth with the other. "Just *horrible.*"

Mark shook his head. It was a tired and resigned gesture. His wife, he seemed to be saying, how could she have done it to them?

"You know," Jiselle's mother said. "I Googled that. It sounded fishy to me, and I started wondering if you might be getting involved with a serial killer. But there it was in the *St. Sophia News*: PILOT'S WIFE STRUCK BY BUS IN FRONT OF HOUSE.

⁓

"This is just the beginning," their neighbor, Brad Schmidt, told Jiselle one afternoon when they met at the end of their driveways after having dragged out their trash cans for the garbage truck. "It's the tip of the iceberg," he said.

By then Jiselle had already spoken to Brad Schmidt several times—always over the hedge or with the garbage cans at the end of the driveway—and he always said something about the Phoenix flu.

"It's *hairs*," he said that afternoon. "They import hair for wigs and extensions, you know. From Pakistan. Korea. And those people they cut the hair off of died of the Phoenix flu."

Jiselle tried to smile politely. She said, lifting one shoulder, "Who knows?"—although she briefly considered pointing out that the flu had started in the United States, that other countries were outlawing imports of all kinds *from* America—blankets, food, clothes, books. Outside the United States, everything American was suspect.

But what would have been the point of arguing with him? Brad Schmidt was elderly. He was pleased with his theory. A week earlier, he'd had to bring his wife, who had Alzheimer's, back from the group home in which she lived. Several of its employees had fallen ill, and they'd closed down. Since then, Jiselle had seen her only once, when Mrs. Schmidt had wandered across their lawns to the front door. Before she'd had time to knock on the door, Jiselle had opened it, and this

63

seemed to startle the old woman, who asked, "How did you know about me?"

"I saw you from the window," Jiselle said.

"You *watch* me?"

"Well, no," Jiselle said. "This is where I live, and I was looking out the window."

"Oh."

Mrs. Schmidt's eyes remained wide, an expression of puzzled alarm on her face, and Jiselle was surprised how much like a ghost she was—thin, white-haired, nearly translucent, like someone who had been snatched back from the other world but who did not quite understand that she was back, or why. The old woman reached out and took Jiselle's hands in her own, and asked, "So, do you know me, young lady?"

64

"Now I do," Jiselle answered as brightly as possible.

"Then, who *am* I?"

"You're Mrs. Schmidt."

"Very nice," Diane Schmidt said, nodding, as if Jiselle had passed a test. Just then, her husband came panting around the hedge—clearly he'd been searching for his wife—and took her home.

That morning at the end of their driveways, Brad Schmidt snorted and said, "Britney Spears. All this bullshit about Britney Spears. Britney Spears isn't even the first of *millions*."

Jiselle nodded. "Still," she said, "it's very sad."

"Sad, sure," Brad Schmidt said. "Better get used to it."

CHAPTER FIVE

Mark chose an afternoon when the children were on a field trip to Chicago with the public schools to bring Jiselle to the house for the first time. He drove down-state and into Illinois to pick her up in his ice-blue sports car. ("A Mazda RX-8. The only midlife crisis car I could pile three kids into.")

Jiselle heard the engine in her driveway before she looked out the window. The car sounded like an enormous cat purring as it pulled in. The top was down.

Mark had been to her house only once, and Jiselle knew he'd been unimpressed. ("Kind of boxy, isn't it? And the neighbors, too many, too close. But I guess what's the point of having a nice place if you never stay in it anyway?") This time, he didn't even bother to step inside. He took her over-night bag out of her hand at the door, walked back to his car, tossed it in his trunk, and then turned to watch as she locked the front door and descended the little cement stoop. After she'd crossed the front lawn to him, he took her in his arms, pulled her to him, and kissed her. For a second, Jiselle let her eyes flutter open. Over his shoulder and across the street, she saw a teenage girl in cutoffs and a T-shirt watching them dreamily, but intensely, from her own front yard.

Of course.

How many times had Jiselle herself fantasized this scene when she was a teenager—a handsome man, a fast car in the driveway, the passionate kiss, the way he would sweep her into the car, drive her away?

In one of Jiselle's earliest memories, she and Ellen had stuffed one of their Barbies into the passenger seat of a Barbie-Mobile, stretching out her long legs stiffly on the dashboard as Ken drove her wildly across the shag carpet in Ellen's basement.

Clearly, that had been Ellen's fantasy, too—except that the driver had been Jiselle's father, who'd driven her drunk in his Roadster straight into oncoming traffic, and the next day Jiselle was called to the wrecking service, shown the car. The blood-soaked upholstery. The collapsed roof. A single high-heel shoe on the floor of the passenger side.

The wrecking yard workers had stood around her, telling her the car was still worth at least ten thousand dollars.

"You can't just junk it," one of them had said. "It's a classic."

But Jiselle had walked away from it with only a few coins she'd found scattered on the driver's seat, believing that they had fallen from her father's pocket and that she should keep them. But she had put them in her purse, where they were scattered among the other coins, and she finally spent them on a parking meter, maybe, or a package of gum.

After she settled into the passenger seat beside Mark, she put a clip in her hair, and as they drove off, Jiselle waved to the teenage girl, who looked away, pretending she hadn't been watching.

⌒∽⌒

They drove for miles without talking. Without needing to talk. Mark kept one hand on Jiselle's knee, the other on the steering wheel. His house was seventy miles north of Jiselle's town, on the diagonal. Like Jiselle, he was required by the airlines to live less than an hour away from O'Hare. His town, St. Sophia, had been one of those on the suggestion list Jiselle had been given when she'd taken her job, but she'd decided against it because she'd thought it was too small. There would be no single men to date.

How many flight attendants, she now wondered, had made the same mistake? Who among them might have been beside this pilot in his sports car today if it had been otherwise?

Mark drove the sports car the way he flew a plane, with total confidence, in deep concentration. Ahead of them, the highway wound blackly through green hills. For a while, they followed the river, which was smooth and dotted with stone-white ducks and seemed to have stopped moving altogether. After a while they came up behind a pickup truck carrying several large birdcages, each cage full of silky white

67

doves. Hundreds of doves. The driver was an elderly woman, who glared at Mark and Jiselle as they passed her in the no-passing lane.

Mark and Jiselle smiled at each other.

They passed a few more cars. An empty school bus. An ice-cream truck. Another pickup—this one hauling a horse trailer out of which a horse's amber tail swished the air.

They crossed rickety covered bridges spanning rocky little streams that bubbled and frothed below them, and then they were crossing the boundary to his town, St. Sophia, where a red-white-and-blue sign stated simply: ST. SOPHIA—AMERICA'S HOMETOWN.

They slowed down.

"We're here," he said. He took his hand off her knee and placed it on the steering wheel. Jiselle nodded and smiled over at him, but he was looking straight ahead, so she looked around.

Gingerbread Victorians lined the shady Main Street. There were brick and clapboard storefronts. The library had Greek columns. The fire station had one shining red truck parked out front and a Dalmatian lounging under an oak tree beside it.

"We moved here to have the kids," Mark said, gesturing around him at his town. "It seemed so old-fashioned. So out of the way. Of course, it's changed a lot since then."

A flag flew from the yard of the school, which was a red brick two-story building with a few gothic flourishes around the doors. The post office had a cupola on the roof, a blue mailbox outside. There was a tidy park with a swing set and a merry-go-round and a wishing well. There was another flag flapping from a pole beside the courthouse.

Jiselle couldn't imagine how St. Sophia had *changed*.

There was about it a sense of time having stopped at some idealized moment—the sun at the highest point in the sky, the season stalled perfectly between spring and summer, the population poised between too few and too many. The happiest hours chiming from a clock tower. The sweetest period of American history reflected in the most romantic of American architecture. Peace, following a war. The kindest politics. A time of prosperity, but not materialism. An era during which people believed in things but were not fanatical.

A little boy riding a red bicycle too large for him waved excitedly as Mark and Jiselle drove by. Jiselle waved back, and Mark saluted. "A school chum of Sam's," he said.

69

They took Main Street from one brief end of town to the other, and then kept on going, until the Victorians slipped away and the trees grew up around them. The road to Mark's house turned to gravel, and then to dirt, and then to clay.

Jiselle had known it was in the woods, at the edge of a ravine, but she was surprised by how deep into the woods it was, how alive the woods seemed to be—fluttering with leaves, and wings, and the fragile airy progress of butterflies.

They pulled into his driveway, and there it was—a small log house, the house Mark had described to her so well that the one in her imagination matched this one perfectly: The covered wraparound porch. The brick chimney. All of it pushed up to the edge of a ravine full of pines and white birches. There were lace curtains in the windows. A chipmunk sat on the front porch, cheeks stuffed with something, munching. It looked up as they pulled in, as if it had been expecting them, and when they stepped out of the car, it didn't run away but waited until they'd reached the mossy cobblestone walk to the front door before slipping into the rock garden.

"Here it is," Mark said. "Your home, if you'll have it."

He took her by the arm and guided her through the rooms to the kitchen, where he presented her with a bouquet of tulips he said the children had picked for her themselves. They were carefully arranged on the kitchen table in a white vase—three black-cupped blooms, each one seeming to burn with a small electric light at its center.

70 "Here," Mark said.

 ⁓⦵⦵⦵⁓

When she woke up next to him in his log house on the afternoon of her first visit, in his big four-poster bed under a Navajo blanket after making love, Jiselle slipped out of his arms to wander into the rooms of his house, and felt as if she recognized them from somewhere deep inside herself, as if the place had grown up like a shell around her dream.

The sun was high in the sky, streaming through the lace curtains and the window shades, making a dappled splash at the foot of the bed, pooling on the wooden floorboards. Jiselle picked Mark's shirt out of that pool of light, slid her arms into it, stepped through the curtain in the doorway into the other rooms, and she saw that all the thresholds were draped with colorful silk cloth instead of doors. It was such a beautiful gesture, those silk curtains stirring peacefully in the doorways to every room.

The house was small and cluttered but very clean. The walls were made of raw logs and planed boards trimmed with brick. The windows were old-fashioned, too—the kind you cranked open. Verdigris iron rimmed the panes. There were real wooden shutters on the outside.

Jiselle walked down the hallway between the bedrooms to the family room, with its comfortable tweed couch, two overstuffed chairs, a coffee table spilling magazines. A big TV took up one wall, and there was a sliding glass door against the other, opening onto a cedar deck.

Mark had told her about the deck—how it was built around an oak tree, how the tree looked, from the family room, as if it grew straight out of the house. Jiselle went to the sliding glass doors and saw that this was true.

The trunk of the oak poured upward through the cedar slats of the deck, and then it branched overhead, gloriously green—an enormous, ancient, tree. She slid the door open and stepped out. She touched the trunk. It was rough and warm.

Mark had also told her that he and Joy had built the house as close to the ravine as they could without having to worry about the house falling into it after forty years of rainfall and erosion. Jiselle stood on the deck and looked into that beautiful abyss. The air smelled pure. She inhaled so deeply it made her feel a little dizzy, and she steadied herself with a hand to the trunk of the oak before turning back to the house. She wanted to see the children's rooms.

First, she peeked around the silk curtain in the doorway and into Sam's room. A stuffed tiger on the floor. A cowboy hat on the desk. The bed was unmade, and the sheets had pirates on them—skulls and crossbones and tall-masted ships. There was a photo of Sam himself on the nightstand. From Halloween? His curly strawberry-blond hair was pulled back in a ponytail. He wore a patch over one eye.

Camilla's room was spotless. Just a row of slim hardcover books on a white shelf. A round green rug on the floor. The clover-covered bedspread was pulled up carefully over the pillows. A dustless desk with a stapler, a laptop, a small bowl of thumbtacks, and a few pencils lined up.

Sara's room, on the other hand, was the typical adolescent disaster. Clothes tumbled out of the closet and onto the floor. There was a half-full bottle of Diet Coke open on the nightstand. Books and notebooks were scattered across the desk. On the wall was an enormous poster of a wild-haired man with a naked torso, holding the neck of an electric guitar with one hand, the other pointed at the camera, middle finger raised. The bedspread was black, as were the silk sheets rumpled on the mattress, which had been pulled off the bed frame and onto the floor.

Jiselle stepped out of the room and back into the hallway quickly, but she wasn't alarmed. Although she herself had kept a tidy teenage room under her mother's vigilant administration, she remembered how teenage girls could be. She remembered Ellen's room. The piles of dirty laundry. The

72

books and magazines scattered across the floor. Having to wade though the debris to get to the bed, where you had to push away more debris to sit down.

She wandered to the kitchen then, where a bowl of red apples sat on the butcher-block countertop. She took one and smelled it before biting into it. Orchards and sunlight in that mouthful of apple. It was crisp. Tart and sweet at the same time. She stood and ate it down to the core in Mark's kitchen, her bare feet on the ceramic tile, before finding the garbage pail under the sink and dropping it in.

Then she made her way to the living room, where she went first to the bookshelf, studied the titles on the spines lined up neatly:

Aviation Through the Ages. Light Aircraft Navigation Essentials. Memoirs of an African Big-Game Hunter. The Art of Chess. The Sibley Guide to South American Birds. Woodcraft.

They were books that spoke of masculine hobbies—large, heavy books with glossy dust jackets, smelling of their own clean pages—and Jiselle thought with some shame of her own shelves, overstuffed with paperbacks. The broken spines and the pages folded over to mark a place to which she'd never returned. The library books were mixed in with the books she owned, so that she was always searching, and her books were always overdue.

She would, she vowed, clear the shelves when she got back, dispose of those books, return the library books, donate all the others to someone, something (a homeless shelter? an orphanage?) before she moved into this perfect house with Mark. She would let someone less fortunate have them. She would *clean up her act*, as her mother used to tell her to do.

She was thinking about that—about her fortune, and her worthless books, and her mother—when she turned and saw it hanging above the fireplace:

A framed photograph.

A full-length portrait.

A wedding portrait.

More than anything in that first moment of recognition, Jiselle was startled that it hadn't been the first thing she'd seen when she walked in the door.

It took up half of an entire wall.

Framed in filigreed silver, it was perfectly centered over the mantel.

In it, Mark looked so much younger that she might not have even recognized him if it hadn't been for his eyes, deep set and dark, and the playful lift of the eyebrows, an expression she recognized—one he'd make boarding a plane, saying, "Howdy, folks," to the flight crew before the passengers boarded and one of the flight attendants, always a woman, came up behind him to help him slide out of his coat. His eyebrows would rise in that casual, inverted *V*, and he'd say, sighing theatrically, "Ah. A good day to die."

But in this portrait he was only a prop. He was an afterthought. Jiselle stepped closer to look more carefully, although her heart was already beating hard. The center of this large photograph was the bride, of course, wearing a wedding gown, holding a blindingly white piece of cake up to the photographer. She was offering that piece of cake to the future, it seemed, on a wide silver knife. Her strawberry-blond hair cascaded over her shoulders in ringlets. She did not wear a veil but, instead, a ribbon of ivory velvet in her hair, wound through a strand or two, tied in a loose knot. Jiselle put her hand to her mouth.

"Oh, dear," Mark said, coming up behind her.

He'd startled her, but she didn't turn around. She couldn't, transfixed as she was by that first bride's gaze.

"Oh, Jiselle," Mark said. "I just keep that up so the children will feel, you know, as if their mother's here. Of course, now I'll take it down."

He took Jiselle's shoulders in his hands and turned her around to look at him.

He pulled her to him and kissed her then with so much gentle longing that her knees would have buckled beneath her if he hadn't been holding her so steadily in his arms.

75

CHAPTER SIX

The spring passed in a blur of anticipation. When Jiselle wasn't flying, she was busy with preparations—the catering, the flowers, the invitations.

She still hadn't met the children, but she'd sent the girls opal necklaces to wear with their bridesmaid dresses, and Sam (not for the wedding) a pirate's three-cornered hat with a red feather. Mark would be bringing her to the house for a week prior to their marriage, and he said, "You can see for yourself then that they're great kids, and they'll adore you. But you'll still have time to back out!"

Until after their honeymoon in Puerto Rico, he would continue to employ the nanny. Afterward, they would "see what the next step should be."

"If you *want* to quit, to be home with the children, of course that's fine. If *not*—"

If not, Jiselle knew, they would need to find another nanny.

She had not met the present nanny, but when she'd called Mark's house once, a bright-sounding young woman had answered and called out to Mark in singsong, "The phone's for you!"

"Where does she sleep?" Jiselle asked.

"When I'm here," he said, "she sleeps at her apartment in town. When I'm gone, I don't know. The couch? Why would I care? I hope you're not jealous. I'm not one of those widowers who's so desperate he sleeps with his children's nanny."

"Of course not!" Jiselle had said.

Who knew better than she that Captain Mark Dorn could have any woman he wanted?

Still, twice in two weeks, Jiselle had tried to make an appointment with her therapist to discuss the issue of quitting her job to take care of Mark's children. She knew she could afford no *fuzzy logic* here, with her wedding only weeks away, but when she called Dr. Smitty Smith's office, she got only his answering machine, on which he'd left a recording saying that his patients should leave a message, which he would return when he was over his illness.

CHAPTER SEVEN

The chapel in which Jiselle had been baptized, the one they'd reserved for the wedding, was damaged by the flooding that started the first week of July, after the long week of relentless rain at the end of June, so Jiselle quickly reserved the small garden behind the restaurant, where the reception was to be held as well.

Both events had to take place outdoors due to the new Health Department regulations requiring at least three months' notice for an indoor gathering of more than thirty people. But the weather was terrible. After the rains, a thick humidity cloaked everything in more gray and stench. Some afternoons, the air was so thick and motionless that it felt like trying to breathe inside an aquarium. Mark and Jiselle decided to be married at twilight.

The afternoon before the wedding, around four o'clock, Jiselle and her mother arrived at the garden behind the restaurant to check on the flowers and the tables and chairs, to make sure everything was in order and had arrived, along with the cooler of champagne.

Jiselle had tried to call Mark earlier from her cell phone, but she couldn't get a signal. She'd wanted to know how the children were. The night before, they'd gone out to dinner after the rehearsal, and Sam had thrown up at Jiselle's mother's feet. He'd been drinking 7-Up. Gallons of it. Every time he finished a large glass of it, the waitress had brought him another. Only Jiselle's mother had been watching this, and later she said, "What do you expect, letting a child drink all that soda? Of course he's going to throw up."

But when Jiselle spoke to Mark that morning, Sam seemed fine. Camilla, however, was lying down, complaining of menstrual cramps, and Sara had not yet broken the Vow of Silence, as Mark had begun to refer to it. She'd begun it the week Jiselle came to stay, and Jiselle knew, from sneaking a look at her diary, that she planned to continue:

> If he marries this stupid bitch, I'm going to make their lives a living hell.
>
> For one thing, I'm never going to say another word out loud to either of them as long as they live.

∽◎∾

After they'd supervised the raising of the canopy over the garden by Perfect Party Rentals, Jiselle and her mother went back to the house together to get dressed. Jiselle's wedding dress, freshly laundered at BC-YU Cleaners, hung on the back of the door of her childhood bedroom, now her mother's sewing room. It was draped in a clear plastic sheet emblazoned with a black cartoon caricature of a ninja soldier with the face of B.C. Yu, the laundry's owner and operator, a sword held high over his head.

Jiselle had known B.C. for years. She'd driven into town with her mother to drop off their clothes at his establishment a thousand times. He'd dry-cleaned Jiselle's prom dresses, steam-ironed her graduation gown, laundered the black dress she'd worn to her father's and Ellen's funerals. He'd cleaned those and wrapped them in the same clear sheet with his face and the sword. It was a perfect caricature, and Jiselle could never decide whether it was, for B.C., a joke (playing off stereotypes—the mild-mannered Korean dry cleaner turned ninja?) or a fantasy.

She was exhausted and closed the sewing room door. The film of humidity and drizzle that had coated her during the wedding preparations had mixed with the smell of her own sweat. She was too tired to take a shower just yet. She had to rest for a minute or two first.

Because there was no longer a bed in her old room, Jiselle lay down on the floor beside the sewing table and closed her eyes. She heard the shower begin in the bathroom, and the sound of the shower doors sliding open and closed, and then she fell asleep to the music of water pelting the naked flesh of her mother, and then she was dreaming—dreaming that she was under the Perfect Party Rentals tent, waiting for a wedding to begin. It was a dream within a dream, and the feeling was so peaceful that it didn't matter to Jiselle whether or not anything ever happened to her again. There was water running somewhere, and the sounds of doors opening and closing politely, and then, "Oh my God, *Jiselle!*"

Her eyes snapped open. She sat up, finding herself in the sewing room again, with her mother standing over her wearing the salmon-pink linen dress she'd bought for the wedding—her ice-blond hair carefully clipped behind her head; her white summer shoes, her matching purse over her arm—and an expression of horror on her face.

"What the *hell* are you doing?" she shouted. "You're getting married in *thirty minutes.*"

"How long have I been asleep?" Jiselle asked. She looked at the gold watch Mark had given her for her birthday and saw that an hour had passed. The hour she'd allotted for dressing, and makeup, and arranging her hair.

"For God's sake," her mother said, "get your dress on!"

And then, still stinking, stripped down to her underwear, having only enough time to drag a brush through her hair, Jiselle was ripping the ninja off her wedding dress, pulling it up over her hips, hearing the fabric rip with a terrible, permanent sound, and realized that she was stepping on the hem of the dress at the same time that she was yanking it on, and then she was in the passenger seat of her mother's car.

"Oh Mom," Jiselle said. She was trying not to cry.

"Don't *talk,*" her mother said.

But Jiselle couldn't help it.

"I just can't believe—"

"I said, *don't talk*, Jiselle. It's just going to make it worse if you start crying now. This whole thing is a fiasco anyway."

Jiselle bit her lip, which tasted like salt, and willed herself not to cry, not to speak, but then, it seemed, her mother's floodgates burst:

"Why exactly, Jiselle, do you think I kicked your father out when you were fifteen?"

"Because . . ." Jiselle said, but then realized she had nothing to say. Somehow, in her mind, she'd connected the dog, Bingo, with her parents' divorce. Her father had come home with the dog, and the next day he was gone. But, surely, the dog could not have been the last straw. Her parents had been married for twenty years by then.

"Because he was sleeping with that little slut already. I caught them in *our* bed in the middle of the afternoon while you were at school. Your little friend was playing hookie."

"No," Jiselle said. "Mom, they didn't start—"

"Oh, for God's sake, Jiselle, be quiet."

Be quiet.

Jiselle's mouth was still open, but she couldn't speak. It was as if her mother had cast a spell over her. Jiselle saw that her mother's hands were holding the steering wheel so tightly that the knuckles had gone from white to red, and she was shaking her head in little snaps. Her lips were pursed, but she was also grinding her teeth.

"I have been keeping my mouth shut about this for the last eighteen years, but didn't it *ever cross your mind*? Do you ever remember your father taking an interest in *anything* about your life except for your friend Ellen?"

Jiselle put her hand on the door handle, as if she might be able to simply step out of the car.

"*Well?* Why do you think he was always so eager to give darling little Ellen a ride home or pick her up for you?"

Jiselle didn't move or swallow. She couldn't.

"And now my daughter's about to make the same mistake I made, marrying a man because he's charming and handsome, without knowing another damn thing about him."

Jiselle had to unroll her window despite the air-conditioning in her mother's car, and still she could hardly breathe. She had to close her eyes. She let the air rushing past her pummel her face like ghosts in boxing gloves. Finally, her mother pulled over, brakes squealing, wheels thumping up against the curb. "Get out," she said to Jiselle as she jumped out herself, in her salmon-pink suit, and disappeared around the corner of the restaurant.

When Jiselle finally managed to get out of her mother's car—carefully, she did not want to risk ripping the hem of her dress even more—and closed the car door, someone behind her called out, "Lady?"

She turned to look. It was the man from Perfect Party Rentals. "Lady," he said again, "there's a problem with your tent."

"What?" Jiselle asked, but he'd already stepped past her to the garden. She followed him, holding her dress off the damp pavement with one hand, trying to hold the hastily tied ribbon in her hair with the other.

The guests were already gathered, murmuring in a blur of colorful clothes. Mark was there. He stepped toward her, and

83

then she saw it—the tent, collapsed onto the buffet table and the folding chairs and the ground. It looked as if a parachute had fallen to the earth with alarming speed, from a great height, directly onto Jiselle's wedding. Her mother's arms were crossed, her jaw set. She was standing in the shadows beside Pastor Gillingham, who had changed so much since Jiselle last saw him that she recognized him only by the way his bushy eyebrows, white now, took up so much of the surface of his face. His left arm dangled limply at his side. He looked back at Jiselle and did not register any recognition at all.

"Jiselle?" Mark said quietly.

He took her arm, peering into her face. His dark hair glittered with silver in the dusk. He appraised her, taking in the ripped seam, the safety pins, her hair wild around her face, the ribbon slipping out of it. Looking from her to the sky, he said, "If we do this before it starts to thunderstorm, Jiselle, we don't need a tent."

She nodded weakly.

She looked around.

Her guests had circled the collapsed tent, and they were smiling apologetically at her. Sam, in his little blue suit, with his long strawberry-blond curls glistening in the hazy sun, had picked up an edge and was looking under it. Camilla, radiant in the yellow satin dress Jiselle had chosen for her, with her long elegant arms shining, brushed her blond hair out of her eyes and smiled. Sara, in a black lace dress, black tights, and black combat boots, stood with her arms crossed, staring at the ground, at her own shadow, it seemed.

"All is well, sweetheart," Mark said, cradling her elbow in his palm. "Nothing to worry about." He motioned with his arm, then, to his children, calling them over, and they gathered behind him—Sam bouncing over, Camilla gliding, Sara shuffling reluctantly behind them.

"Doesn't Jiselle look lovely?" Mark asked them.

"*Pretty!*" Camilla said. She was still smiling brightly, not a shred of sarcasm revealing itself on her face.

"Jesus," Sara said, breaking her vow. "You stink."

Somehow, the storm waited to explode overhead until after Pastor Gillingham had pronounced them man and wife. It was no longer dusk, but actual dark. Still, the sky, starless and clouded, reflected the lights of the town and glowed over them, and when Mark leaned down to "kiss the lovely bride," as Pastor Gillingham instructed him, Jiselle opened her eyes wide, realizing that *she* was the lovely bride.

The kiss went on and on. The guests laughed and clapped and stayed long enough under the darkening sky to raise a toast. They gathered around Mark and Jiselle. Even her mother looked peaceful, pleased, by then. She took Jiselle's hands in hers, leaned into her, and whispered, "I'm sorry, Jiselle. You're a lovely bride, and he's probably nothing like your father."

"Thank you," Jiselle said.

"And what I said about—"

"It's okay," Jiselle said.

The guests stepped gingerly around the collapsed tent and raised their glasses, just as the warm rain began to fall in fat drops on their heads and arms, and said in unison, as if it had been planned, "To the perfect couple!"

CHAPTER EIGHT

In Puerto Rico, their plane skidded to a stop in the midst of a driving storm. Thunder, sounding like far-off artillery, rolled in off the Caribbean in one unbroken wave of sound. They'd flown through the night, and Mark was still heavily asleep beside Jiselle. His small airline-issued pillow had fallen onto her lap.

On the flight from Newark to Ponce, there had been only a dozen other passengers, and these all seemed to be native Puerto Ricans, going home, speaking Spanish. The flight attendants never bothered to give their announcements in English, except for the standard warning that North American travelers who displayed suspected symptoms of the Phoenix flu could be turned away at their ports of entry without forewarning.

Mark and Jiselle were alone in first class, separated by twenty rows from the rest of the passengers.

When they deplaned, the flight attendants didn't smile.

❧

While Mark went to fetch the rental car, Jiselle waited inside the little terminal and watched the baggage carrousel lurch in circles, bearing its suitcases and bags—an eternal loop slipping through and under the fringed rubber curtain, returning from that mysterious beyond with a new bag every few minutes. She watched as bag after bag passed by but didn't see theirs. Finally, Mark came up beside her and said, "There's no car for us, and apparently there's not one fucking vehicle for rent on this entire fucking island."

❧

They decided to make the best of it.

It was their honeymoon!

What else could they do?

They laughed in the empty airport terminal. Mark made some calls to airline personnel, who said not to worry, they'd find the bags. The bags would be on the next flight. They'd be delivered to the resort.

After numerous cell phone calls, a driver was procured who was willing to drive them to their resort, and Mark and Jiselle sat together on a bench outside the airport waiting for him. The air was warm, sultry. It smelled of seawater and the rot of weeds in seawater, but it was pleasantly pungent—a kind of necessary and utterly natural decomposition taking place offshore under turquoise waves. Eventually a rusted white van that read NORTH AMERICAN

TRANSPORTER on the side, in stenciling that looked far newer than the van, pulled up.

"*Hola.*"

The driver was an elderly man. He bowed to them and said in a heavy Spanish accent what sounded to Jiselle like "Welcome to Purgatory" but must have been "Welcome to Puerto Rico." Then he held out a wet towel and said, "*Por favor,* you must wash your hands."

Mark looked at Jiselle, amused. They shrugged, smiled at each other, and passed the towel between them, wiping their hands. It was warm and sodden and smelled of bleach. When they tried to hand it back to the driver, he only shook his head at it, and nodded toward a trash can. Mark stepped over and dropped it in, and they followed the driver to his van.

The drive to the resort was quick. The freeway followed the seashore, which was lapped by azure water. The sky was radiant. The old man turned on the radio, and someone seemed to be reading poetry, in Spanish, in a monotone. The words washed around Jiselle with the breeze through the van windows. She put her head on Mark's shoulder, closed her eyes, and when she opened them again, she found that she was no longer resting on Mark's shoulder but had her temple pressed to the armrest between them, and Mark was outside of the parked van arguing with the driver, whose thin empty hand was held out.

"No one takes North Americans in a van now! No one but *me!*"

"It was a thirty-minute drive!" Mark said.

"Well, it would have been a longer walk, *señor*. Two. Hundred. Dollars."

Mark stared at the old man in disbelief, and then looked into his open hand. After a few slow seconds, he reached around for the wallet in his pocket, took it out, counted ten twenty-dollar bills, and placed them in the open hand, where they disappeared instantly into the old man's pocket.

❧

The Hotel Paradiso—which Jiselle and Mark would begin, over their seven-day honeymoon, to refer to jokingly as the Hotel Limbo—was nearly deserted except for another couple from the United States, also there on a honeymoon, and a family from New Jersey with three small children named Cato, Caitlin, and Calli.

Except for those three occupied suites, the rest of the rooms seemed to be empty. The whole resort had the feel of something that had been abandoned abruptly. There were empty lounge chairs placed carefully around the pool. The hot tub bubbled forsakenly.

Their luggage never arrived, so they bought bathing suits, shorts, and T-shirts in the dive shop on the beach.

The other honeymooning couple from the United States was younger than Mark and Jiselle and spent much of their time strolling along the beach. By the middle of the week they were both sunburned almost beyond recognition. Their faces were red and swollen—eyelids, lips, bloated with burn.

"I think they sold us phony sunblock in the dive shop,"

the young woman said. "We were both slathered in SPF forty-five, and *this* happened." She gestured to her face. "Joe can't even lie down," she said, nodding at her husband.

"It wouldn't surprise me," said the mother of the three Cs from New Jersey, sauntering over to their table. "They hate us here. Have you seen all the buttons and bumper stickers?" She was referring to the red circles with slashes through the outline of the United States—similar to the ones Jiselle had seen in Denmark months before and in every country outside the United States she'd been to since.

"Our kids wanted to snorkel," the father of the three Cs said, scratching his large, hairy stomach, "so we asked about it in the dive shop, and the old woman said, 'Well, you have killed our coral reef, so there can be no snorkeling.' And I said, 'Hey, *señora*, I'm not responsible for your coral reef . . .' I mean, you can't blame Americans for *everything*."

"But they do," the honeymooning wife said. "They blame us for the coral reefs, and the fish, and the hurricanes, and the flu. All of it. A plane crashes, and it's our fault. Some species of bird dies out, and we did it. You name it, they blame it on us."

There was a moment of silence.

A bird high in a palm tree made a screeching sound, but otherwise there was just the white noise of waves washing onto sand.

The mother of the three Cs agreed, nodding vehemently. She said, "You know, that witch at the front desk gave me the evil eye. She accused me of *stealing* my children."

"What?" all the others, including Mark and Jiselle, cried out at once.

90

"Yes," the woman said. "She said, 'Look, you stole them all from different countries. They aren't your children.' I said, 'We *adopted* our children from different countries— *poverty-stricken countries*. We didn't *steal* them.'"

"What did she say then?" Jiselle asked.

The mother shrugged.

"Well, I tell you," the honeymooning wife said, "that's unforgivable. And so is this." She pointed to her sunburned neck.

"And look at *this*," her husband said, holding out his arms. "If they did this to me, it's tantamount to attempted murder."

"That's true," his wife said. "This much sun can kill you. I tell you, I'm not coming back to Puerto Rico in this life-time."

Jiselle looked out at the ocean. The undulating turquoise, and cobalt, and indigo. A pelican was riding an air current just over the water, looking black and prehistoric. It plunged into a wave, emerged with something silver and wriggling in its beak.

Still, the days of Mark's and Jiselle's honeymoon were full of quiet luxuriating in each other's company. They strolled alone along the ocean. They swam alone in the pool. They sat alone in the swirling vortex of the hot tub. They rented a kayak and stroked their way in perfect coordination out to the dead coral reef, where they snorkeled side by side.

Just beneath the surface of the Caribbean, wearing that snorkel mask, Jiselle could hear only her own steady breath-

91

ing. The sunlight turned the pale blue water on the ocean floor to dancing, electric brainwaves. And the ghosts of the coral, like a white forest, were spread out beneath her for what seemed like miles and miles of serenity. The rictus of cacti, bleached to bone. Or the bare branches of winter trees, coated in snow—blameless, voiceless, motionless peace. She cast her own floating shadow down on it, as if she were a cloud passing over the shared dream of a million vanished people. Mark, beside her, fluttering in his fins, reached out and caressed her through the water. She was so happy she shed a tear or two, but the tears simply slipped out of her snorkel mask and joined the salty, abiding tears of the sea.

Part
Three

CHAPTER NINE

I t seems your son has head lice," the woman on the other end of the line said.

At first, no part of the sentence registered.

Head lice.

Your son.

But when Jiselle leaned down to look at the Caller ID, she saw that the woman was phoning from Marquette Elementary, where she'd dropped Sam off a few hours before.

"You need to come and get him, I'm afraid. School policy."

When Jiselle arrived at the school, Sam was sitting alone in a corner of the main office. He was scratching his head, pulling the fingers of both hands through the long strawberry-blond curls. The secretary looked up at Jiselle with what seemed to be skepticism or disapproval. "Are you the nanny?" she asked.

"No," Jiselle said. "I'm the stepmother."

The secretary raised her eyebrows.

"Here," she said, sliding a piece of paper over to Jiselle gingerly, as if she, too, might be infested. "You need to sign him out."

Jiselle signed her name *Jiselle McKnight*—and then remembered, scratched it out, and wrote *Dorn* over the last name. The secretary took the clipboard, looked at it, and then looked up at Jiselle again, as if trying to see through her, to read something on the other side of the room, something Jiselle was blocking her view of. She said then, "You know, no one *knows*, but *my* thinking is that this virus could just as easily be spread by lice as by anything else. If he were my son, I'd shave his head right away."

Jiselle nodded at the woman and mouthed the words *thank you*, although no sound came out of her mouth.

In the parking lot, Sam slid onto the passenger seat of Mark's Cherokee, slouched over the backpack in his lap, and said, "This sucks."

Jiselle nodded at him, started up the car. "Yeah," she said, and then, as an afterthought, quietly, "Sam, I think you're not supposed to say 'sucks.'" Wasn't that one of the admonitions she'd heard Mark give him?

Sam nodded with the infinite weariness of a very old child.

They drove to the drugstore. The school receptionist had given Jiselle what looked to be a Xerox of a Xerox of a Xerox of a handout on head lice, and a list of the products you could buy to rid your child of them. Sam held that list in his hand beside Jiselle as she drove.

It had rained hard the night before, and the weather—still like early autumn although it was the first week of November—had the feel of the tropics, although the leaves had fallen from most of the trees. Humid, bright air lingered over everything. Blue puddles of rain and oil dotted the drugstore lot. After she parked and picked up her purse, Sam said, "I don't want to go in."

"No one can *see* them, Sam," Jiselle said.

"Mrs. Hicks saw them."

"No, she didn't *see* them. She just—figured. Because you were itching."

"No," Sam said. "She *saw* them."

Jiselle looked at Sam's head.

In truth, she thought perhaps she *could* see something black, and maybe moving, in the silky part in the hair at the top of his head.

She said, "Okay. You can wait here if you want."

Inside the drugstore, Jiselle scanned the shelves for a few minutes for something with the word *lice* on it, until, finding nothing, she had to ask the girl behind the counter, who called across the store to the pharmacist, "Where's the head lice stuff?" She felt relieved that Sam had waited outside.

It took a minute or two, but the pharmacist came out from behind his glass cage and led Jiselle to the shelf for "pests and critters." To get to it, they had to walk past the cardboard displays of flu "cures." Life-size cut-outs of healthy-looking men and women holding bottles of Immune Master. Pink-cheeked children running across a green field overlaid with the words *Dr. Springwell's Secret!*

They made their way through the leftover Halloween costumes and candy and decorations displays, and a variety of gags, such as battery-operated plastic hands that scooted across the floor, tarantulas and bats on strings. That year had been like no Halloween Jiselle ever remembered, festive and commercial beyond anything she would have imagined for what had, at one time, been the simplest, briefest of holidays.

Mark had been home Halloween weekend. He'd donned a top hat, Jiselle had worn one of his trench coats, with black sunglasses, and they'd walked door to door with Sam, who had dressed as a soldier. Red vest over a white T-shirt. White pants and black boots. A tall red hat with a blue feather in it. He'd carried a pillowcase. By the end of the night, it weighed forty pounds.

Not only were the children out trick-or-treating that night, but adults were, too. Alone and in crowds, with their children and without, wearing elaborate costumes—beggars, prostitutes, Abe Lincolns, Grim Reapers—they were swigging from flasks, passing the flasks to strangers, exactly the kind of germ-sharing they were constantly warned against. But they were happy, friendly. Raucous with laughter and polite at the same time. Some of the houses in town had absurdly elaborate Halloween displays. Enormous inflatable cartoon animals on their front lawns. Hundreds of them. Pranksters had taken to stabbing them with screwdrivers and box cutters. All over town, deflated decorations littered lawns. Their owners, playing along with the pranks, erected tombstones over them. R.I.P. SCOOBY-DOO. HERE LIES SNOOPY, STABBED THROUGH THE HEART BY A HEARTLESS KILLER.

There were light displays, too, and someone had strung naked baby dolls from telephone poles all along one street. Someone else had built a scaffold in the elementary school parking lot and hung an effigy of the president wearing a witch's hat. One family had dangled hundreds of plastic bats from the birch tree in their front yard.

The regular codes of conduct were being pleasantly broken or ignored that night. People walked in the middle of the street, unwrapping candy and discarding the trash on sidewalks. Despite the public service announcements about not eating candy the origins of which you were uncertain, children and their parents were gobbling it down even as they collected it. Teenagers were handed cans of beer by homeowners. A few macabre revelers wore zombie masks and nurse uniforms in reference to the Phoenix flu. One tall, frightening boy sauntered alone, without bothering to collect candy, from door to door in a black cloak and a long-beaked bird mask. People smiled at him, and he nodded somberly back.

99

. . .

The pharmacist joked about the lice—"How big are these bugs? Can you fry 'em up for supper?"—but when Jiselle was apparently too flabbergasted to respond, he explained to her soberly what she needed to buy and what she needed to do, and she left the store with a small comb and a bottle of something called Nix, with a horrifying cartoon of a beast with eight legs on the label.

∽

"You okay?" she asked Sam when she got back into the Cherokee with her paper bag.

He was staring straight ahead. "Look," he said when she was behind the wheel, and he pointed to something in the parking lot.

She put on her sunglasses to see what it was through the glare on the windshield. She leaned forward, squinting.

There, in the middle of the nearly empty drugstore parking lot, was a small group of dark furred things. Moving but not scurrying. *Milling.*

Animals, clearly. But what kind?

She rubbed her eyes and leaned forward to see them better. There were eight or nine of them. Tails. And paws. Black.

"Listen," Sam said.

Jiselle held her breath and listened, and even through the rolled-up windows she could hear them making a quiet high-pitched sound, like childish chuckling, or singing. She turned to Sam and asked, whispering the question to him, "What *are* those?"

"Rats," he said.

"Oh my God," Jiselle said, putting a hand to her mouth and seeing them, then, clearly. Their naked tails. Their sharp pink ears. Her heart sped up. She started up the engine of the SUV, and the rats, seeming to have heard it, turned their horrible faces in its direction but didn't run off. They simply stared at Jiselle and Sam in the SUV. As she drove out of the parking lot, she was careful to make a wide loop around the rats, which did not leave their tight circle but seemed, instead, to stand their ground even more stubbornly, watching them drive away.

❧

Back at home, Jiselle read the directions on the bottle of Nix, while Sam ate the grilled cheese sandwich she'd made for him. It was the one thing she'd mastered in the kitchen since moving into Mark's house. The *only* thing. She'd gone so long in life without learning how to cook, it seemed that she had lost the capacity to learn. She'd burned omelets and served up pink-centered chicken breasts a few times before the girls took to cooking for themselves, Lean Cuisines and pot pies.

("None of the other nannies could cook, either," Sam said to her once, and then stammered an apology when he saw the look on her face.)

The few dinners she'd made that had actually succeeded—lasagna, seafood manicotti, chicken and dumplings, an enchilada casserole—had displeased the girls as much as the ruined ones. Too spicy. Or not spicy enough. Sara would say she was a vegetarian some days. Camilla would claim to have allergies she'd failed to mention until a certain meal was served. And although Sam was always willing to eat anything she made, all he really wanted was grilled cheese, and that, at least, Jiselle had finally figured out how to make exactly as he liked it.

Browned but only slightly. The cheese soft and warm but not gooey in the center.

She'd put the sandwich in front of him on his favorite plate—pale blue with a faded picture of Scooby-Doo in the center—and poured him a glass of milk. She unscrewed the top of the bottle of Nix and sniffed it, and realized she must have made a face when Sam said, "Is it super bad?"

"Well," Jiselle said softly, "it's not great."

In truth, it smelled like tar and also formaldehyde.

"We'll do this a little later, okay?" she offered.

"Okay," Sam said, tearing parts of his sandwich off before eating them. Jiselle put the bottle of Nix on the table and folded her hands. Sam was going to hate this. This boy who squirmed away from his father when he simply tried to wipe some ketchup off his face—who, once, when Jiselle had suggested cleaning out his ears with a Q-tip, had looked at her with wide, horrified eyes and said, "Are you *kidding*?"

She watched him eat. She tried not to stare at his hair— all those beautiful curls, and what might be crawling among them—but she leaned a little to the left, considering the shape of his skull. He had beautiful cheekbones. A pleasing jaw and brow. She said, "Have you ever considered having your head shaved?"

Sam looked up brightly from his Scooby-Doo plate. "Wow," he said. "You mean, like a total skinhead?" Sam knew about skinheads. They'd been the latest bad news. Burning down Chinese-owned businesses. Burning crosses on the lawns of Jews, African Americans, Muslims—anyone they chose to blame at the moment for the Phoenix flu.

"Well, yeah," Jiselle said. "I guess. Like a skinhead—but *nice*."

"That would be *so cool*," Sam said, holding a piece of his grilled cheese aloft. His eyes were wide. In them, Jiselle could read the clock on the microwave behind them blinking 11:11, 11:11, 11:11.

103

❧

Jiselle told herself she was not shaving Sam's head because of the advice of the hysterical secretary at his school, but what could it hurt?

It was just hair. It would grow back.

So, after lunch, she stood behind him at the kitchen sink. First, she used scissors to cut the strawberry-blond curls off his head—soft, beautiful handfuls—and then she shook the satiny strands off her fingers into the trash can. They clung to her arms, her shirt, her jeans, and the static electricity actually crackled when she brushed them off in little jumping sparks. She wet what was left of his hair by leaning him forward over the sink, filling her hands with lukewarm water, splashing it over his hair, and then she patted shaving cream onto his head. Finally, she used Mark's razor to carefully smooth the last of it from his scalp, and afterward they both went into the bathroom and stood in front of the mirror so Sam could see.

The skin on Sam's scalp was pale, but it looked healthy—and without hair, it was possible to really see how handsome his features were. The nose was Mark's, but the eyes were deep set and olive-brown. At his temples were subtle and delicate blue veins just under the surface. The head was a beautiful shape, and the back of his skull felt solid and satisfying in her palm. Touching it—the weird, beautiful, wonderful nakedness of it—Jiselle could imagine what it had been like for Mark, and for Joy, to bring him into the world for the first time, the way the skin of a newborn might really feel like the organ that skin is: breathing, alert, warm and cool at the same time. She had the impulse to kiss his head, but she had never actually kissed Sam before, except for the kind of air-blown kiss to the cheek her mother had always given her, and she had no idea how he'd react, so she settled for smoothing her fingertips along the beautiful ridge behind his ear, tickling him a little. He laughed. He moved his head around so he could inspect himself from both sides in the mirror, and asked, "How do I look?"

"You look perfect," Jiselle said.

Because of head lice and the public school's policy on them, Sam and Jiselle had the whole day free, and it wasn't even noon.

A hike? Monopoly? A trip to town to the hobby shop?

Since the children had started school in September, Jiselle had mostly spent her afternoons alone in the house, moving through its rooms, feeling baffled as to how to begin to clean them up.

The dust she'd dispersed a few days before would have either settled again or redistributed itself with maddening genius. Sam's plastic action figures would be everywhere. The girls' shoes, jewelry, magazines were scattered across every flat surface, and Jiselle knew that if she picked those up and moved them there would be shrieking later—*Where the hell's my bandana? What did you do with my magazine?*

105

And the *floors*.

The floors seemed magnetized—eternally capturing or *creating* long clouds of lint and hair held together with dust, which were spirited into corners when Jiselle turned her back. She would have just finished with the broom, turned around, and there those clouds would have gathered again.

On the phone from upstate New York, Annette said, "Get a fucking housekeeper. For God's sake. You're not his *maid*, Jiselle."

But how, Jiselle thought, could she justify her days to herself or to anyone else if she had a housekeeper, if someone else were coming in to do the few things she had to do?

And what would *she* do while the housekeeper did these things? And what would she do with the time left over?

Sometimes the vacuum cleaner sounded like the dual engines of a jet starting up. Or Jiselle would hear, overhead, an actual jet—a distant needle in the sky—and she'd imagine her past still taking place up there. The metal cart. The drawer of ice. The faces looking up at her. The way turbulence or exhaustion, or simply being thirty-five thousand feet in the air, could turn even the most self-satisfied businessmen and women into needy children.

They were scared.

They did not have wings. They did not know how to fly. They were incredibly grateful for the calm smile, the foil packet of pretzels.

But of course there had been the other sort of passenger. Drunk on miniature bottles of Jack Daniel's. Punching their flight attendant buttons for more. There had been the woman who'd said to Jiselle once, when she'd had to rouse her from a drooling sleep to put her tray table back up for landing, "I hope you *burn in hell*." She didn't miss that.

But, since quitting, the *days* could last so long. Sometimes Jiselle would sit down at the kitchen table and will the phone to ring. *Call me, Mark.* When it did ring, she'd jump, heart racing, but it usually wasn't Mark. Once or twice, it was Brad Schmidt calling from next door, asking if Jiselle had heard this or that bad piece of news on the radio. Although their houses were separated by a long, tall hedge, Brad Schmidt seemed able to see through it, to know when Jiselle was sitting by the phone.

No, she would not have heard the news. She didn't listen to the news. Why would she? Whales washing up on beaches. Chickens being burned alive, and some man who

106

called himself Henry Knighton killing prostitutes in Seattle to "cleanse the earth."

The news had to *happen* to her before she knew about it—and even then she wasn't always sure what it was, like the afternoon when, while folding laundry in the bedroom, she heard a crash in the kitchen.

No one was home. Mark was flying; the children were at school. Jiselle stepped cautiously out of the bedroom and went to the kitchen, where she found that the cupboards had all swung open. A broken dish lay on the ceramic tiles. A coffee cup had rolled off the counter and into the sink. She stood with her hand to her chest for what must have been several minutes, feeling her heart beat hard, trying to get used to this new order of things, this unfamiliarity, the idea that the kitchen cupboards could open on their own and spill their contents. Then she heard Brad Schmidt shout, "Hey!" from the other side of his hedge, and she hurried to the kitchen window and looked out to see him standing in the side yard, his arms parting the branches, looking through them. "You know what that was, Mrs. Dorn?"

"No," Jiselle called back, opening the window to hear his answer.

"*That* was an earthquake!"

Indeed, a rare Midwestern earthquake had shaken the whole region. Gently but surely, it had registered itself with a few framed photographs falling off walls, some cracks in a freeway overpass, that dish Jiselle had to pick up off the kitchen floor, and the cup out of the sink. Not terribly damaging, just surprising.

"This is just the beginning," Brad Schmidt said to her

later at the end of their driveways. "Tip of the iceberg. Tornadoes. Tsunamis. Hold your hat on. Ever read about the Black Death? It was all there. Before the plague did its worst work—the floods, the winds, the earthquakes. You wait." There was no mistaking the tone in his voice for anything but excitement.

⤞⤝

After considering his options for his free afternoon, Sam decided on a hike into the ravine behind the house.

He loved a hike. Loved the ravine. He and Jiselle had already taken a few hikes together since she'd moved in. There was a good trail, and Sam knew every inch of the ravine and liked to dispense his knowledge. Jiselle was the ingénue. Everything surprised her. Rabbits surprised her. *Ferns* surprised her. The occasional deer crashing away through the trees. Raccoons.

That afternoon, the pine trees pulsed with light under a blank white sky. Following the path into the ravine, Jiselle had the sense of entering a vast emptiness. Something abandoned. Many species of birds had migrated south. Animals were hibernating. The only sound was the watery, distant call of a pigeon. There was not a plane in the sky, as far as Jiselle could see. Not even a contrail fraying above them.

Sam walked ahead of her on the path. She'd made him wear one of his father's fishing caps—a smashed khaki thing that was too big for him—because the exposed flesh on his freshly shaved head looked so pale. Now, trudging ahead of her in the cap, he looked comical, top-heavy, like some car-

108

toon character, with his bony shoulders, his long gait, that hat.

She was looking from Sam's back to the treetops, thinking what a perfect day it was (warm but not hot, the whole afternoon ahead of them) when *it* ran across the path only a few inches in front of her.

A warm-blooded darkness. A sneaky, wild, black furred thing, slipping between herself and Sam.

If she hadn't frozen instinctively, Jiselle would have tripped over it. But after freezing, she jumped backward, screamed, and Sam turned just in time to see the rat scurry off, and Jiselle's boot (which was all wrong for hiking, she realized at that moment, the heel of it too smooth and high) and the path slide out from under her. And suddenly she was slipping backward into the muck, arms windmilling ridiculously around her as she tried to regain her balance, not regaining it, propelling her instead farther and farther off the path until she finally fell with a thud, and then was simply sitting in the muck, on her butt, the dampness seeping in. She looked up.

The expression on Sam's face was bright with shock. His eyes were wide, his mouth an exaggerated zero.

"Ji-*selle*?"

They stared at each other for a few seconds before they both started to laugh, laughing until they were gasping with it. Sam, holding his stomach, doubled over, finally managing to ask, "Are you okay?"

"Well," Jiselle said, wiping the tears from her eyes, "my *pride* is a little wounded."

She tried to push herself up, but her hands slid out from

under her, and then, when she slid through the muck again, she just gave up and lay back laughing. What difference did it make now? She was covered by then with the stuff.

Sam reached down to offer her a hand, and Jiselle said, taking it, "This sucks," as Sam pulled her to her feet, and her body emerging from the muck made a genuine sucking sound, and they started to laugh so hard again that Sam lost his grip on her hand, and she was lying on her back in the muck again.

∽∾

"What were you thinking?"

She looked up. She hadn't heard Mark pull in the driveway, although she'd known he was on his way home. She and Sam were sitting beside each other on the couch, reading from the Hans Christian Andersen collection, "The Happy Family," in which a family of naive snails foolishly envy their cousins, the escargots. Mark stood in the center of the family room holding his bag in his hand as if he might not bother to set it down.

Jiselle tried to keep her voice from trembling as she said, "He had head lice, Mark."

She had already told Mark this news over the phone. Camilla had gotten home from school, seen Sam's shaved head, and gasped, "Does *Dad* know about this?" She let her mouth hang open, staring at her brother, and then looked at Jiselle.

Jiselle had flushed. Hot. Sweaty. Except for the most casual criticism ("Our mother used to squeeze the orange juice herself"), Camilla had never said anything before to Jiselle's face that wasn't full of sugary approval—*Great! Thank you! How cool!*—and Jiselle felt now, seeing her look of deep disapproval, that something shameful was being exposed. Dirty underwear, smelly feet. That shameful thing was, she realized, her own willful naiveté. Jiselle had known (how could she not?) that the girl hated her, had overheard what she had to say to her sister from behind the curtains of their rooms, but she had let herself pretend it was something it wasn't, anyway, and that determined ignorance had made her even more detestable, she realized now as Camilla walked swiftly out of the room.

Sara had simply come in, looked at Sam, and turned around. Her shoulders, Jiselle thought, seemed to be shaking. With laughter?

A few minutes later Jiselle heard Camilla whispering from her bedroom on her cell phone, "She just totally shaved Sam's head, Dad. She's gone *crazy.*"

A few minutes after that, Mark called Jiselle on the house telephone, pretending he didn't know. He started by telling Jiselle that he was in an airport lounge in Newfoundland. That there was so much wind that a corporate jet had been tipped over on the runway. He asked her how she was, how the kids were, how the weather was, and finally she couldn't stand it anymore and just blurted out, "I shaved Sam's head because he had head lice."

There was a sigh, and then a clearing of the throat, and then, "You're kidding, right? Jiselle? Tell me you're kidding?"

"No," Jiselle said, and even to herself, it sounded like pleading. "He would have hated the shampoo."

She did not, and never would, tell Mark about the secretary, and what she'd said. *If he were my son, I'd shave his head.* She knew what Mark would say about that—about superstition, about hysteria, about the flu.

He said, sounding weary, "I guess, Jiselle, we'll have to discuss this when I get home."

Now, still holding his black leather bag, Mark walked over to Sam, took his son's chin in his palm, moved his head around, inspecting, and then he looked over at Jiselle, and said, "There are ways to get rid of head lice without shaving the kid's head, Jiselle. Jesus Christ." He shook his own head. "Surely," he said, "you must have thought . . ." He trailed off.

"Thought what?" Jiselle asked, but no sooner had the words come out of her mouth than she realized, suddenly, clearly, *what*.

Joy.

Her curls.

Those cascades of strawberry-blond ringlets ribboned with satin on her wedding day. What that hair must have looked like beside Mark, stretching from her pillow to his in the mornings. The smell of it after she'd washed it. Rain. There was a rain barrel in the backyard, and Camilla had pointed it out one day and said, "Our mother used to wash her hair with rainwater."

Maybe she used to let the girls brush it. Like handmaidens. In the evenings. Sitting at the little vanity table. The sparks flying off the brush into the air. Maybe Mark used to gather it in his hands and kiss it. Maybe Sam, still a baby, would have taken it in his cereal-sticky fists and shoved it into his mouth.

Oh my God, Jiselle thought, full of understanding:

Sam's hair had belonged to Joy.

She could feel her lips quivering. She couldn't speak.

Mark exhaled.

"Look," he said, seeing the expression on her face. "It's okay. It's okay, Jiselle. You just . . . didn't think. What's done is done. It's just hair. It'll grow back." He shrugged, but then he turned away. It was the first time he'd ever come home without taking her in his arms.

"*Daddy!*" Camilla called then from her bedroom, dancing out from under the cloth in the doorway. She threw her arms around her father. He lifted her up off her feet, swung her around. "How's my princess?" he asked.

Jiselle watched them from the couch. The light from the sliding glass doors shone on Camilla's golden hair, and a kind of pure white light flashed from it. Her cheeks were flushed. The little pearl studs in her ears looked damp, iridescent, freshly plucked from the sea.

"It was my idea!" Sam shouted then, loudly.

Jiselle looked down at him, startled, and Sam pressed his eyebrows together, elbowed her sharply.

Mark turned to look at him, and then at Jiselle. How was it that the tears sprang up so instantly, so unbidden, into her eyes, as if they'd been there all along, waiting?

"Sweetheart," Mark said to Jiselle. "I'm sorry. I know you only did what you thought was best."

Camilla stepped away, disappeared back into her room, as Mark came over to Jiselle on the couch and kissed the top of her head, as if she were one of the children. Still one of his children, if not his favorite.

"But," he said softly, "it *was* a bit thoughtless."

Over his shoulder, Jiselle saw Sara, who'd been absent for the whole homecoming scene between Camilla and Mark, standing in the shadows of the hallway, looking back at Jiselle, a half-smile on her face.

CHAPTER TEN

Jiselle suggested to Mark that, before the holiday season started, maybe they should all go down to Florida so that she could meet his mother.

"Jesus," he'd said. He was lying on the couch reading a magazine called *Aviation Today*. He put the magazine down, open on his chest, and said, "Why would you want to do that?"

"Because she's your mother?" Jiselle offered.

Sara in her bedroom had overheard them and shouted out, "She's *my grandmother*, and *I've* never met her."

Jiselle, blinking, looked down at Mark on the couch. He shrugged and said, "She's a drunk, Jiselle. Completely out of her mind. She lives in a trailer with ten cats and a pet alligator. I would never subject you or my children to her."

He was wearing a black T-shirt. His uniform was laid out on the bed. He was leaving for the West Coast in five hours.

"So—"

Jiselle sank into the plaid chair across from him, about to say it—*So, the children did* not *have a grandmother who could have taken care of them?*—when Mark stood. He said, "As soon as we have a chance, I'll take you somewhere wonderful, sweetheart," and knelt down and held her face like a precious object in his hands.

For the three days he was gone, Jiselle rehearsed in her mind what she would say when he returned:

So, there never was a grandmother?

So, you always knew you wanted me to take care of the children?

So, would you have married me if there had been no children?

But Mark was delayed for twenty-four hours, his plane grounded at the gate at LAX. One of the ticket-holding passengers, it seemed, was exhibiting symptoms of the Phoenix flu, according to an airline employee at the kiosk where he'd checked in—coughing, broken blood vessels on his cheeks, a watery-bloody discharge from the eyes.

But the passenger was a lawyer, traveling with his wife, who was also a lawyer. He said he had pinkeye, a severe case, and that without evidence to the contrary it was illegal, discriminatory, to refuse to let him on the plane.

Mark called Jiselle off and on from the airline lounge during the first six hours of the stand-off, but then his cell phone died. The whole thing went on for hours before the security guards ushered the passenger out of the airport and into a waiting police van and drove him away. By then, the flight crew had been dismissed, and Mark called her from the hotel. "I miss you, sweetheart," he said. "All I want is to hold you in my arms tonight. To have to wait until tomorrow seems like torture."

By the time he finally got home again and stepped through the door in the dark, a shadow of beard on his jaw, a bouquet of roses in one hand and his leather satchel in the other, Jiselle had forgotten what she'd planned to say about his mother, or why, and in the morning he had to leave again.

~∽⊘∼

"Well, things will get better," Annette said over the phone when Jiselle told her about the haircut and also about Sara's diary.

117

> She is going to go the way of all the other bitches
> he's brought home—RUNNING OUT OF HERE SOB-
> BING INTO HER LITTLE FUCKING HANKIE.

"Don't read the diary if you don't want to know what she thinks of you," Annette went on. "Or, I guess you could say, would you really not know what she thinks of you if you quit reading the diary?"

"She leaves it out," Jiselle said, "like I'm *supposed* to read it. She leaves it *open*."

In fact, the day after their bedroom door was installed, Sara had left the diary on Mark's and Jiselle's *bed*.

She thinks she can ruin everything. She thinks she can erase my mother. She can't!!!!

"Mark? Can we install a door?" Jiselle had asked him in a whisper one night after they made love in such total silence and darkness that Jiselle had felt briefly bodiless, and disoriented, under him.

"Well." Mark hesitated at first, and then said, "Sure. I guess."

Jiselle had suspected that the girls might not like it, but she'd had no idea how angry it would make them until they came home and stood in front of it—Camilla with a hand covering her mouth, and Sara with her fists balled at her waist. "Is this so you guys can make noises while you *fuck*?" she'd shouted at the door.

"Well," Mark had said later to Jiselle. "It'll take them a while to get used to it. They liked the curtains. Their mother put those up."

Why? Jiselle had wondered. Admittedly, she, too, had liked the curtains when she'd first seen them. Those flimsy pieces of silk draped in the doorways had seemed like a sweet, strange, new kind of privacy—a privacy made out of fabric woven in Asia, some land where the air hung too heavy, was too precious to restrain with anything as cumbersome as a door.

But she soon realized that you could not be an American newlywed in a small house full of children without a bedroom door.

But neither could you be an adolescent girl making the

kind of final, smashing accusation that the slamming of a door accomplished until you actually had one. Even if it was not the door to your own bedroom.

"Nothing's perfect," Annette said, and then laughed.

The holiday season began with a blizzard the day before Thanksgiving—but Mark, stranded in Minneapolis, rented a car and was home before Jiselle had put the turkey on the table.

Her first turkey. Ever. She'd spent the whole morning peeking in at it. Covered in its crinkled tinfoil, it made sizzling sounds, but it was deathly pale, and every time she saw it again through the glass in the oven door, she felt her heart sink—literally felt it *sink*, as if her torso were filled with water and her heart were a sodden sponge. Sinking. What was in that oven did not look like the turkey of her fantasies, which would have been browning, plumping with juices, somehow generating its own golden gravy in the roaster.

This turkey looked, instead, like a very large, very dead, bird. It had cost eighty-seven dollars because of the turkey shortage. So many had been killed (senselessly, it was said, because they were not carriers of *Yersinia pestis*, but killed nonetheless), and no one had anticipated that Americans would stick so stubbornly to their traditions, that millions more turkeys would be demanded than would be available, and that the price of a turkey, when one could be found, would be whatever a person was willing to pay.

119

Jiselle's mother had gone to visit a sister in Albuquerque for the holiday. She'd done it, Jiselle knew, to avoid the new arrangements. It was the first Thanksgiving since her parents' divorce that she and her mother had not gone to Duke's Palace Inn together, except for one time when Jiselle had been flying. But when Jiselle invited her to the house for Thanksgiving dinner, her mother was utterly silent for several long seconds on the other end of the phone before she said, "No. Thank you. I'm going to New Mexico."

Right beside her relief, Jiselle had felt a surge of panic. She had, she realized, no idea how to make a Thanksgiving dinner, and although her mother hadn't made one herself in decades, surely she knew more about it than Jiselle.

120   She did her best. She read an article in a magazine suggesting she put sage and walnuts in the dressing. So she did. She boiled cranberries for cranberry sauce according to the directions on the plastic package of cranberries, and marveled at the way the skins of the berries split and spilled their deep burgundy syrup into the saucepan. Who, she wondered, had first thought to do that? They were such tough little berries, and so sour. Who would have guessed that sugar and boiling would change them so completely? Jiselle tried to picture the inventor of cranberry sauce—some woman not unlike Jiselle but wearing a pilgrim's black dress and white apron, hair pulled back in a bun, peering into a pot with grim determination.

Jiselle was just pulling the turkey out of the oven when Mark stepped in the front door. His hair and the shoulders of his black leather pilot's jacket were dusted with snowflakes, and he was holding a bouquet of orange tiger lilies.

"Happy Thanksgiving!" he said.

He didn't even take the jacket off before standing at the head of the table and carving the turkey, which was somehow miraculously browned on the outside, steamily moist as he sliced into it. Outside, the snow continued to fall, and except that Sara was wearing black lipstick and a ripped T-shirt, and Camilla had said she wasn't hungry and so was lying on the couch in the other room watching MTV, they were, Jiselle thought, a kind of Norman Rockwell painting—a healthy American family gathered around the Thanksgiving table.

121

The Christmas season came fast on the heels of Thanksgiving, faster than Jiselle ever remembered it coming. For weeks the newscasters had been announcing that there had never been such a lavish holiday season. Money was being thrown to the wind, credit cards maxed out. Shelves were being emptied. Some said the cause was a renewed confidence in the economy. Others said it was fear of a coming depression, or a fatalism brought on by the flu, or the anticipation of the end of the war or the start of a new one. One historian Jiselle heard interviewed on NPR said, in a voice so low it sounded like the source of gravity itself, that a return to traditions often preceded the complete collapse of a culture.

Jiselle had driven into St. Sophia one Saturday afternoon. It was a week until Christmas, and she needed to mail something to her mother, because her mother again had made other plans. This time she was going to visit an old high school friend in Maine. Jiselle decided to buy her a bracelet at the local jewelry store and FedEx it to her.

She parked Mark's Cherokee outside the store, and was surprised to see how many shoppers were strolling through St. Sophia's tiny downtown. They wore expensive parkas and sunglasses and carried shopping bags. A fluffy snow, looking like feathers, was falling from a few marble-gray clouds in a blue sky. The air was so still that the flakes seemed to hang, weightless with patience, before drifting down in long pendulum arcs through the air, resting on the branches of the trees and the ground, sometimes surging upward again before settling. She looked up at the sky, where she thought she could see, up near the clouds, a few white balloons traveling overhead. But they were too far away to be sure. She saw them so often now that she might have been imagining them.

Jiselle had to wind her way carefully down the sidewalk crowded with shoppers. Surely they were tourists from Chicago (visitors who wanted to be part of an old-fashioned small-town Christmas scene for a few hours on a Saturday) because there were more people downtown today than there were *houses* in St. Sophia.

And the town did look like the quaintest of villages in the snow that afternoon. Garlands hung from the brick façades of the stores. Tinsel and lights were strung in the trees, swaying between the street signs. When Jiselle reached the jewelry store, she was surprised to find a real reindeer tied by a red velvet ribbon to a lamppost outside. Beside the reindeer stood an old-fashioned Santa—thin, wearing a maroon robe and hood—with an antique sleigh. Children had crowded around, petting the reindeer, which raised and lowered its head with such dignity it seemed as if it might address the crowd: *I'm honored to be here with you today.* . . . A garland of silver beads and cranberries was strung over its antlers and draped down its shaggy flanks, and a red velvet blanket covered its back.

Jiselle stopped, too, and gazed at the strange sight. The reindeer's antlers looked so heavy she wondered how he held his head aloft. She imagined what it might be like to feel the first stirring of those bones growing out of your skull—the ache, the itching, the excitement. And this St. Nicholas, Jiselle could tell, had a real beard—long, gray, and authentic. His eyes were startlingly blue. He looked Old World and serious, nothing like the mall Santa Clauses of Jiselle's childhood, who'd been the kind of Santas you might glimpse later in their red felt costumes smoking cigarettes in the parking lot.

123

No, it seemed impossible to her that they'd ever been fooled by those, but they had. Somehow they'd managed to believe that each one of those costumed men was Santa despite the impossibility—the identical red felt and plastic and the tin buckles of their belts. As children, they'd whispered their secrets to him. They were sure he'd grant their wishes, even when he didn't.

The jewelry store was crowded. Customers in their parkas elbowed one another politely out of the way. A teenage girl went from glass case to glass case with a bottle of Windex and a paper towel wiping off fingerprints. Under the glass counters, row upon row of diamond rings flickered with their tiny, cold fires. Strand after strand of gold was laid out on a black velvet tray. Loose gems were scattered around in the display case—rubies and emeralds and sapphires. Some perfect pearls glowed in a half-shell.

Jiselle picked out a slim, bright silver bracelet for her mother. She held it against the underside of her own wrist to look at it. It was like a silver vein traced against the skin there. A man and his wife looked at it, too, waiting, it seemed, for Jiselle to put it down.

"Are you buying that?" the woman asked impatiently. "If you're not buying that, I'd like it."

124   Jiselle ignored them, signaled the woman at the cash register, and said, "I'll take this one," holding it up. The couple huffed and walked over to another display case.

The saleswoman wrapped the bracelet for Jiselle in pale purple tissue paper, tying it with a scarlet ribbon. By the time Jiselle was back on Main Street, outside Starbucks, St. Nicholas and his gathering of children were gone. A dwarf in a green velvet elf costume, bells jingling on his cap, was sweeping the reindeer's droppings into a paper bag.

❧

Christmas morning, Sam was up first. At daybreak, he came to Mark's and Jiselle's door and knocked until they got out of bed. "Presents!" he shouted. "Now!" When he was certain that Jiselle and Mark were up, he went into his sisters' rooms, pulling them by their arms, groaning, yawning, into the living room.

While Jiselle went to the kitchen and made coffee, Mark started a fire in the fireplace, and the smell of the Christmas tree mixed with the coffee and the sulfur smells of the fire, which roared up quickly—a few black ashy stars from the newspaper drifting among the dancing flames.

Sam was wearing his thermal underwear. Camilla, a long white gown with lace at the sleeves. Mark had his black velvet robe pulled around him, socks on with his plaid slippers.

Sara wore a black slip. Dime-store satin. She perched herself on the arm of the couch, and from where Jiselle sat on the floor, she could see that Sara was again wearing that pair of panties trimmed in black lace that Jiselle had bought for herself in Paris.

"I have to warn you," Mark had said after Thanksgiving. "Christmas. It was Joy's favorite holiday. She was very *elaborate* about Christmas. As you can imagine, for the children, well, it can be a difficult day. For the girls, at least. Sam was so young. I'm sure he doesn't even remember those years, but . . ."

Jiselle didn't speak as he shared this information with her, but later she tried to get more details. What had Joy done for Christmas? How had she decorated? What did she cook? But Mark dismissed the questions, saying, "Joy's been gone a long time by now, Jiselle. It would be worse if you tried to . . ."

He didn't have to say it: *Be Joy*. Behind him Jiselle could hear the kitchen clock ticking like a little hidden bomb.

But if the children were thinking of their mother on Christmas Eve, they didn't show it. Bobby Temple came over and watched TV with Camilla, and Sara listened to her iPod, sprawled on the family room rug. Sam helped Jiselle frost cookies, and they ate together what was left of the frosting, sitting at the kitchen table with spoons and bowls until Jiselle's teeth ached with the sugar and Sam's face and hands were sticky with it. Mark arrived, like Santa Claus, in the middle of the night. He slipped into bed beside Jiselle, smelling of snow and sky. She fell back to sleep in his arms, and then Sam was pounding on the door, and it was Christmas morning, and they were unwrapping presents.

For Jiselle, there was a clay mug from Sam with her initials drawn into it. It had been a class art project. It was a beautiful, solid, turquoise mug, the kind of thing you might find in a museum. Circa 800 BCE. Jiselle held it up for everyone else to see and said, "I love this, Sam!"

She did.

From Camilla, a paperweight with a daisy captured—floating, immortalized—at the center of the heavy globe. As Jiselle looked at it, Camilla said, "You said they were your favorite flower," smiling.

Jiselle didn't remember saying that daisies were her favorite—truly, roses were—but she was touched. "Thank you," she said, "so much," holding the satisfying weight of it in her palm.

From Mark she received a pair of jade earrings from China—exquisite, breathtaking, something an empress might wear, and she said, "Oh my," holding them up to her earlobes. "Oh. Mark."

"Do you like them?"

"Of course!"

And then there were the gifts for the children.

Mark had left the buying of their presents to Jiselle. ("Oh, you know what kids like better than I do," he'd said. "It'll be easier for you. I'll just pick up a few things at the airport if you don't mind doing the rest.")

Sam had been easy. He'd happily made a very specific list for Jiselle, all the details, down to the manufacturer of the plastic toys he longed for. On Christmas morning, he ripped the boxes open, exclaiming over each one, shouting out the names, the model numbers.

The girls, however, had not been easy.

Jiselle had shopped for them for weeks, and every time she picked up a sweater, a book, a board game, she imagined the look of exasperation on Sara's face, or the cool acceptance on Camilla's. In the end, she decided to shop by material. Cashmere. Linen. Pure silk. How, she'd hoped, could anything made of the right material be scorned?

But the girls' reactions to Jiselle's presents were perfunctory. "Thanks," they said, and then exclaimed brightly over the perfume their father had picked up for them at the Duty Free shop the day before. But that little injustice, Jiselle felt, was to be expected. She herself remembered the thrill of the small afterthoughts her father would sometimes pick up a few days before a holiday—the way the exotic wrapping paper, no doubt chosen for him by a woman at the store, outshone her mother's dependable efforts. She could still smell the sweet watery little-girl's perfume he'd bought for her the Christmas she was sixteen, and the way the soft bristles of the vanity brush had felt in her long hair when she pulled them through it, and the weightless feel of the matching gilt-handled mirror in her hand—although she remembered, too, that the gold of it had flecked off on her hands within a few weeks. Still, it had been her favorite gift, and it did not matter that her mother had given her a stereo, the best one at the store.

"This is for you," Sara said after everything else had been opened. She handed Jiselle a small box.

It was the size of a ring box or a box for a pendant. Beautifully wrapped, in silver. A large white bow. A little glittery tag hanging from it. *For: Mommy. From: Sara.*

"What is it?" Mark asked. He was sitting on the couch pulling up the wool socks Camilla had knitted for him. Jiselle was still on the floor, her flannel nightgown spread out around her.

The tape along the wrapping seams was gummy. She had to shake it off her thumb and forefinger. She took off the white ribbon, peeled away the silver paper, and opened the box.

Sam leaned over to look. He said, "Huh?"

"Well?" Mark asked, looking up from his socks. "What is it?"

Sara started to laugh then. A high, cackling laugh at first, and then a deep wild hiccuping. She slid off the arm of the sofa and onto the floor, holding her stomach with one hand, covering her face with the other, laughing and gasping as

Mark and Camilla watched. Gently, Camilla kicked her sister with the toe of her slipper and said, "So what *is* it, idiot?"

Jiselle stood up fast, snapped the lid of the box shut. She tried to swallow, but her mouth had gone so dry she had nothing to force down her throat.

"What?" Mark asked, and then looked down at Sara, writhing on the floor. She was still laughing, but it was silent laughter now. Her mouth was open. Jiselle could see her tonsils. The wet red entrance to a cave. "What's up here, Jiselle?" Mark asked, but Jiselle still could not speak and could not take her eyes off Sara.

"*Sam?*" Mark asked then. "What's going on here, Sam? What was in the box?"

Sam shrugged. He cleared his throat. He said, "It looked like a big booger to me."

129

Jiselle walked quickly out of the room then, took the box to the kitchen, and tossed it into the trash under the sink. She stood, holding tightly to the edge of the sink for a minute or two, and then she started to run water into it, rinsing the dishes they'd left there the night before. A high ringing started in her ears, as if she were at the end of a long metal tunnel and someone outside of it was pounding on it with a metal spoon.

"Honey?" Mark said, coming up behind her. "Honey?" he said again, burrowing his face in her hair. "Oh, Jiselle. Jiselle. I'm sorry."

Jiselle said nothing. She continued to rinse the dishes. After a few seconds, she had to break free of his embrace to put a rinsed dish—Sam's Scooby-Doo plate—into the dishwasher.

"Sweetheart," Mark said into her hair, and then into her neck. "Sweetheart, you know Sara's just a mixed-up kid. She'll be so ashamed of herself in a few days. But this is a tough time for her. Having a stepmother. Christmas. All the adjustments."

Jiselle continued to rinse dishes.

Camilla's ice-cream bowl. Sara's orange juice glass. Then she let a few pieces of silverware slip out of her hand, clatter into the sink, and let her hands rest at her sides. She drew a trembling breath. She opened her mouth but closed it again. She cleared her throat. Finally, with her back to Mark, she was able to say, in a tone she wanted to snatch back even as it traveled out of her into the air above the sink, "Of course, it's so easy for me."

130 "Oh," Mark said. "Oh, of course. I know, my darling. My *darlingest*. Of course. Of *course*! It's hardest of all for you."

Jiselle swallowed but could say nothing more, and Mark said nothing but kept his head on her shoulder as she began to rinse dishes again, moving with her as she went from the sink to the dishwasher, keeping his arms around her waist. He had to shuffle to stay attached to her, and it was ridiculous, comical. On the way back from the dishwasher, holding her waist as she moved in front of him, he stumbled, and when Jiselle started to laugh, reluctantly, he whirled her around, pulled her to him. She let go against him then, kissing, and being kissed, and laughing and shedding a few hot tears at the same time, while outside, the actual sound of sleigh bells seemed to jangle somewhere close by.

CHAPTER ELEVEN

One morning, Camilla leaned over the bowl in which Sam's sea monkeys were swimming in languid, microscopic circles for the first, and only, week of their lives, and stated, both casually and profoundly, "They're dead."

It was the second week of January, and the sky was deep purple now every day. Low clouds, looking like steel wool, skimmed over the tops of the trees in the ravine. There was no snow on the ground, but the wind blew it in hard little flakes sideways past the windows. Jiselle, eating Cheerios at the kitchen table, looked up when Camilla spoke.

"No," she said. "They're not dead. They're just—"

"Yeah, they are," Camilla said. "They're dead."

Jiselle stood up from her Cheerios and walked toward the counter, still shaking her head.

No.

Only an hour had passed since Sam had so carefully changed the water, taking a clean bowl from the cupboard, rolling up his sleeves, gently tipping the dirty water into the bowl. Jiselle watched as he did it. He bit his lip. He rinsed out the dish—the green scum swirling around in the sink before it disappeared—and tested the water from the faucet with the tips of his fingers, and then filled the plastic dish, and then scooped the sea monkeys out of the dirty water with a teaspoon, and put them in the fresh dish.

She went to it. Sam stepped into the kitchen then. He'd overheard. He walked straight to the dish, and he and Jiselle both looked down.

"Oh, Sam," Jiselle said, rubbing his back in tiny, nervous circles.

"Camilla's right," he said. "They're dead. The change in water temperature killed them."

"Oh," Jiselle said. "It's—"

"It's my fault," he said. He shrugged.

"No!" Jiselle said.

But Sam walked out of the kitchen to the living room, and Jiselle listened to his footsteps cross the wood floors to his room.

"Jesus," Camilla said. "They were just sea monkeys."

When Mark was gone for more than a few nights in a row, Jiselle began to *pine*. She had not, she realized, really known before what that word meant or the feeling of it—to long for something or someone to the point of physical suffering. She would close the door to their bedroom and lock it behind her, and go to his closet, where she would gather up his uniforms in her arms and breathe them in. The blood around her heart seemed to ache. She would close her eyes, and sometimes she had to get on her knees—doubled over with a pain in her stomach, as though she had been shot with a poisoned arrow.

It was even worse during the day, when the children were at school, and the hours seemed to hover around her like some sort of exquisitely heavy gown. When they were home, the girls barely spoke to her, but even their angry outbursts at each other were a distraction from the longing. Sara's scream-ing music behind the curtain in the doorway of her room filled the house with a kind of ear-splitting clutter that was mind-numbing and, therefore, somehow comforting. Ca-milla's boyfriend, Bobby, would come over sometimes, and if he wasn't on the couch in front of the TV with Camilla, he might get on the floor with Sam, and the two of them would move action figures across the rug, sputtering out artillery noises.

133

There was Sam.

Sometimes Jiselle wasn't sure if he was suggesting Mo-nopoly or a walk in the ravine or a card game for his sake or for hers, but she never turned him down. Why would she? What else did she have to do? It had taken her these months in St. Sophia to learn that, despite the brick and clapboard storefronts and the shady streets of the town, no one really *lived* in St. Sophia. They slept there, and they dropped their children off at schools there before heading for the freeway ramps. People from the cities and suburbs nearby drove in for quaint small-town lunches and antiquing on the weekends, but Jiselle was, she realized, never going to make friends in St. Sophia. There would be no reading groups or knitting circles. She'd be invited to no tea parties. There was no one in the park or at the library during the day, and the only people she'd met so far had been the Schmidts, next door, and Camilla's boyfriend's parents, Paul and Tara Temple. Still, even in her loneliest hours, she could barely tolerate the television, and the radio was full of music she didn't like, or paranoid ranting:

"Dr. Springwell has been broadcasting his show from the Canary Islands for the last three months," the woman on the radio said. "*That's* Dr. Springwell's secret!"

Laughter followed from a small studio audience.

That morning they'd announced the resignation of the secretary of state, the suspension of interstate Amtrak service, the death of a basketball star, the president's plans for military action against the Alliance of Nations embargo.

"We cannot allow our nation to be destroyed during this brief troubled period. We have been a friend to the nations that would turn their backs on us now, and we must now demand their friendship in return."

But there were no more white balloons, and the federal government had ordered all flags to be flown at full mast. *No more doomsday thinking.* This had been a strategy that had helped the country survive two world wars—the careful manipulation of information to the public and the suppression of pessimism.

"These *frauds*," the woman on the radio, sounding happy and full of excited energy, said about Dr. Springwell and his ilk, "should be executed when this is over and they try to get back into this country."

❧

One Friday afternoon, when Mark was flying to Australia, and then to Hawaii, and would not be back until Monday, Jiselle, on her knees in his closet, began to feel around on the bottom of it. If she was looking for something, she didn't realize it, until she came upon a shoebox in the back, beyond his tennis shoes and snow boots and a pair of shower shoes she'd had no idea he owned.

She pulled out the box, brought it to the bed, and opened it. 135

On top were a dozen photographs. Mostly, they were of Joy. Jiselle recognized the curls, the tilt of her head, the slightly crooked smile. But there were others. A woman with a short blond bob standing with a surfboard at the end of a jetty. Another with brown tresses pulled back behind her head; this one had an arm thrown around a much younger Camilla, who wasn't smiling. Another one Jiselle recognized as the nanny who'd come to the house to retrieve a pair of flip-flops she'd left on the deck. Jiselle had come out of the bedroom to be introduced to her but could not fail to recognize the girl's coldness as anything but hostility. Mark hadn't been home, and Sara was the one who handed over the flip-flops with a smug smile. "See ya!" she said, closing the door on the girl.

Jiselle had assumed the hostility was because the nanny had been displaced from her job by Jiselle's marriage to Mark. But, looking at this photograph, Jiselle understood what she had found. The girl, lounging on the couch in the family room—her straight brown hair hanging down over her shoulders in a glossy cascade—had a smile of such radiant pleasure on her face as she stared into the camera that there was no mistaking what this box contained. And it didn't surprise Jiselle to find, under that photograph, one of herself in a black silk blouse, in Copenhagen, outside the Round Tower.

Jiselle's hands were trembling, and coolly damp—but why? If Mark had searched through her own things back at her old house, he could have found a similar stash of old images of boys and men Jiselle had been with. There was a Polaroid, she knew, of Stephen in her bathtub, with his wet hair streaming down his face. Aaron, just waking up in her bed. She could hardly complain that Mark had photographs of old girlfriends, or that he had old girlfriends. Could she?

She was about to close the box when she decided to look at the newspaper clipping at the bottom of it. It was yellowed and softened, and she opened it carefully. It was an account from the *St. Sophia Gazette* of Joy's "untimely death."

Local Mother Killed While
Attempting to Protect Her Child

Joy Dorn, of 1161 Forest Glen Road, was laid to rest today at the St. Sophia Cemetery, following services. Mrs. Dorn was killed on Monday after being struck by a school bus outside her home. Her older children had already boarded the bus when her two-year-old ran into the road. In an attempt to prevent him from being hit by the bus, Mrs. Dorn ran into the road after him. Paramedics who arrived on the scene told reporters that the mother was killed instantly.

Jiselle folded the clipping up again carefully along the original creases, put it back in the shoebox, with the photographs on top of it, and put the box on the floor in the back of the closet where she'd found it.

∽

That afternoon, Jiselle waited until she saw Brad Schmidt at the end of his driveway before she went, herself, to retrieve the empty trash can. "Hello!" she called out to him. He turned and waited for her to reach him.

He wanted, as always, to talk about the flu: "Don't kid yourself that the rats don't have it. And the mice. Protect yourselves."

Jiselle nodded. She said, "Well, we're doing what we can."

"What kind of traps do you have?" he asked.

"Live traps."

Brad Schmidt shook his head, as though at very bad news or at foolishness so vast there could be no other response.

. . .

The exterminator thought it might be the unusually mild winter, the early spring and summer weather, that was causing all the trouble with the rodents—a complaint across the Midwest and the eastern states. By the last week of May, you couldn't cross a room without having a mouse dash in front of you. Every morning, when Jiselle came into the kitchen for her first cup of coffee, something small and dark and alive would flee from her. She'd scream—a high, unfamiliar yelp that seemed to come straight out of her subconscious— heart pounding, all her senses jolted to high alert.

As with the birds, there was a barrage of public service announcements about the rodents. They were not carriers of *Yersinia pestis*, just as hemorrhagic zoonosis was not the bubonic plague. The stories of corpses found in abandoned buildings and in ditches gnawed to pieces by rats could certainly have been true, but this did not link any particular illness to the presence of rodents. Rats had always eaten dead bodies. The usual care was needed to keep rats and mice out of homes and businesses, but panic was unnecessary and unproductive, and even un-American. Some of the announcements on television showed a flag waving at full mast against a blue sky, while the voiceover cautioned the public against panic.

A decision to use poison or traps, the exterminator told Jiselle, would depend on whether or not anyone in the house would be willing and able to empty the traps—live or otherwise. The poison was slower, he said, and less predictable, but the mice would usually go elsewhere to die. You didn't have to see them or dispose of them. The traps, however, required "cleaning" and maintenance. Clearly, he'd noticed the absence of a man in the house.

"I'll take care of it!" Sam insisted. "I want to do it!"

"We're not going to *kill* them, are we?" Sara called from her room.

Jiselle hadn't realized Sara was listening to the exterminator talk to her and Sam at the kitchen table, but when Sara shuffled out wearing her black Saturday morning pajamas—already (or still) in her black makeup—it would have been impossible for the exterminator not to notice her resemblance to a rodent.

Sara said, "I'm not going to live here if we're going to kill innocent creatures."

Jiselle held up a hand to try to keep Sara from saying anything else, but it might also have looked as if she were waving goodbye.

The exterminator looked at Jiselle.

"Live traps?" she asked.

"I can do live traps if you can do live traps," he said.

As it happened, Sam was perfectly happy to hear that the traps would fill up fast, that some of the mice might be diseased, or "biters," and that he would have to wear mesh gloves so he could grab the ones that refused to vacate their cages. Over the next few weeks, like an apprentice exterminator, he took complete responsibility for the mice, for the cages and their maintenance, for the whole operation of trying to keep the mice from taking up permanent residence in the house, or taking it over. Jiselle would wait in the living room as Sam

Laura Kasischke

ran through the family room each morning and out the back
door with a cage full of mewling and fur. He quit sharing
the details with her—their numbers, the state of their health,
their attitudes toward their captor—after the first tale of an
albino mouse "the size of a baseball" that had bled from its
nostrils and— "Stop," Jiselle had said, trembling, placing her
coffee spoon down on the kitchen counter.

"I'm sorry," Sam said, looking apologetic but smiling at
the same time.

"I hope you're burning them," Brad Schmidt said, and Jiselle
decided there'd be no point in arguing with him about why
she would have live traps if she was going to burn the mice,
except to be sadistic.

"Can I ask you a question?" she said instead.

"Go ahead," Brad Schmidt said.

"So. You were here when . . . ?" Jiselle looked toward the
road, unable to finish the question.

"When Mrs. Dorn was killed? Sure! We took care of
those children until Mark got back."

"Did she—how did it happen?"

"He never *told* you?" Brad Schmidt's eyebrows shot up as
if he'd caught someone in a fantastic crime.

"Well, he told me of course about the bus, but of course
he doesn't like to talk about it."

"That little Sam," Brad Schmidt said, "he tried to dash
away from her, into the road; the bus had just started up, and
she went after him." He slammed his left fist then into his
right hand to show the impact. "She was a saint, that woman.

Not just because of that. Because of *everything*. If there was ever a mother who would have wanted to die taking care of her children, that was Joy Dorn. It's the only comfort any of us can have."

"Thank you," Jiselle said, "for telling me."

                                                      —∾∾—

Before she went to pick up the children at school that day, Jiselle stood for a long time at the front door, looking out.

There, she thought, looking to the end of the driveway, is the place where Joy died.

There.

There was nothing there.

Why, she would ask Mark when he got back, hadn't he told her that part of the story? The part of the story in which his first wife had run in front of a bus to save his son?

But would *knowing* have changed anything?

If not, why had he left the details so purposely . . . *fuzzy?*

Perhaps, Jiselle thought, she should try to call her therapist again. She'd left several messages in the last two months, but he hadn't returned her calls. She turned from the front door and went to the telephone and dialed Smitty Smith's number, which she knew by heart.

After several rings, a woman answered. "Yes," she said when Jiselle asked if she'd reached Dr. Smith's office.

"I'm calling to make an appointment," she said.

"That's too bad," the woman said. Her voice sounded full of bitter irony. "He died three weeks ago."

"What?"

"Dr. Smith died three weeks ago. This is his wife. I'm just here cleaning out the office. If you'd like a memento—say, a paperweight, or the Phoenix flu—I can send you something. But you won't be having any more talks with Dr. Smith. I suggest you try solving your own problems for a change."

Jiselle heard the woman laugh—loudly, unhappily, sounding nearly insane—before the line went dead, and then she stood looking at the phone in her hand for a long time before she put it back in the cradle.

Impossible.

There was some mistake.

Some sort of horrible joke was being made. She would try the number again in a few days.

142 Surely, if your therapist died—a therapist you'd seen regularly for over a decade—there would be some sort of official notice. A telegram? Perhaps no one would expect his patients to come to his funeral—after all, how many patients must Dr. Smith have had?—but surely, there would be *something* shared with her, expected of her. The man was the receptacle of her whole life. He could not simply have *died*.

Perhaps she'd dialed the wrong number, or his number had changed. Had he ever told her, anyway, that he *had* a wife? It had somehow never occurred to Jiselle that he might. Thinking back now of his hands on his knees as he listened to her, she was sure there had never been a wedding ring there.

She went to the front door again, squinted toward the end of the driveway, and past that to the other side of the road—

the place Sam must have dashed to, the place Joy never made it. From her side of the screened-in door, the silence and the stillness out there seemed accusatory, like the nail above the mantel where the wedding portrait had been—that protected square of wall that had stayed pristine through all the years that had passed while the portrait hung over it, while the rest of the wall darkened and faded at the same time around it.

Greater than nothing. That empty space made Jiselle feel like a voyeur, an interloper, a rubbernecker, a nosy neighbor:

If you're so curious, come out here yourself and see.

What choice did she have?

Jiselle walked out of the house in her bare feet, down to the end of the driveway, where she stood very still before she stepped into the road, thinking, *Here.*

She looked down at her feet and then behind her.

No one.

Nothing.

She seemed, herself, not even to be casting a shadow in this place. In this shaft of space and light, she seemed to cease to exist. She turned around, and then turned around again, looking for that shadow, but if it was there at all, it was managing to stay behind her, to sneak away when she turned to look, shifting out of sight when she tried to find it. She turned around so many times she finally grew dizzy, and felt foolish—what if Brad Schmidt was watching from next door?—and went back into the house.

143

Part
Four

CHAPTER TWELVE

The night before Valentine's Day, Jiselle took the children, for the second time, to meet her mother for dinner at Duke's Palace Inn. Mark was in Munich, but he was scheduled to be home in time to take Jiselle out for a romantic Valentine's dinner the next night. They had reservations at the Chop House. She'd seen, in his sock drawer, a small package wrapped in red tissue with her name on it. For him she'd bought cuff links—gold, simple squares with his initials.

An ice storm was predicted for the evening, but by the time Jiselle left with the children for downtown Chicago, the sky, although dense with dark blue clouds, was spitting out only a bit of thin snow. It glazed the windshield of the Cherokee, glistened in the bare branches of the trees, shone palely in the light of the early moon, but it melted by the time it hit the pavement.

Sara wore a plaid skirt, like a Catholic schoolgirl, except that the skirt was so short it barely covered her panties. White knee socks. There was a black garter around her right thigh. Jiselle had asked her to wear something "appropriate" when she'd come upon her lounging on the couch in a T-shirt that read, *Fuck You, Justin Timberlake*, but when she came out of her room in the plaid skirt, her white blouse unbuttoned down to the snap at the front of her black bra, Jiselle had not had the energy to ask her to change. There was, she felt certain, nothing Sara would find to wear that would not horrify her mother, but if Sara did not come along to dinner at all, her mother would note the absence, taking it as proof of Jiselle's impossibly foolish choice, marrying a man with such a daughter.

148   "You can wear my shoes," Jiselle had said, looking at Sara's bare feet.

Sara had rolled her eyes but didn't object when Jiselle brought out the beautiful shoes she'd bought in Madrid. They slid perfectly onto Sara's feet. Even Sara looked down at the shoes in appreciation.

They'd driven about forty miles from the house and were still ten miles from their freeway exit to downtown when Camilla, in the passenger seat beside Jiselle, pointed out how dark it was, except for the moon's white light bleeding between cracks in the clouds. "Why aren't the streetlights on?" she asked.

Jiselle leaned forward to scan the distance beyond her windshield.

Yes. The streetlights were completely dark against an ever-darkening sky. The signs that usually lit up the billboards were off. The only light besides the shredded bits of moon overhead came from the headlights streaming toward them on the other side of the freeway.

Why?

Then Jiselle noted not only the absence of streetlights but also the absence of traffic headed into the city. It was all headed out.

"Weird," Jiselle said, more to herself than to Camilla.

She kept driving until they reached their exit, ten miles later, and pulled off the freeway to find that the city streets were nearly empty. No pedestrians. All the store and restaurant windows were dark.

Jiselle was just slowing down outside Duke's Palace Inn, noting the unlit sign outside, when her cell phone rang. The Caller ID read, MOTHER.

"Don't tell me you drove all the way into the city. For God's sake, Jiselle, don't you listen to the radio?"

No, she didn't. It was impossible, in one car with Camilla, Sam, and Sara, to find a station, or even a CD, they could agree on. They always rode in silence.

"No," Jiselle said. "I'm here."

"Well, go home, and hope *your* power's on. I'm on my way back. Unlike you, I heard it on the radio and turned around."

"Oh," Jiselle said. "Should I—?"

"You should go *home*," her mother said. "All the sane people are on their way home. Nothing will be open in the city."

149

Jiselle said goodbye then, and Happy Valentine's Day, and that she would call in the morning—by which time the power would be back on, surely, and she and her mother would, perhaps, make plans to meet somewhere for lunch. She flipped her phone closed, cleared her throat. "Okay, kids," she said, looking first to Camilla, who'd rested her head with her eyes closed against the fogged window, and then into the backseat, where Sam was twiddling his thumbs across his Game Boy, utterly absorbed. Sara was scowling. "Power outage," Jiselle said. "I guess we're heading back. Let's hope we have power at home."

❧

150   But getting out of the city was nothing like getting into it had been. Everyone was headed out, back to the suburbs and the small towns beyond them, where they lived. Hundreds, *thousands*, of cars were idling in a line that began a mile or two away from the ramp.

The frozen rain had begun to fall even harder, ticking and snapping onto the windshield and roof of the Cherokee. The traffic was a confused jumble of vehicles driving less than a mile an hour, but in a frantic rush, like a marathon for snails, nearly unmoving or moving imperceptibly. The squeaking of bad brakes. The impatient revving of motors. Emergency lights blinking.

Jiselle kept the defroster blowing, because her breath, mixed with that of the children, was beginning to condense on the windows, fogging everything. She glanced behind her. Only Sara was awake now. She was still staring out the window with an angry smirk. Sam was slumped against her shoulder. Beside Jiselle, Camilla was breathing steadily, eyes closed, rosebud lips parted, oblivious.

It took a full hour to get to the freeway. By then, Sara was asleep, too, her eyeballs twitching back and forth beneath her black-painted eyelids.

Jiselle rubbed her own eyes, trying to stay awake herself, finally passing that red Yield triangle at the entrance to the freeway, and spilling with the other cars out of the congested queue. Although the traffic here was also backed up for miles, at least it was *moving*.

As she drove, Jiselle could see to the left and right that the streets sprawling out around the freeway were completely dark. The windows of the houses were black, causing her to waver a bit in her hope that the power outage had affected only the city, that they would reach home to find heat, lights, television. How long, if the power was out, might it *stay* out?

151

Jiselle closed her eyes briefly, and then snapped them open when a truck pulled up next to her and blew its bullhorn— impotently, furiously—waking the children. Sara sputtered to life, coughing. Camilla blinked, looking around as if she had been peacefully asleep for many years. Sam, still holding his Game Boy, sat up and said, "This scares me."

Jiselle reached behind her, patted his knee. "Nothing to be scared of, Sam," she said. "People just don't know how to behave when something unexpected happens. The power will be back on soon. And your dad will be home tomorrow."

Sam nodded, as if Jiselle knew what she was talking about.

She tried to speed up then, but she had only just managed to bring the Cherokee up to twenty miles per hour when she had to come to a full stop again, when the traffic got too thick, too slow, merging into two lanes from three to avoid a lane of orange cones. She drove a few more miles slowly until Camilla said, "What if the power's out at home?"

"Well," Jiselle said, trying to sound optimistic, "we'll have to light some candles. Do you kids have any flashlights?"

"No," Camilla and Sara said in unison.

"There's a Wal-Mart," Sam said, pointing into the distance.

Jiselle looked in the direction of his index finger, and saw it. Somehow, surrounded by darkness, the Wal-Mart sign had remained lit. Its prisonlike cinderblock had faded into the night, but the parking lot was crowded with cars, and there was no mistaking the brilliance pouring through its automatic glass doors for anything but business as usual.

"There's always a Wal-Mart," Camilla said, "and it's always open."

Jiselle glanced over at her. Like so many things Camilla said, it was completely noncommittal, completely lacking in emotion or judgment. A statement of fact.

"We'll get off here," Jiselle said.

"Good thinking," Camilla said.

Camilla and Sara waited in the Cherokee while Sam and Jiselle went into Wal-Mart, where flashlights and candles were being sold faster than they could be hauled out of the stockroom. The workers in their red vests were harried and troubled looking. No one understood, it seemed, how the generator that kept the store lit up and operational worked, or how long it would last. A few of the employees seemed to feel cheated.

"Damn," a pregnant girl in one of the red vests said. "Every store closed for miles around, and Wal-Mart's still up and running."

"It *can't* last," an older woman said as Sam and Jiselle stood waiting for the teenage boy who'd gone to the stockroom for more flashlights. "Power's out from here to the city."

"I know," Jiselle said. "We just came from the city."

The woman continued. "I have a salt-water fish tank at home. Tropicals. They've got to have just the right temperature to survive. When I get home, they'll all be dead."

"My sea monkeys died," Sam said sympathetically.

"Oh, poor little boy," the woman said. "What's a sea monkey?"

Sam didn't have time to explain. The lights overhead surged. The cash registers all bleeped and buzzed at the same time. A cheer, and a sigh, and the pregnant girl's audible groan went up through the store: The real electricity, not the generated electricity, had come back on. The fish tank woman turned away from them, back to the rack of bungee cords she'd been arranging, as if the electricity had flipped a switch somewhere inside her, too. No more time to waste. In fact, the whole celebratory strangeness of the atmosphere of Wal-Mart ended abruptly. The hubbub subsided, and with it the sense of rush and excitement. The crisis was over. Sam said, "Can we still get some flashlights?"

Jiselle looked at him. The rims of his ears were red. She could see his scalp through the soft hair that had grown back on his head. She said, "Of course." There was nothing Sam liked more than a new gadget. A can opener would have sufficed, but Jiselle said, "Let's get a whole bunch."

"Cool," he said.

When the stockroom boy emerged from behind the aluminum stockroom doors, bearing nothing, not even looking in their direction, Jiselle called out to him, "Excuse me!"

He turned. "Yeah?"

"Were there any flashlights back there?"

The boy looked at her blankly. "You still want 'em?"

"Yes," Jiselle said.

Of *course*—for the next time, or just in case. Shouldn't that be obvious? Wouldn't anyone who'd come into Wal-Mart during a power outage, owning no flashlight, still want one?

No, it seemed. The boy in the red vest pointed to the shelf that had been empty of flashlights only moments before. They were back, returned by customers who'd decided they weren't needed. The plastic packages had been shoved sloppily on to the hooks they'd been taken from or thrown down below the hooks. "Well, there you go," the boy said. "Help yourself."

· · ·

Sam picked out two red ones, two blue ones, and a yellow one. Jiselle grabbed some matches and batteries on the way to the front of the store, to the register, where there was no line. The cashier was a small man, shorter even than Sam, with a long gray beard and a brilliant flash of gold in the center of his smile. "Somebody's thinking ahead," he said to Sam and Jiselle approvingly. He took the money, slipped it into the cash register, handed Sam the bag of flashlights. "Just you wait, folks. You're going to be needing these."

He said it with such authority that it crossed Jiselle's mind that this little man in his red vest was the one in charge of the power grid. That he knew something they didn't.

No sooner had they reached the electric doors to Wal-Mart, bearing their plastic bags, than the power surged, brightening strangely, before the lights went out again just as the door slid open, this time plunging Wal-Mart into total darkness.

Jiselle grabbed Sam's arm, hurrying him away from the doors, which hesitated once and then closed with an electrical finality behind them. "Shit!" someone shouted from inside the store, and there were more shouts following it—curses, cries of dismay, protest, exasperation, disbelief muffled by the glass between the world and Wal-Mart.

155

∾ℰ

At home, as Jiselle had feared, there were no lights. She used her flashlight to make Sam and herself some peanut butter sandwiches for dinner in the kitchen. Camilla and Sara both said they weren't hungry and disappeared into the darkness of their rooms.

Jiselle lit a candle, put it on the table, and turned on the radio. Apparently the outage had swept the Midwest to the East Coast. A power grid problem. "The infrastructure of this country is collapsing!" a caller to WAVT shouted. "This isn't the weather; this is a collapse of a culture!" On another station a caller blamed the outage on the flu. "People are dying! We're not going to be able to keep the lights on!"

Jiselle snapped the radio off so Sam wouldn't hear. In the flickering light across from her, he looked like a figment of a fevered imagination—the light leaping around on his face giving him the appearance of something made of fire, made of pure energy.

"Won't it get cold?" he asked.

"I'll build a fire," Jiselle said, "after it gets cold, if the power doesn't come back on. It'll be cozy."

She tried to sound like someone with a plan, but she was hoping that the power *would* come back on before she needed to build a fire, since she'd never built one before—and, in fact, Mark had warned her not to. "There's something wrong with this flue," he'd said one day, leaning into the fireplace, looking up. "I don't want to risk the ashes or flames blowing back on you. Don't use the fireplace if I'm not here, okay? Until I have a chance to get it fixed." Obviously Mark hadn't anticipated that there would come a time when a fire would be the only source of heat.

"Do I have to sleep in my room?" Sam asked, and Jiselle remembered then—his night-light: a frog plugged into the electrical outlet next to his bed. Sam couldn't sleep without that.

"No," she said. "We can camp out. On the floor. In the living room. Until the power comes back on."

His eyes widened, and he smiled.

After Sam and Jiselle were done with their sandwiches, they took their flashlights to the linen closet and hauled out the spare blankets and a couple of pillows. Sam held the flashlight while Jiselle made pallets for them on the rug on the floor of the family room.

They didn't bother with pajamas. Sam lay down on the floor in his khaki pants and green sweater, and Jiselle lay beside him in her black slacks. He'd brought the book of tales with him from his room, and Jiselle rolled over, opening it beside her, holding the flashlight on the page they'd marked the night before:

> *They stopped at a little hut.*
>
> *The roof sloped nearly down to the ground, and the door was so low they had to creep in on their hands and knees.*
>
> *There was no one at home but an old woman, who was cooking fish by the light of a train oil lamp.*

"Sam?" Jiselle whispered after another page or two.
No answer.
He was asleep.
She closed the book and snapped off the flashlight. It

surprised her how total the darkness was. And how quiet. From the girls' rooms there was no sound at all, and outside there was nothing but the tick-ticking of icy rain on the deck. She closed her eyes, and after what seemed like a long time listening to the sputter and hiss of rain on wood, she fell asleep, dreaming of sitting beside the old woman from the story, who was cooking a fish. The fish glowed with a kind of reflected light from the oil lamp beside the woman—silvery, like a moon in the shape of the fish—and she was leaning over it with a knife when a sudden, brilliant, digital, pealing music slammed into the silence, and Jiselle's eyes snapped open, and she caught her breath and sat up fast, recognizing her cell phone theme, "The Blue Danube," and found herself jumping, moving toward it instinctively, still mostly asleep—but where the hell was it?

Stumbling toward the music into the family room, she banged her shins against the coffee table. "*Fuck.*" She got on her hands and knees and scrambled toward the music, which was apparently coming from somewhere deep in the couch—a tiny technological box with a relentless orchestra stuffed inside it. "*Shit.*" Sara must have taken it when they'd gotten back to the house in the dark, talked on it in whispers in her room. This happened every few weeks, when, Jiselle suspected, Sara's own monthly minutes were used up. Afterward, she'd stuff it into the cushions of the couch so Jiselle would think she'd misplaced it herself.

Jiselle felt around among the upholstery and crumbs until she touched something solid and cold, pulled it out, opened it, and held it to her ear. "Hello? *Hello?*"

"Jiselle?"

"Mark?"

"Jiselle, I—"

"Mark," she said. "Where are you? The electricity's gone out. Completely out. What do I do if . . ." She did not know how to finish the question, so she just listened, waiting for an answer, which didn't come. In the silence, however, she thought she heard Mark sigh. She did hear him clear his throat, she was sure of that, but still he didn't speak. Finally, to the silence, Jiselle said, "Mark?"

Crackling between them, she suddenly understood, was an ocean. She could hear the waves. There were ships on that ocean, she thought, listening to the silence. Ships bearing good news and bad. False documents. Stowaways. Silk flowers. Parrots in cages. Diamonds in felt sacks. But before the static of all that ocean was yanked away and replaced by the true silence of a connection gone completely dead, Mark said, "Jiselle, I don't know when I'll be back. They've got us detained here. We—"

"What?"

"Yes," he said. "Detained."

"Detained?"

"Well," Mark said, "that's what I just said, Jiselle. *Detained.* Don't you know what *detained* means?"

There was an exasperated huff, and Jiselle felt tears spring into her eyes. Her heart rose into her throat. Of course she knew what *detained* meant, but it wasn't like Mark to speak in jargon. If there had been mechanical problems, he'd have said, *The fucking incompetents can't get their plane put together.*

159

If it had been political, *The fascists snatched our passports.* If there had been a strike or a storm, *We're stuck on this toilet until tomorrow.*

Detained? He was supposed to be home in twelve hours. He was going to take her out for Valentine's Day. They had reservations. She'd pictured champagne and candlelight, and their knees touching beneath a white tablecloth, opening that small red package he'd spirited away in his sock drawer—a silver bracelet or gold. She could barely speak, but she finally managed to say, "Of course I know, Mark. But—Mark?"

He didn't answer.

"Mark?"

Nothing.

Jiselle took the cell phone from her ear then and looked at it.

Dead.

Some kind of blind hope made her bring it to her ear again and say his name once more, but still there was no answer. Only the sound of her own ear.

And that ocean.

Ships going down in that ocean. Swallowed without a sound.

CHAPTER THIRTEEN

Jiselle didn't sleep again that night. She tried over and over to call Mark at the number he'd phoned her from, but there was never any answer. She let it ring for what seemed like hours, and then she went into the bathroom and closed the door so she wouldn't wake the children, and tried to call the airline.

"We don't have that information," she was told, and Jiselle knew the airlines well enough to know that, if this was what they'd been told to say, it was hopeless—that she could dial a hundred numbers, explain who she was, invent stories *(His mother's in the hospital, his children are missing, the house burned down, we have to get in touch with Captain Dorn . . .)* and it would make no difference. They weren't going to tell her anything whether they had anything to tell her or not.

She lay back down beside Sam on the floor, keeping her cell phone on her chest, and tried to go back to sleep, but the phone never rang again, and she never fell back asleep, and the power never came back on. When the sun finally rose high enough that she could see to make her way through the house without stumbling, she went to the bedroom and opened the little red package in Mark's sock drawer.

She couldn't help herself.

It was Valentine's Day.

Inside the box, it turned out, were both the gold bracelet and the silver bracelet she'd imagined. Jiselle put them back in the box, wrapped it again, put it back in Mark's sock drawer, and then stood for a moment practicing the bright smile she'd flash when he gave the gift to her.

∽✲∽

162 The power was still out later that morning. Jiselle went to the refrigerator, somehow surprised when the light didn't come on when she opened the door. She had spent most of her childhood believing that the light in the refrigerator was always on, until her mother explained it to her, showed her the darkness inside by opening the door only a crack and telling Jiselle to look in.

This time not only did the light not come on, but the smell of spoiled milk, bacteria, and lunch meat gone bad had filled up the darkness. Jiselle took out a garbage bag and started dumping the things she was sure couldn't be salvaged.

She took the bag to the garbage can outside and marveled at how warm and bright the day had turned out to be after the rainy ice of the night before. What snow there was before the storm had been washed away by the rain, and the ice had melted. The lawn rolling toward the ravine, which had been covered in slush for a month, looked like a carpet of crushed green velvet.

Perhaps, Jiselle thought, she'd better go over to the Schmidts' to see if they were okay over there without electricity. Who knew what kind of special needs the elderly might have that depended on electricity?

She went back in the house to get a sweater and saw that Sara was awake, standing barefoot in front of the refrigerator, with the door open, staring into its emptiness.

"Where did the food go?" she asked, and then, "Why isn't the light on?"

Pulling on her sweater, Jiselle considered explaining to Sara, as her mother had to her, that the light in the refrigerator was not always on, but she felt sure this was something Sara, so full of her own inner darkness, would have been born knowing. She said, instead, "Well, *no* lights are on, and the food was rotten."

"When's Dad getting back?"

Jiselle decided to wait to say anything about that until she knew more. "Soon," she said, and went out the sliding doors to see to the Schmidts.

Brad Schmidt opened the door wide enough to let Jiselle in, but he didn't invite her to sit down. "Sure *we're* okay," he said, waving his hand in the air as if to wave her concern away. He said he'd grown up in a sod house in Nebraska. He was prepared for the inevitable. He'd always known the electricity was going to be the first thing to go. Gas was going to be next, then food, and then water. "When's your husband getting back?"

"I don't know," Jiselle said. "He's been"—for a few seconds she couldn't think of the word—"detained."

Brad Schmidt's eyebrows leaped, as they always did when he heard bad news. "That right?" he said.

"Yes. I mean, I guess. He called last night, but I haven't been able to get in touch with him since."

"Where's he at?"

"Germany," she said, and Brad Schmidt snorted through his nose, a kind of knowing chuckle. "He'll be back when—"

"When hell freezes over!" Brad Schmidt said. "They warned us! You gotta give 'em that. The Krauts aren't like Americans, you know. They're not just gonna let a bunch of foreigners in and tell them they can spread their disease all over the place."

"Well, they'll send them back in that case," Jiselle said. "Why would they keep them?"

"It's obvious!" Brad Schmidt said. "To teach us a lesson!"

"That would be against the law," Jiselle said.

"Whose law? What law? You think the Europeans have any sympathy for *us*? Ha! We burned that bridge, and all the other bridges are burning as we speak."

"I don't think—"

But he cut her off, seeming to be gesturing to the door or to the world, suggesting with the gesture that she should go. "Good luck, Mrs. Dorn. I suggest you get yourself a rifle. *I've* got one, and enough water to last me a year."

"I'm not worried about—"

"Of course you're not," Brad Schmidt said, smirking. "You don't seem like the worrying type. But, in the meantime, you need a weapon."

Jiselle was just turning in the doorway when Diane Schmidt wandered out of a back room wearing what looked like an old wedding dress and curtsied to Jiselle.

Before she realized she was doing it, Jiselle was curtsying back.

∞

Back at the house, the children were gathered around the kitchen table eating peanut butter on bread and drinking warm Coke.

"What the hell is going on here?" Sara said when Jiselle slid into a chair at the table with them.

"I don't know," Jiselle said. She suggested that they listen to the radio. Did they own a radio that didn't have to be plugged in? Sam and Camilla left the table to try to find one, but Camilla came back with the only thing they had, dangling it by its electrical cord.

"Call Dad," Sam said.

"Well," Jiselle said, trying to use the voice she'd needed so often (and so often failed to have) on planes, during turbulence, during lightning storms, during snowstorms, "everything is fine, but your father called last night, and he's in Germany. He's been"—again, the word escaped her for several heartbeats—"detained."

"What's that mean?" Sam asked, his mouth full of peanut butter sandwich.

"Well, they seem to be holding the crew—and, I don't know, actually, maybe the passengers. I think it probably has to do with—"

"How long?" Camilla asked.

"We'll find out," Jiselle said. "Later. He'll call. I'll call. If I can't reach him, I'll call the airline."

It seemed to her that, as she looked at them, the children were exchanging a look among themselves.

∽⬥∾

When it got lighter outside, the house was bright enough to clean it up a bit. Sam was playing with two small soldiers and a truck on the family room floor. Camilla was reading on the couch. Sara was in her bedroom, and it sounded to Jiselle as if her pen were scratching wildly across the pages of her diary, the pages flipping fast. She tried not to think about what Sara might be writing.

She picked Camilla's sweater up off the floor.

Sara's balled-up white knee socks.

She could find only one of the shoes from Madrid she'd let Sara borrow—lying abandoned on the floor of the family room, as if Sara had stumbled out of it.

Jiselle got on her hands and knees, looking under the couch, under the chairs, for the matching shoe, finding nothing.

"Sara?" she called.

"*What?*"

"Where's my other shoe?"

"How the hell should I know?" Sara called back. "We were in the dark when we came home. Maybe it fell off outside."

"Well, if it fell off your foot outside, wouldn't you have noticed that you were wearing only one shoe when you came *inside*?"

"*No*," Sara shouted, as if the question were absurd. "It wasn't my idea to wear *your* shoes."

Jiselle closed her eyes for a moment. There would be, she knew, no point in continuing the conversation. She held the one shoe in her hand before taking it to the bedroom and placing it carefully at the bottom of the closet. Afterward, she went to the front door and looked out to see if she might find the other shoe, discarded on the lawn.

No.

A little while later, when she heard the shower running and Sara complaining, "The water's *fucking freezing*," Jiselle hurried into Sara's room, to her closet, and opened it.

Her heart was pounding with the thrill and anxiety of it, as if she were a safecracker or a cat burglar. She got down on her knees and moved her hands around through the shoes scattered on the closet floor, feeling for her own. It was too dark without the overhead light to see well, but each time Jiselle felt a shoe she thought might be hers, she picked it up and looked.

No. No. No.

They were all Sara's.

167

Her sandals. Her flip-flops. Her combat boots and stilettos and slippers.

She was feeling around farther in the back of the closet when she heard the shower go off—and then, as if somehow it had been kick-started by the end of Sara's shower, the lights blinked, and blinked again, and then blinked back on, and everything in the house seemed to come alive at once—the television, the stereo, Sam whooping with happiness, Camilla calling out in surprise, the clocks beeping, every light blazing, and Jiselle looked up from the shoes, seeing everything in Sara's closet vividly and brightly at the same time, and she gasped, finding herself staring directly into the deep green eyes of Joy Dorn.

Who was smiling.

Who was dressed in white, holding up that piece of white wedding cake. Beaming. Lovely. Full of light, as if she'd been the source of it, or had absorbed it and was letting it back into the world now.

The portrait. Sara kept it in her closet.

"What the fuck are you doing in my closet?"

Jiselle turned to find Sara standing over her, wrapped in a towel, mouth open wide in astonishment and outrage, but just at that moment she heard "The Blue Danube" coming from the other room and hurried past Sara to answer her cell phone without trying to explain.

⁓

"Oh my God, Mark," she said. She was crying before she could say anything else.

"Look, Jiselle," he said. "I'm not going to be able to talk long. They're holding the whole plane here, and not telling us how long. Quarantine. But the airline's lawyers are on it like piranhas. This can't go on for longer than a week without an international—"

"A week?"

"Jiselle. Please. I need you not to be hysterical, okay. This is bad enough. You need—"

Jiselle said, "I'll come *there*." The whole plan spun out around her as she held the phone to her ear. The children could stay with the Schmidts. She would fly to Munich. If they wouldn't let him come out to her, she would go in to be quarantined with him.

"Don't be ridiculous," he said. "Now, I love you. I have to go."

"I love you, too. Mark. Please, don't—"

But he was gone. She tried to call the number he'd called her from, but it rang a long time and no one answered.

She had just hung up the phone when she looked up to find Sara standing in the hallway. The bedroom door was open, and she was looking in at Jiselle. "So," she said, "when are you leaving?"

"What do you mean?"

"Come on," Sara said. "Just tell me. You think we didn't know the second you realized how much Dad's gone you were going to be outta here? You think you're the first one who got fed up with Dad being gone all the time?"

Jiselle put the phone beside her on the bed. "I'm not going anywhere."

"The hell you aren't," Sara said. "I thought you looked clueless enough that it might take you nine or ten months, but I guess this time Camilla won the bet—although, to be fair, *Mommy*, you pretty much set the record for the longest he's managed to keep a girlfriend around. I guess he was right that getting married might be the way to go this time."

"Sara?"

But she was gone.

CHAPTER FOURTEEN

Jiselle called Mark every day. On the other end of the phone, he always sounded no farther than a few yards away. He sounded as if he were in the other room, or as if he were out in the street, in the backyard—but when Jiselle went to the windows, holding the phone in her hand, listening to Mark's voice on the other end, she'd see that the backyard was empty, as was the front yard, and, at the end of their driveway, the road.

He sounded close, but Mark was in Munich.

Mark was detained.

∾⊘∾

By the middle of March, he'd been detained for a month.

Some days, she *nearly* pined, lingering at their closet, trying to conjure the feeling she'd had that used to make her knees weak when she took his uniforms in her arms. But there was so much else to do. She certainly did not have the luxury of locking herself in the bedroom to cry now that the power, when it was on, could only be counted on to go out again. During these brief spells with electricity, Jiselle had to prepare for the much longer periods during which there would be no refrigerator, no lights, no outlets to use to recharge the little appliances one relied on. There were so many things to gather and prepare—and, at the same time, as always, the children needed the usual things they needed.

The schools had closed early for spring break due to the power outages and fears of the Phoenix flu. But, after spring break, they did not reopen, and it was not made clear when they would open again.

172

"What is it like there?" Jiselle asked Mark.

"Efficient," Mark said.

But she had meant the weather. At home, it was the kind of weather you would invent for a perfect early spring. On their walks into the ravine, Sam and Jiselle saw chipmunks under every leafy, unfurling fern. Their fat, cartoon cheeks looked full, and they were all but tame, scampering toward the two of them on the path, looking up expectantly. If Sam and Jiselle knelt down, the chipmunks would come right to them, seeming content to gaze into their eyes for as long as they liked. Sam and Jiselle started bringing bags of nuts along on their walks, and the chipmunks took them shyly, graciously, right from their hands.

When Jiselle told Mark about the weather at home, Mark told her it was dreamlike in Germany, too. The windows didn't open in his room, but he could see that outside the Gesundheitsschutzhaus (which, he said, roughly translated to "Good Health House"), it was sunny, with a blue sky, day after day.

Jiselle tried to picture the scene he described. The distant snowcapped mountain, the foothills surrounding it. The way those hills appeared in the evenings to breathe slowly— sleepily, deeply, purple. There was a train track, Mark said, looking like a silver stream up the side of the mountain. He could see it shining sometimes in the early mornings, behind the pines. At four o'clock every afternoon the rushing glint of a train passed over the tracks.

"I'm learning patience," Mark said. "And studying German."

In the background she sometimes heard a woman say something—to Mark?—in German.

"It can't be too much longer," he told Jiselle. "Since not one of us has even shown symptoms, they're not going to be able to justify quarantining us forever."

"I love you," she said. "I miss you."

"My dearest," he said. "My princess. My darling. Imagine I am kissing you."

She closed her eyes.

She tried to imagine it, but the phone made an unnerving humming in her ear.

"*Herr Dorn?*" someone called in the distance.

The woman.

"I have to go now," Mark whispered. "It's morning here. Time for breakfast."

❧

Bobby's father, Paul Temple, gave Jiselle the extra generator he kept in his garage, and if Bobby wasn't already there, he would come over during the longer outages, hook it up, fill it with gas, start it.

"Feel free to call on my son for anything you need," Paul Temple said. "There's nothing worse than a population of young men without enough to do. It's the reason they launched the Crusades."

As always, Paul Temple, the high school history teacher, seemed unable to keep himself from sharing his knowledge, and was embarrassed to have shared it. He looked away from Jiselle and scratched his sandy hair.

"Thank you," she said.

Except for the mechanical purr under the kitchen window and the darkness of the neighbor's house, it was as if nothing were different.

Every few days Jiselle would go over to the Schmidts' to see how they were faring, but Brad Schmidt always waved her away.

She called her mother, who said, "Don't worry about me, Jiselle. *You're* the one with the problem."

❧

One morning, the first week of April, a flock of thousands of blackbirds flew out of the ravine behind the house, over the roof. The sound of them woke Jiselle, and even Sara roused herself to come onto the deck, look out. The sky was dark but shivering—all wings and fretful energy, as if the morning had been peeled back to expose its nervous system.

"Whoa, whoa!" Sam called, waving his arms over his head as if trying to stop them.

Sara said, "Holy shit."

"Where are they going?" Jiselle wondered aloud, and the children looked from the birds to her as if they were surprised that she didn't know.

As it turned out, they didn't *go* anywhere. They flew from one end of the ravine and back again, and then they dispersed.

On the radio it was said that people in Chicago had reported the same thing. The birds went from park to park, circled, flew over the lake, and then were gone.

This incited some panic.

The birds looked healthy, but who knew what sort of secret viruses they carried, or what their circling and disappearance portended? Parents kept their children indoors and out of the parks—although flyers were posted all over the city and delivered door to door explaining that fear of birds was superstitious, not scientific.

But who was delivering these flyers, people wanted to know.

The government?

And why? To keep people from panicking or because there was something to hide?

The movie *The Birds* became the number one movie download of all time, and television psychologists had a hard time explaining its popularity. You would think no one would want to see a movie that so closely paralleled the fears of the time. But they did.

◦≫⊘≪◦

A week after the blackbirds, a white goose took up residence in the backyard—some escaped farm fowl, it seemed. At first, Jiselle considered shooing it away. It could be diseased. But it looked harmless and lost in the backyard. Its orange beak matched its orange feet, and it came and went from the ravine without flying, just waddling. When Jiselle and the children went out on the deck to watch it, the goose would look up and honk.

Sam wanted to make a pet of it, but whenever he stepped off the deck to try to approach it, the goose turned and headed down the slope into the ravine, disappearing in the shadows. Once or twice, Jiselle heard it outside in the middle of the night, honking right under the bedroom window as if it wanted something, but when she went to the window to look out, the goose seemed only to be wandering in awkward circles in the dark—a bright patch of reflected moonlight.

◦≫⊘≪◦

Within a few days of the blackbirds and the arrival of the goose, a small flock of swifts took up residence in the chimney, and they whirled and screamed, glistening blackly, like living ash, from the roof of the house to the leafy trees, coming and going all day long. And some finches built a nest in the oak that grew out of the deck in back. Soon there were eggs in the nest, which seemed to have been pieced together with twigs and toilet paper and also hair—Camilla's? Golden strands of it glistened when sunlight hit the oak in the mornings.

Jiselle ignored Brad Schmidt's advice to clear the birds out. He stood at the edge of his own yard, looking up. "They might as well be living in your house," he said. "Whatever diseases they've got, you've got."

But Jiselle could not bring herself to be worried about the birds. There were stories every day on the news now about celebrities who'd fled the country, entering other countries illegally. Jodie Foster was living with a long list of fellow celebrities in the Canadian wilderness. No one had seen the wife of the governor of California for months, so she was presumed to be dead of the flu. Reportedly there were hygienic bunkers built under Washington, D.C., in which the Supreme Court justices were being housed.

Closer to home, it was said that thousands of people had started an encampment at Millennium Park in Chicago to get out of the apartment buildings where there was illness and where the air was presumed to be infected, and that the Beluga whales at the Shedd Aquarium were refusing to eat. Marine biologists all over the world had been consulted,

177

without success. Nothing could be done. A twenty-four-hour candlelight and prayer vigil was being held outside the aquarium, which had been closed to the public for weeks, for the whales, who were said also to be singing whale songs that had never been heard before. "They know what's ahead for us," one Chicago evangelist had told a television reporter, "and they are calling out to God."

This theory was widely repeated, as if it were a fact, and poets and popular song writers had banded together in a movement called the Whale Prayer Project, which was dedicated to expressing in human language what the whales were trying to sing to God in their own language.

In the morning, the swifts sounded like wind chimes in the chimney, and Beatrice (the goose—Sara had named it, and the name stuck) heralded morning with a discordant squawk, and then waddled off across the yard into the ravine, disappearing in the dark foliage for the day and coming back after the sun set to walk in circles in the backyard. They never saw her fly.

In truth, they had no idea if Beatrice was female or male, but Camilla pointed out that the goose had a kind of feminine posture. She held her head high, as if proud of her neck, as if she thought it was much longer than it was. She had a habit of holding her wings away from her body an inch or two, shivering them in the sunlight. It seemed coquettish. Obviously, Beatrice *couldn't* fly or she would have, but she enjoyed having wings nonetheless.

After Jiselle and Sam did some research on what geese

liked to eat, they learned that the bread crumbs they'd been leaving were no good. The bread swelled up in the goose's stomach, making her feel full without actually giving her enough nutrition to survive, so they went to the pet store and bought a sack of something that was supposed to be better: Fowl Feed Deluxe. In the morning, Sam hurried out of bed when the goose honked, ran out to the backyard, sprinkled the feed on the ground, and although the ingredients listed on the side of the bag seemed to be mostly oil and ash, Beatrice pecked happily at it before strolling back to the ravine.

∽৵৶⌒

On Tuesday, Mark sounded wistful. "Do you remember Paris, my love? Zurich? Copenhagen? Will we ever see places like that again?"

Indeed, those places seemed far away, impossibly remote, charming villages from another time.

It was hard to hear him over the noises of the household. Camilla and Bobby were starting up the generator again, and it made high whining noises outside the kitchen window. Sara was listening to her music in her bedroom—a man shouting obscenities over the sounds of guitars and garbage can lids being smashed together. Sam was waiting in the family room for Jiselle to get off the phone so they could go for a hike in the ravine. Mark told Jiselle not to tell the kids that she was talking to him. He said he didn't want to hear their voices, that it only depressed him.

. . .

But Wednesday he was angry. "The world's going to hell. I could be stuck here forever."

"No!" Jiselle said. "Don't—"

"I'm sorry," he said. "But you don't understand. Every fucking day here seems to last a week."

"I love you," Jiselle said.

He said, "I know that."

CHAPTER FIFTEEN

For Easter, Jiselle and Sam dyed hard-boiled eggs, and stuffed candies into plastic eggs, and hid them all around the house and the front and backyards, all the way to the edge of the ravine. It took Sara and Camilla two hours to find them all—wandering barefoot through the bright green grass in the late morning sunshine, languid, but laughing.

That afternoon, Jiselle took them in to the city to meet her mother at Duke's Palace Inn. The power had been on for a week without interruption, and the weather was glorious.

The restaurant was decorated in pastels for the holiday. There were pots of hibiscus and paperwhites everywhere, and pale green and pink papier-mâché eggs were strung from the ceilings. The brunch tables circled the entire dining room. Crystal bowls overflowed with sweet rolls. There was a fresh fruit platter—melon balls and mango, gigantic strawberries. At the center of it all, a chocolate fountain bubbled: three tiers of melted chocolate spilling over, gathering in a rich, dark pool.

The fragrance of that fountain wafted through the whole restaurant like a decadent, delicious pall, while a young woman in a yellow chiffon dress floated from table to table with a white cloth and an ever-replenishing bottle of champagne. She poured champagne into Camilla's glass, and Sara's, and even tried to fill Sam's glass, until Jiselle's mother fixed first Jiselle and then the woman in the yellow dress with an outraged stare. "You're going to let the boy drink *champagne*? He can't keep *root beer* down."

"Of course not," Jiselle said, putting her hand over Sam's champagne glass. The woman shrugged noncommittally and sashayed to another table.

182   The rest of the brunch was uneventful. The girls, perhaps a little tipsy, laughed out loud at the story Jiselle told of the woman on the flight to Scotland who'd grabbed her hand and told her fortune. Sara had agreed that morning, grudgingly, to wear a white T-shirt with her black leather miniskirt, and because her bare legs in fishnet stockings were under the table, from the waist up she looked like a girl dressed for Easter brunch, if informally.

They took the back roads and highways home instead of the freeway, which was congested with all the post-Easter brunchers (the lights at Duke's Palace Inn had flickered twice during brunch, and Jiselle presumed this had happened all over the city, and people were worried, heading for home), and Sam and the girls laughed at the enormous inflated bunnies in front yards as they passed through each small town.

There were neon-bright plastic eggs strung from trees. Plastic rabbits hanging from clotheslines. Pink and yellow streamers waving from telephone poles. Newscasters had linked the serious outbreaks of the flu in California and the rumors of war on a second front to the extra significance given this year to the Lenten season. Believers weren't just giving up candy; they were giving up sex. They were giving up cell phones. They were giving up pleasures and conveniences of all kinds. The police had been called in to end a parade of flagellants in San Francisco on Ash Wednesday. In New Mexico, three men had been roped to crosses outside a church and left there overnight. The nation was looking forward to Easter and to the end of this nonsense.

They passed through one town at the Illinois-Wisconsin border where there had apparently been a parade earlier in the day. It had left shredded pink and purple paper all over the road. A few Easter baskets rolled, lost, along the sidewalk. A kind of throne had been built outside the courthouse for, it seemed, the Easter Bunny—a trellis decorated with tissue roses and green crêpe paper and a chair draped in pink and purple velour. It was empty now, but there was still a trail of crushed candies and pale blue candy wrappers where the children must have stood in line waiting for a chance to sit on the Easter Bunny's lap.

Driving through that little town with the pastel trash and the spring flowers in bloom—the daffodils and tulips and all the flowering trees in their whites and pinks—reminded Jiselle of the sugar Easter eggs her mother used to buy for her when she was a child. You would look inside the bright sugar cave to find a perfect little village with emerald green grass and cozy bungalows for rabbits and ducklings made of more sugar.

Usually, Jiselle had kept those on a shelf until her mother, around the Fourth of July, would point out that they were attracting ants. But, one year, she'd decided to taste the egg.

Although the first broken-off bit of the bric-a-brac on the eggshell had tasted stale, Jiselle couldn't resist another nibble, and another, until eventually she'd managed to nibble away the whole exquisite egg and the peaceful scene inside it, too.

⁓

184

As the length of his detainment dragged on, Jiselle began to call Mark several times a day. If he didn't answer, she left long messages on his voice mail:

"I'm sitting on the deck. The kids are inside. Sam's been building a tower in his room out of Legos. Sara and Camilla have been downloading songs, now that the power's back on. I baked a loaf of bread and washed the sheets. Every night I hold your pillow in my arms and pretend it's you."

"Sweetheart," Mark said. "It's important not to ramble on the voice mail. It costs just as much as talking to me in person, and I think we should be as conservative as we can. Who knows how long this will go on."

"But . . . what about the lawyers? I thought you were sure—"

"What's *sure* in this life, Jiselle? I love you, and I know this is hard for you, but it's harder for *me*."

"Of course," she said. "I know that, Mark. It's—"

"*Shhh*," he said. "I love you. You are the love of my life. I have to go."

~❧~

Summer came in early, mild and sweet. The air smelled of cake, yeasty and moist. There was the usual seasonal sense of something new beginning again, except that with the weather growing warm and humid so early, it was as if a step in the process of the seasons had been skipped. By the middle of May, teenage girls and their mothers had taken equally to wearing what looked like lingerie in the middle of the day—to the grocery store, to the bank. Black camisoles. Satin halter tops. Short shorts.

Seeing them in St. Sophia, with its tulips lined up in straight rows outside the public buildings and its flags flapping overhead, those girls and women looked to Jiselle as if they'd stumbled on to the wrong set—parading their call girl costumes through the filming of a 1950s TV show.

The power outages, it seemed, and the shortages, and the fears of the flu had inspired a portion of the population to toss off its old morality and to live for the moment. Drug use and promiscuity were said to be at an all-time high among teenagers. Small communes were forming, in the Western states especially—enclaves devoted to free love, spiritual growth, and the pleasures of the flesh. It was said that Dr.

Springwell was not, after all, in the Canary Islands but on a ranch in Wyoming, where he led a cult of young people who were devoted to sexual experimentation.

But other groups formed, too.

After it was noted in the press how few Phoenix flu deaths had been reported among the Amish, the New Amish groups sprang up. They blamed cell phones for the power outages and the flu: the radiation emitted by the towers was blanketing the country in poisonous, invisible vibrations that disrupted the environment, driving the birds into a frenzy. This was also the reason for the visibility in recent months of so many rodents. They had been driven out of the ground. They had lost all sense of direction because of the effect of the vibrations on their inner ears.

186 The radiation was causing the human immune system to go haywire, the New Amish said. They lived in sod houses and made their own clothes and utensils from found materials.

But most of the people Jiselle saw around town simply seemed bored. There had never been so many people in St. Sophia. Stuck in St. Sophia. Spending their days in St. Sophia. Without school, without sports, without work, without the malls in the city and suburbs open, they were wired with energy and exhausted at the same time. They actually sat on the park benches, which had seemed to be merely decorations to Jiselle until then. Mothers pushed children on the swings in the park. They walked on the sidewalks.

One morning, as she stood in line at the St. Sophia Credit Union (Mark had told her to go, to make sure the airline was still depositing his checks and to get some cash "in case"), she saw ahead of her in the line, which snaked out the door and around the corner of the bank's brick façade, Bobby's mother, Tara Temple. She was wearing patent leather high heels. Black, they glinted in the sun bouncing off the sidewalk and sent thin beams of light straight up the insides of her long, tanned legs. She was wearing shorts so short that Jiselle could see the fold between her thigh and her buttocks, and, on the inside of one sleek thigh, a little rose, which looked like either a temporary tattoo or a brand-new one.

Tara Temple had met Jiselle only those two or three times (the last time was when she'd brought over the Wholeness book) and didn't appear to recognize her. Between them, a man in a necktie and Bermuda shorts stood very close to Tara, and Jiselle watched as, saying nothing, he reached behind Tara and smoothed three fingers down the small of her back to the place where her tailbone clefted into her tight shorts.

Jiselle looked quickly away. Bobby's mother had to have been at least ten years older than she, but standing behind her in that line, wearing flat black sandals and one of Mark's baggy T-shirts over a pair of worn-out khaki shorts, Jiselle felt old, and maternal, and disapproving. She liked Paul Temple, Bobby's father, who had stopped by several times recently to help Bobby with the yard work, which Bobby had agreed to take on for forty dollars a week. (He'd wanted to do it for free—because "I eat like five meals a day here!"— but Jiselle had insisted on paying him.) Because Paul Temple taught history at St. Sophia High, he'd had nothing to do since the schools closed down. A week earlier, he and Bobby had spent the whole day cutting down dead brush between the lawn and the ravine for her, and then they'd burned it in a barrel in the backyard. It had been an especially great day for Sam, who adored Mr. Temple, who liked to punch Sam in the shoulder and call him Bud.

A bank teller came out then and announced that the computers had frozen, and the wait could be "days." She strongly suggested their leaving and coming back another time.

Jiselle watched as Tara Temple turned to look at the man behind her.

They smiled sleepily at each other and left the line together.

GOODBYE TO THE NECKTIE was a news bulletin for days. Men were being encouraged to go without them. The "New Businessman" had an open collar and short sleeves. He wore cargo pants or shorts, carried a satchel instead of a briefcase. There was some joyful speculation that the days of eight-to-five were over forever, replaced by siestas, long vacations—an entirely different way of life having been glimpsed in this brief, strange period. It was a side benefit to the collapse of the economy, the devastation wrought by the Phoenix flu. The rules for behavior of all kinds had changed overnight— or changed while Jiselle had been making grilled cheese sandwiches for Sam and reading novels at home.

Camilla had hauled out all the books she'd been assigned in her Advanced Placement English course that year, lining them up in the order she thought would be most educational and appealing. Jiselle had just finished *Tess of the d'Urbervilles*, which had left her weeping in the bathtub the night she'd finished it. Now, she was halfway through *Mrs. Dalloway*, which kept her in a kind of dreamy reverie long after she put it down.

"I can't believe you didn't read this stuff in high school," Camilla said, and Jiselle felt the familiar prickle of her skin at one of Camilla's seemingly harmless observations. "Or at least in college."

Jiselle looked up at her. Camilla was looking at her curiously from the couch. For the first time, perhaps, Jiselle noticed that the girl had a very fine, blond down on her shoulders and arms. She was wearing a sundress with thin straps, and no makeup, and Jiselle felt as if she were looking at a stranger.

"I never finished college," Jiselle said. She opened her mouth again and realized that she was about to tell Camilla about her father, about Ellen, about the accident, as if that explained why she'd left college, but then she closed her mouth again and gave a little apologetic smile.

"That's no biggie," Camilla said. "Some of the dumbest people I know finished college."

The second week of May, there were the first officially confirmed reports of massive outbreaks of hemorrhagic zoonosis in Arizona, Nevada, and Idaho. Some newscasters used the word *hundreds*. Others said *thousands*. All nonessential government services nationwide were closed down by executive order, although there was grumbling about this in the Midwest and on the East Coast. Wasn't this clearly, mostly, a Western disease? Wouldn't the most prudent thing be to limit travel over and across the Mississippi until the cause of the illness, the source of the contagion, could be determined? Why shouldn't people in Ohio be allowed to keep their post offices and libraries open if they wanted to? *They* weren't infected with hemorrhagic zoonosis.

People in the Western states thought the same things about the East.

"During the Black Plague the English called it the French disease, the French called it the Italian disease, and so on and so on. People blaming other people for the plague is nothing new," Paul Temple said. He'd started coming by most days around five o'clock, if he wasn't already there working on the yard, walking the two miles from his own house. He'd knock politely on the door and wait for Jiselle or one of the children to open it for him, although Jiselle had told him it was fine just to come in. When she opened the door, he'd smile apologetically and say he was "just looking for something to do. With the schools closed, not a big demand for history teachers in St. Sophia."

When the power was on and there was cold beer, Jiselle would offer him one. Often, sitting across from her on the deck in his T-shirt and jeans—looking rugged, Jiselle thought, like an outdoorsman, not a historian—he'd seem as if he were about to tell Jiselle something or ask her for advice, but he never did.

There was no denying now that people were dying in large numbers, all over the country—and that even if it was not being called a plague, it was a plague. The suppression of information until recently had not been a conspiracy, the public was assured, but rather a *complexity* that had kept those numbers from being interpreted and disseminated in an accurate manner. And although no one had called it the Phoenix flu or hemorrhagic zoonosis, there had been deaths in St. Sophia as well—a child who'd gone to Sam's school, a woman who'd worked at the library, an elderly couple and their disabled son. When Jiselle and Sam went into town for the goose food, she had seen graves being dug in the St. Sophia Cemetery, and then the fresh dirt mounded over them. Despite the ban, a white balloon had managed somehow to snag itself in one of the tallest trees in the center of town. It blew around there erratically in a high breeze for a couple of days before the Fire Department came with a truck and ladder and took it down. Apparently, it had been upsetting residents of St. Sophia.

191

"It's hype," Mark said over the phone. "The whole thing. The pharmaceutical companies and the European Union have a lot of money to make over this hype." He no longer sounded anxious on the phone. "The airline is paying my salary, right? As long as the checks don't bounce, everything'll be okay."

The checks were not bouncing. They continued to be deposited directly into Mark's and Jiselle's shared account every week. So, Mark pointed out, there had been no hardship, really, had there? The Gesundheitsschutzhaus was clean, comfortable, he said. The food was good. They were allowed to go outside into a small fenced garden. There was a gym for exercise. No one had gotten sick. They would soon be allowed to leave. He might even miss it. Germany was an amazingly efficient and beautiful place.

"I miss you," Jiselle said. "I can't tell you how much—"

"Keep yourself busy," Mark said. "That's what I'm doing. This'll be over before we know it."

Sam taught Jiselle how to play chess.

It took her days to learn and memorize the fundamentals, only to find that she was the kind of player who might make a fine move that set in motion a long series of self-defeats, unable as she was to think more than one move ahead. But Sam was patient, and Jiselle was learning from her mistakes. When she made a good move, he was delighted: "Yeah!" he'd shout when she took his pawn.

For her part, Jiselle could not believe that after a lifetime of looking down at the mystery of a chessboard (all of her previous lovers, and her father, had played, and none had ever suggested teaching her), she understood now what was being enacted on it. For the first time, she understood what *checkmate* meant and what it meant to be a *pawn*.

They played some nights at the kitchen table by candle-light when the power went out, and, those nights, Jiselle sometimes had the feeling that she was a woman from another era, another life. That she had gone back to some step she'd skipped in a process she hadn't recognized as a process:

Candle flickering. The child's face, deep in concentration over a wooden board and its simple wooden pieces. Through the open windows, the crickets' excited confessions to the dark. Next door, she might hear Diane Schmidt singing folk songs to herself in a high, girlish voice.

One day, Sara put down her leather-bound black diary, in which she sometimes spent hours writing in tiny letters ("I'm trying to save space") and took up one of Jiselle's half-finished afghans and finished it. After that, she began and finished another. Then, a flowing winter scarf, and then she started to crochet a shawl with the exotic yarn Jiselle had bought in Rome but never used—gossamer, fawn-colored. Sara sat for hours on the couch in the family room, intent on the task of pulling the fine, pale stuff through the silver eye of her crochet hook, spinning it out on the other side as an intricate orderliness spilling softly around her.

Jiselle picked up the edge of the shawl and smoothed her hand over the downy floss and lace of it. The stitches were perfect.

"Sara," Jiselle said, "you're so good at this."

Sara looked up. She said, "I heard you reading that story to Sam, the one about the girl who had to make a shawl so thin it could be pulled through a wedding ring before the prince would marry her."

193

Jiselle said, "Are you looking for a prince?"

Sara snorted, rolled her eyes, went back to work. She alternated between the careful crochet work and the tiny printing in her journal. When she wasn't doing one, she was working on the other.

Camilla took up jogging.

Mornings, she'd head out the front door in her running shoes and silky shorts, come back an hour later soaked with sweat, scarlet-cheeked, panting. Her legs began to look stronger, the calves chiseled, defined by the muscles in them. Bobby might be waiting for her in the family room. Sometimes Jiselle would find him moving Sam's action figures across the arm of the couch even when Sam wasn't around. He'd laugh when she caught him at it, and say, "The boredom's making me regress." His father was spending more and more time on the lawn than it required, mowing it into a perfect chessboard pattern of crisscrosses and squares while Bobby, displaced, sat on the couch with the action figures or on the deck drinking lemonade.

"I could make a nice brick path for you," Paul suggested to Jiselle one afternoon. His T-shirt was soaked with sweat, and Jiselle could see how physically fit he was. His muscles were different from Mark's, which were hotel-gym muscles, and more defined. Paul's body was solid, sinewy. His hair was damp around his forehead. "From the deck down to the ravine. I've got the bricks left over from a project. It would give me something to do, and it wouldn't hurt Bobby to keep a bit busier, if you know what I mean." He nodded up to Bobby, who had fallen asleep in a lawn chair while Camilla was out running. "Keep our kids out of trouble."

He showed Jiselle where he would lay the bricks. He said he thought that at the end of the path he could even make a few steps down the bank and into the ravine. "What do you think?" he asked.

"Well, a path would lovely," Jiselle said. "I'll need to ask Mark, but I think—"

"Oh, of course," Paul said. "Ask Mark. See what Mark has to say."

They walked back across the lawn together. That day, the backyard was a riot of midsummer flowers and leaves, and overhead in the sky the contrail of a jet had dissolved across the clear blue. Planes were still flying sporadically, despite the restrictions and the drastic diminishment in flight offerings, the lack of fuel. Passengers were required to produce a statement of purpose to be approved thirty days in advance of travel, and even some of the most desperate were being denied. A woman in Oregon was trying to get to her son in New Jersey. The boy was twelve years old and had gone to visit his father and stepmother, both of whom had fallen ill and died within a week of his arrival. The boy was in the hospital in Newark now, also ill, and although she was willing to pay up to ten thousand dollars for a one-way flight, the mother could not get a seat on any airline. The last report Jiselle heard on the news was that Tom Cruise had arranged a private plane to take the woman to her son. There was footage of the woman on a tarmac climbing the stairs to a small jet, her hair whipping behind her in the wind.

195

Now a jet was flying over the house, and the stream behind it looked like a white ribbon that had frayed and then been pulled to pieces.

It was impossible, she thought, but Jiselle considered briefly that the jet held that mother. She was alone up there, looking down, hands clasped in her lap. Behind her, a plume of desperation and relief. Soon that disintegrating path behind her would be invisible overhead.

〜

When Jiselle spoke to Mark about the brick path, he said, "Tell him I said that was fine."

"You're sure?" Jiselle asked.

She could hear what sounded like a party taking place behind Mark's voice. Ice dropped into glasses. A violin. Mark said that they'd been bringing in entertainment, catering nice meals paid for by the airline, subsidized by the European Union, which was insisting on their continued quarantine. Sometimes Jiselle thought he sounded drunk. He slurred the occasional word. *Zhizelle.*

"Why not? Brick path," he said. "Sounds great."

So, the next week, one morning, Paul and Bobby arrived with a load of bricks and stacked them neatly at the side of the yard while Jiselle watched from the deck—Sam running between Paul and Bobby, a blue jay shrieking down from a tree branch, the sweat on Bobby's and his father's T-shirts soaking through the cotton. A cross of sweat on

196

Bobby's back. The dark silhouette of a Victorian widow on Paul's.

For three days in a row, the midafternoon heat had topped ninety-nine degrees. The power had come back again, and Jiselle turned on the air-conditioning when it grew so uncomfortable that she felt she couldn't stand it. The sweat pooled on her eyelids and onto her eyelashes.

But the heat didn't dampen Bobby's and Paul's and Sam's enthusiasm for working on the brick path.

"They're bored," Camilla said. "They're going nuts. They're not like us."

She'd come back into the house from her run. Jiselle had implored her not to run in the heat. ("You'll pass out. Heatstroke. You'll get dehydrated.") But Camilla just shook her head, smiling. "It's nice of you to worry, but I'll be fine."

And she did seem fine. Flushed, glowing. After her shower, Camilla lay on the couch in the family room in the air-conditioning with her hair wrapped in a towel, watching CNN. Jiselle sat down beside her.

Usually now, when she watched it, the news was good. No one expected severe power outages since the government had intervened. China was backing down. The war in the Mideast was all but over. The oil embargo would not last, but new developments in alternative fuel sources were being made every day. Researchers were on the verge of finding the cause of hemorrhagic zoonosis, and although this wasn't a cure or a vaccine, it was the first step in that direction. Angelina Jolie and Brad Pitt had been married on a boat in the middle of the ocean so that the wedding could be attended by guests from every corner of the globe—the many foreign dignitaries who loved them but who could not have flown in to the country for it because of the travel restrictions. According to CNN, thousands of large and small boats had crowded around the *Angelina* for the occasion. There were fireworks. There were photographs of the couple wearing white, waving to helicopters circling them on a calm ocean in a perfectly blue sky.

One afternoon Jiselle was both shocked and strangely gratified to hear a CNN reporter mention, almost offhandedly, that there'd been some speculation that the Phoenix flu was being caused by the importation of hair from developing countries, and Jiselle looked forward to telling Brad Schmidt the next time she went over to their house to see if they needed anything. She would congratulate him on his prescience. He would be pleased, especially if he'd made a believer out of her—and, in truth, suddenly this theory seemed no more farfetched than some of the other things being blamed: Herbal supplements. Global warming. Contaminated grapes. Germ warfare. Bad Karma. Infected cats. Infected dogs. Teenage sex.

On CNN, it was Britney again, dancing on a hilltop in the sunlight wearing a spangled bikini top, blond hair flowing behind her. Sara walked into the room. "Jesus," she said. "Like, how many people have died since *her*, and they're still going on about this?"

Camilla turned the television off, pointing the remote at it like a handgun. The screen went black. "*Really*," she said. "It's pathetic."

Part
Five

CHAPTER SIXTEEN

He had been quarantined in Germany for twenty-two weeks, and Jiselle was having trouble picturing Mark's face.

Every night, she'd stare at his photograph on top of their dresser—the photo in which he, in his pilot's uniform, had his arm around her, in her flight attendant's uniform, and the Pacific Ocean was an infinity of gray containing only one small sailboat behind them.

But as soon as she closed her eyes and tried to call up the features of her husband's face without the help of the photograph, they would melt in her imagination, as if he were a runner, blurring by. Or on that speeding train up the side of the mountain in Germany.

"Well, Jiselle, you barely knew him before you married him, and he's been gone most of your marriage anyway," Annette said.

It felt like a slap across the face—some thin, feminine

hand made of air and disapproval smacking her cheek. Annette made a sound on her end of the line, something like air being snorted out of her nose. She'd had a difficult delivery—hours of labor followed by a C-section—but the baby was healthy, a little girl named Paulette, who was three months old. Annette was still so weak from her pregnancy problems that they'd had to hire a nanny to look after the baby, but Annette had been able to get out of the house a few times in the last couple of months.

"Don't worry," she said when Jiselle's silence went on long enough that it was clear she wasn't going to say anything else, "it'll all work out when Mark gets back."

202

"I need you," Jiselle said to Mark one evening when the phone connection was unusually crisp over the ocean between them, and when he responded, she could hear every consonant, perfectly pronounced. She could even hear what sounded like swallowing, and the sound of his tongue passing over his teeth when he paused.

"I don't want to hear that right now, Jiselle," he said. "I'm helpless over here. I have to believe you're okay there, and that you're up to the job of taking care of the kids and yourself. I can't deal with any soft-minded stuff."

"What?" Jiselle instinctively put a hand to her throat, pressed the phone closer to her ear.

"You know what I'm talking about, Jiselle. Try to rise to the occasion, okay? This isn't Disneyland for any of us anymore. Now, I have to go. It's the middle of the night here. Goodnight, my darling."

Jiselle mouthed the word *goodnight*, but Mark hung up before she could say it aloud.

She stood looking at the phone in her hand for a long time.

∽⦵∾

After it became clear that there would not be time left in the school year for schools to reopen before September, the children had begun to stay up until well into the early hours of morning—1:00 AM, 2:00—and to sleep until noon, even during the week, which had, without the routine of school, become indistinguishable from the weekends. Often, Bobby Temple did not leave for his own house until the sun came up. Those nights, Jiselle fell asleep to the low murmur of his and Camilla's voices on the other side of the wall.

She thought that, perhaps, as the stepmother, as the adult in the house, she was supposed to ask Bobby to leave, but he was so polite, so helpful—emptying the garbage and then hauling the can to the end of the driveway on Fridays, playing with action figures on the floor with Sam, emptying the rodent cages with him. It was a comfort and a relief having a nearly grown man in the house. When the county stopped garbage pickup, Bobby helped Jiselle burn what couldn't be composted. (He'd started the compost himself, behind the garage.) When the electricity went out, he would go through the house gathering up the flashlights they'd left lying

203

around since the last power outage, and then he'd start up the generator.

In the middle of April, Bobby drove Jiselle to the airport in his father's car to pick up Mark's Mazda from airline employee parking, where it had been since Mark's fateful flight to Germany. Jiselle drove the Mazda back, and Bobby followed in the Saab.

They parked the Cherokee in the garage and closed the garage door.

"Do what you have to do," Mark had said disapprovingly over the phone when she told him that she was going to start driving the Mazda instead of the Cherokee now because of the SUV attacks. "Let the thugs run the world," he said. "But be careful with my Mazda."

Jiselle didn't respond. His disapproval didn't change her mind. She had responsibilities—his children. She had to take precautions. The attacks were becoming more and more common, moving inexorably from the city to its fringes. Drivers were being hauled out of their big vehicles and beaten. The SUVs were toppled, smashed with baseball bats, set on fire.

"We've got to blame *something* for the Phoenix flu," Paul Temple said. "We're like the flagellants during the Black Death. What we're whipping is ourselves. We're not a God-fearing society, so if it isn't God who's punishing us for our sins, it must be the environment punishing us for our gas-guzzling vehicles."

That afternoon, Paul had walked over to get his Saab

back, but Bobby and Camilla had already taken it out again to pick up some things for dinner, so Jiselle invited him in, offered him a beer. The electricity had been on solidly and without interruption for four days, so the beer was cold. He took the bottle gratefully and settled into a chair on the deck, gazing out at the ravine, which was still glistening and dripping from the rainstorm earlier. The air was warm and humid. Paul Temple was flushed. His forehead was beaded with sweat. He leaned on his elbows with the bottle of beer on the table between his arms and held his head in his hands.

"It's a secular society," he went on, "so it's not God; it's global warming. But it's the same idea. The idea is that we brought this on ourselves. That cult in Idaho, the one where they all killed themselves to erase their carbon footprint— that could be straight out of the Middle Ages."

Jiselle had seen photos of the cultists—more than a hundred dead men, women, and children in rows in their compound outside of Boise. They had all had white sheets pulled up to their chins, and their bare feet dangling from the ends of their cots. Such organized mania, she'd thought, looking at the photographs on CNN. How had they managed it?

Paul looked up at Jiselle and said, "These are strange times."

Jiselle nodded. She saw bewilderment and despair in his expression, which she felt sure had to do with his wife, Tara. That day at the bank returned to her. She was afraid she might betray her own knowledge then, and looked away.

Overhead, she heard a plane and looked up to see a pinwheeling bit of silver in the haze. Not a commercial airliner. Those had been grounded for good in the last two weeks. It was, instead, one of the small, fast military or corporate jets that had been crisscrossing the sky lately—quiet and suspiciously high, gone in a blink, although Jiselle continued to stare at the silver spinning place it had been until the sun in the haze over the treetops appeared to double itself.

⚬⚬⚬

That afternoon, Jiselle realized they were low on everything. The milk was gone. One of the children had used the last of it and put the empty carton back in the refrigerator. The peanut butter was mostly gone, and there was a green spot of mold on the last slices of bread in the Wonderbread bag.

Outside, Bobby and Paul were hauling bricks, placing them in careful rows beside one another, while Sam ran back and forth from the deck to the edge of the ravine, occasionally flapping his arms. Jiselle called to Sara and Camilla, "Anyone want to go to the store?"

They both did. It had already become a rare treat to go into St. Sophia. Gas was eleven dollars a gallon, and they were trying to conserve what was in the car for emergencies.

They drove in Mark's Mazda—Camilla beside Jiselle, Sara in the backseat. Jiselle put the top down, for the hard breeze of it, and turned the radio on to the oldies station—happy, stupid songs about being a teenager in a perfect world. Even the car crashes in that world seemed safe, predictable. There were never any special announcements on the oldies station. The only chatter was about a contest in which the naming of a songwriter could win you a thousand dollars. Sara and Camilla nodded along to the songs, seeming content enough. "Take a Letter, Maria." "Hey There, Lonely Girl."

Although it had been dry, the rains had been relentless the month before, so the flowers were as vivid as Jiselle ever remembered them. Along the side of the road the wildflowers waved their caution-yellow faces at the sun. Red-winged blackbirds darted among the blooms and grasses, landing on long blades, not even bending them, appearing to be weightless. Butterflies and moths swarmed around the purple-blue of cornflowers. The Queen Anne's lace made a webby froth in the ditches.

Sara let her elbow rest on the car door and opened and closed her fingers in the wind as the car flew through it, as if she were trying to hang on to the air. Camilla leaned her head back on the seat and closed her eyes, her face lit up by the sun. Jiselle watched the road in front of her spinning out like a black ribbon. There were almost no other cars on the road.

"If you don't want to hear the bad news out there, folks, you've finally found the right station!" a man with a deep voice, which managed to sound girlish in its excitement, shouted over the radio. "We're just playing music and telling really stupid jokes!"

. . .

207

When Jiselle finally reached the edge of St. Sophia and pulled up to the Safeco, the parking lot was nearly empty. There were just a few small cars parked at the edges—employees' cars? A couple of motorbikes were on the sidewalk outside the store, and an empty wheelchair, looking abandoned, sat by itself next to the Dumpster. There was one truck parked out front, and a man in a blue shirt was tossing crates out of the back of it onto the pavement. He didn't look at Jiselle and the girls when they passed by, but after they'd already started to pass through the automatic doors, Jiselle heard him mutter, "Hot babes," as if it were an accusation. When they were on the other side of the doors, which had closed, Jiselle looked back.

208   The man had a wild black beard and bright blue eyes. He was staring at her with his chin lifted. She turned away again fast.

Inside the supermarket, Sara and Camilla parted, heading down different aisles, pushing their separate carts. Jiselle took a red plastic basket and said, "Let's not forget to get Saltines and 7-Up for the Schmidts."

Saltines and 7-Up seemed to be all Mr. and Mrs. Schmidt ate. It was the only item from the store they ever requested when Jiselle offered to pick something up for them.

What were they living on otherwise?

They never took their car out of the garage anymore, but they looked healthy enough. Like the water Mr. Schmidt said he had, did he also have a stockpile of food? Was he setting traps—eating possum, squirrel? There were apple trees in his backyard, but they had only just begun to grow small, hard

fruit. Even if he'd managed somehow to plant a vast vegetable garden, not much could have come up there yet either.

Jiselle would buy them, she decided, some cans of tuna
and sardines, if there were any, but she went to the cracker
aisle first to get the Saltines, which were plentiful and light to
carry in her basket. She took two boxes and moved on.

Freshly mopped, the floors of the grocery store were wet
and streaked, but there seemed to be no one working there
except for one girl behind one cash register. Many of the
things Jiselle wanted—eggs, fresh vegetables, and fruit—lay
behind the glass doors of the padlocked freezers or under
the heavy yellow contamination cloths. Still, there seemed
to be more things on the shelves that afternoon than there
had been the week before, when they were still cordoning
off the bakery aisle. Now, some of the bread was moldy, but
Jiselle found the best loaf she could and put it in her basket.
And she was glad to see that there was milk. Many gallons
of it. And cheese. And even yogurt, which she'd been learning to live without but still loved. She was happy, passing the
displays of canned soup and stuffing mix, to see the plenty.
There was still more than enough in the grocery store to feed
them for months—*years*—if need be, until the energy crisis
ended and normal shipping routes were reopened.

She tracked down peanut butter for Sam, Frosted Flakes.
She shook the box just to hear the flakes inside. Sam would
be so happy about the Frosted Flakes. She took the last box
of Raisin Bran off the shelf, too, but put it back when she saw
that the bottom had been ripped and the waxy pouch inside
was open. She picked up a box of Pop-Tarts instead.

. . .

At the checkout line, they stood and waited for the girl behind the cash register to finish a phone conversation before scanning their purchases.

"That's none of her business," the cashier hissed and whispered. "She can *kiss my ass*."

She had her back turned to them, as if they would not be able to hear her words if they couldn't see her mouth, so they waited in the lane, surrounded by the usual magazines and tabloids, which were covered with the usual headlines:

PRESIDENT THREATENS WAR OVER

EUROPEAN VACCINATION HOARDING

LOSE TEN POUNDS IN TWO WEEKS.

MOTHER SCREAMS, "DON'T LET MY BABY DIE!"

Every one of those magazines was at least two months old. Sara picked up a *People* and put it back down, shaking her head.

Finally, the girl behind the cash register got off the phone and rang up their purchases wearily. Each time she scanned an item she seemed to also glance at her watch. She looked pregnant and was wearing a green apron over her protruding stomach and, under the apron, a dress with yellow tulips on it.

Was it possible that she smelled a bit like whiskey? Could that sweet, hot scent be her perfume, or did the smell drift over only when the girl opened her small, glossy red mouth?

When she'd finally scanned the last item, the cashier

looked at her watch for several seconds, as if timing something internal before she looked up, sighing, and asked, "That it?"

"Yes," Jiselle said, and paid in cash.

The man who had been unloading boxes from the semi was sitting now, unmoving, behind the wheel of his truck in the parking lot. He blared his horn when they passed in front of him, and it felt physical, that noise—Jiselle and the girls stumbled a bit, their cart veering slightly out of control. Sara was pushing, Camilla was walking beside her, and Jiselle quickly stepped between the two of them, linking their arms through hers, hurrying to the Mazda. "Fucking asshole," she said, and she saw the girls exchange amused looks. It crossed Jiselle's mind to say something to them then—about men, about being careful, now that they were a house without a man in it, but when she began to form the first part of the first sentence, she could not find the words. Instead, she kept their arms hooked around hers.

211

~∾~

Jiselle turned the radio back on to the oldies station. She was about to turn right into the road when she realized that the long stream of vehicles passing the Safeco exit was a funeral procession. "Shit," she said before she could keep herself from saying it. The procession was, of course, going in her direction. Who knew how long they'd have to wait? Sara took a fingernail file out of her purse and began to file her nails. Camilla opened a months-old *Elle* she'd bought at the store and began to page through it. Jiselle took a deep breath and listened to the song on the radio until she realized that it was—maybe loud enough for those slow-moving mourners to hear—"Na Na, Hey Hey, Kiss Him Goodbye."

She snapped it off.

She bit her lip.

When she looked over, Camilla was also suppressing a smile, and then they all three started to laugh at the bad joke of it, the morbid coincidence, as car after car continued to pass, headlights shining garishly in the bright sun, little funeral parlor flags snapping from their antennas, until finally the last one, a Mazda just like Mark's, passed, and the driver, a middle-aged man in a black suit, waved to them as if to let them know the procession was over. He was smiling brightly, not like a mourner. Still, Jiselle hesitated before following him into the road, joining the procession.

"Oh, forget it," she said, turning left instead of right. "Let's take the long way, or we'll be behind them for days before they turn off at the cemetery."

"Definitely," the girls agreed.

"Can we turn the radio on again?" Sara asked from behind her.

Jiselle turned it on again. The song was, "Baby, It's You."

❦

The long way home took them past the car dealership—where a salesman was sitting in a lawn chair, seeming to be staring up at the sun—and past the library, closed down with the other nonessential public services, and then past the high school, where the flag had been taken down. Nothing flapped there but a loose gray piece of rope.

Then they passed Sam's school, Marquette Elementary, where the statue of Father Marquette stood in an overgrown garden with his arms open. A white plastic grocery bag was snagged around one of his wrists. The bronze plaque below the statue appeared to have been hacked away from the base, a gouged square in its shape left behind. (Was it simple vandalism, Jiselle wondered, or was there some value in bronze?) She remembered, months before, getting out of her car while waiting for Sam after school to read that plaque. She had learned that Jacques Marquette had stopped in the area during his explorations, due to poor health, and had written his journals there.

She thought, then, of Sara's journal. All those hours she spent now hunched over, when she wasn't crocheting, the tiny little letters spilling out of her furiously across the pages.

"Maybe that girl will be the great chronicler of these times," Paul Temple had said. "Keeping a record of it all. You've heard of Brother Clynn, during the Black Plague in Ireland? He was the last monk alive in his cloister, writing a letter to the future he assumed no one would live to see. The last sentence of his journal was 'Waiting among the dead for death to come,' and then, written in another hand, 'And here it seems the author died . . .'"

"Oh, Paul," Jiselle had said, "don't tell me that."

"I'm sorry," he'd said, laughing as he apologized. "But at least talking doesn't make anything happen."

. . .

213

They drove home along the ravine, dark and leafy-green at the same time. When they were only a few miles from home, they came upon several police cars and a fire engine idling and, along with them, a double row of parked cars. A small crowd of people had gathered, standing in a little huddle, almost as if they were posing for a photograph but looking down into the ravine instead of at a camera.

"Stop," Camilla said. "Shouldn't we see what it is?"

"I don't know," Jiselle said, but she was slowing down as she said it. "I mean, do we—"

"We have to see," Sara said. "We can't just drive by. Something's going on."

Jiselle pulled the Mazda over. She put the car in park, and she and the girls got out and walked over to the little gathered group.

No one was speaking. The only sound was the raspy call of a crow overhead and the sound of the fire engine idling, wasting fuel.

Jiselle and the girls came up behind the small crowd and stood on their tiptoes but still could see nothing, so they walked beyond them to the edge of the ravine and looked down.

At first, Jiselle thought she was looking down on flowers—a blurred garden, a wall of flowers built around a heap of flowers—roses and peonies, perhaps covered with a thin sheet of frost so that the flowers shimmered. An enchanted garden. Then she blinked.

No.

This was something else.

Down there in the shadows and among the foliage, she recognized first the face of a goat turned up to her. Its hollow eyes. Its jaw hanging open. Its implacable expression. And then others came into focus:

A bloated cow and what seemed to be a lamb tossed onto its side. Kittens, curled into a mass—or were they rabbits? A scrawny dog or a coyote. A small horse, which seemed to be bowing on its knees like a circus animal performing a trick.

The smell of it, also flowery, overpoweringly sweet and rotten, drifted up to her on the breeze, and Jiselle put her hand over her face and mouth but didn't gasp until she saw movement—the black shadow of a rat darting under the horse's pale corpse.

"What the hell is it?" Sara asked, holding on to Jiselle's upper arm. Her hand was cold. She was breathing hard. Jiselle couldn't speak. A woman in front of them answered.

"Animals," she said. "Dead. You know, they dump them. The diseased. Farmers, I guess. Or someone. Or a bunch of someones."

"Jesus," Camilla said, backing away.

CHAPTER SEVENTEEN

Back at the house, Jiselle and the girls unloaded the groceries in silence. From the glass doors, Jiselle saw that Sam, Bobby, and Paul were filling a narrow black dirt path with bricks. They had their shirts off now, and their backs were shining in the sun. Sam was holding a brick, waiting for Paul or Bobby to take it from him.

Unlike the other two, he wasn't sweating. He'd taken off his shirt only in imitation. When Bobby or Paul wiped his own brow, Sam did the same.

Jiselle made lunch from what she'd bought at Safeco. Bread, canned ham. She made lemonade from powder and bottled water, poured it, set out a glass for each of them, and called them in for lunch.

The conversation around the table concerned trips they'd taken. The Taj Mahal, the Grand Canyon. The time Jiselle's plane to Sweden had been rerouted to Iceland.

Nothing was said about the animal dump. The girls ate heartily. They seemed to have forgotten the shock of it.

Back near the Mazda, Sara had vomited. Camilla had held her hair. They'd opened the trunk and gotten out one of the dozens of bottles of water they'd bought, and Jiselle had poured some of it onto a paper towel, wiped Sara's face for her, given her the rest to rinse out her mouth, spit, drink. When they were back in the car, Camilla said, "What the hell is going on? Did those animals get the *flu*? Is something going to happen to *us*?"

"Of course not," Jiselle said. "Humans and animals don't get the same diseases. It's just—like the woman said. Farm animals. It's convenient. Like people who dump old refrigerators in the woods. You don't have to pay to—"

"They weren't all farm animals," Sara said. "How did they get there? Why were all those people standing around? Why were the cops there?"

Jiselle said nothing. She could not think of any explanation for the animal dump that was not completely absurd. There *was* no explanation. Finally, she said, "We should have asked the fireman or the police."

But then she recalled the look on the fireman's face—stern, unapproachable, the expression the guards at the queen's palace wore. An expression that forbade the asking of questions.

Now Sara was eating, looking pink-cheeked again. Sam told a joke about a monkey on a bicycle. There was laugh-

217

ter. They lingered long enough for Jiselle to make a second pitcher of powdered lemonade, and when they were done eating, Bobby and Camilla sat down on the couch to watch television together, and Sara went to her room, where Jiselle could hear one of her own old Joni Mitchell CDs playing. She'd told Sara weeks before to feel free to borrow anything she liked but hadn't really imagined she owned any CDs Sara would like. Apparently, she did.

Jiselle and Paul took their glasses of lemonade to the deck, along with Sam, and they sat for a while looking out at the ravine, at the half-laid path down the lawn to the edge of it. Not until Sam went back inside for a cookie did Jiselle tell Paul about what they'd seen—the animal dump.

He nodded. He bit his lower lip. He didn't speculate but said, "I wish I could say I'm more surprised. Something's headed in our direction. The year before the Black Plague did its worst damage, people said they saw herds of horses in the sky. Whole crowds would gather together to stare up at them."

Jiselle was about to protest that this hadn't been a hallucination, that there were actual animals—dozens of them—dead and dumped at the side of the road, but Sam came back out then with a cookie for each of them on a small white plate, and Paul and Jiselle each took one and ate them in the sunshine.

"Jiselle," Paul said to her when she stood to go back in the house.

"Yes?" she said.

But there was a look in his eyes that she understood to

mean he had only been saying her name, not asking anything of her.

◦∽◦

"Mark?" Jiselle asked.

"Yeah?"

These days he simply sounded distracted when she spoke
to him. He said there'd been no progress whatsoever made
on their release. "No one's going anywhere," he said. "Anywhere. For God knows how long."

"I love you, Mark," she said.

"Love you, too."

"The children are doing fine," she said.

"Good."

Everything must have seemed so far away to him, she
realized. What was there to talk about? What were the mice,
the birds, the animal dump, the weather in St. Sophia, or
even the children, to Mark, detained on the other side of the
ocean? When she could think of nothing to say, she said,
again, "I love you."

"I love you, too." He said the words as if she'd badgered
him into saying them.

◦∽◦

By the end of the week, they'd finished the path.

"Do you like it?" Paul asked her. He was standing a few
feet ahead of Jiselle. He crossed his arms over his sweaty

T-shirt. He worked his tongue around near his back molar, the one that had been bothering him for a few days, and waited for her to answer.

It was a perfect path, straight down the back of the lawn into the leafy distance. It divided the backyard into two interlocking halves. It meandered a little, but it was a clear path. Already a bit of moss was growing in the cracks. "It's beautiful," she said.

It was.

Nights, under a full moon, it glowed. There was something in the bricks—ground glass?—that couldn't be seen in daylight but that became luminous in moonlight.

Standing on the path ahead of her, Paul Temple said, as if it hurt him to say it, "You're so good to his children. And so lovely. I hope he appreciates you."

Jiselle inhaled and put a hand to her mouth, before turning back to the house.

"Jiselle!" he called after her. "I'm sorry . . ."

The weather had been so warm and sunny and so wet so early that all the flowers were already at the height of their blooming, and then starting to die already by the beginning of July. The magnolias looked soggy, littering the grass with petals. The branches of the rose bushes sagged with roses. The daffodils lay prone on the earth, their stems having slumped over under the burden of their enormous flowers.

That day, Tara Temple came to the door. Jiselle opened it,

surprised to see how plump she was—certainly she'd gained fifteen pounds since Jiselle had seen her in line at the bank—and how scantily clad. She was wearing a silvery sundress, and it plunged between her large, loose breasts, even revealing a shadow of the aureolae around her nipples. The dress floated over her thighs in the breeze, threatening, it seemed to Jiselle, to fly right off.

Yes, she said to Jiselle as she stepped through the door, she'd love to step in and have a cup of coffee. She'd stopped by to tell Bobby she was going to need to go to Virginia for a week. "Grandma's sick."

But Bobby and Camilla had taken Mark's car into town, on Jiselle's request. The electricity had gone out for three days, spoiling everything, but it had been back on for a day now, and the refrigerator was working, and it seemed to Jiselle that if there was milk and butter at the Safeco, they could risk a few things in the refrigerator again, and that it would be worth the gas to stock up while they could.

221

While Tara Temple sat at the kitchen table, Jiselle made coffee, poured it into mugs, and, after punching holes in the top, handed the can of evaporated milk to Tara, who added it to her cup.

"It's so important, you know," Tara said, pouring the milk into her coffee. "Vitamin D."

"Oh," Jiselle said, but she had never liked evaporated milk and did not want it in her coffee, which was now a rare enough treat that spoiling it seemed like a crime. Like so many other things, coffee had become harder and harder to come by. Luckily, Jiselle had thought to buy several cans before the shortages, and now she limited herself to one cup every other day, because who knew how long it would have to last?

She looked disapproving when Jiselle set the can back down on the counter without pouring any into her cup, and Tara picked the can back up herself before following Jiselle out to the deck.

They sat together with the evaporated milk between them, both women holding their coffee to their noses, taking deep breaths of it.

"It's not a healthy addiction," Tara said, but she closed her eyes when she sipped.

So did Jiselle.

"*My*," Tara said, and rested the cup on her knee, "that tastes good."

She sat with her legs crossed, swinging one over the other, and her dress was so short that Jiselle could see her black lace underwear as she rested her head on the back of the chair, her face to the sun.

"Dairy products," Tara said. "And sunlight. This disease preys on people who aren't getting enough vitamin D, which is almost impossible to get in sufficient quantities because of the diminished sun function. Did you know that?" She looked at Jiselle.

"Really?" Jiselle asked. It was all she could think of to say. Tara Temple had delivered this news with such an air of authority that Jiselle found herself both intimidated and comforted by it. Someone, she thought, at least *thinks* she knows what's going on here.

Tara reached over and handed Jiselle the can of evaporated milk, urging it on her. "You really must," she said.

Obediently, Jiselle poured some into her cup. The coffee was strong—stronger than she would usually have made it back when she'd taken coffee for granted—and the evaporated milk made a little mushroom cloud in her cup. "Thank you," she said, placing the can back down between them.

"That's why the quarantines are so shortsighted," Tara Temple went on. "It only keeps people indoors, when the problem in the first place is not enough sunlight."

"Oh," Jiselle said.

"We're not *catching* this," Tara Temple continued. "We're *developing* this. The subtle changes in the environment are signaling changes in our bodies, our nutritional needs, and it's happening too fast to adapt."

This was something Jiselle had heard Dr. Springwell say, back when he was still broadcasting his show.

"Do you meditate?" Tara asked, leaning toward Jiselle, looking directly at her.

"No," Jiselle said, sipping from her cup, avoiding those eyes. So blue. So full of certainty.

"You *should*," Tara said. "Clarity in a time like this is extremely important." She paused and looked at Jiselle as if she were inspecting her for disease. "What are you eating at least?" she asked.

"Well," Jiselle said. "I'm just trying, you know, to keep us all fed."

Tara Temple shook her head. "You need to be very conscious of what you're eating," she said.

223

"Yes," Jiselle said. She nodded as if she understood, as if she would try to be more conscious of what she was eating. But how? It was so much harder than Jiselle had ever guessed it would be, keeping her small family fed. All those years, dashing from kiosk to kiosk, drive-thru to convenience store, she'd never once imagined how much time it would take to make a meal, to serve it. Without a stove. With a refrigerator that couldn't be counted on. No gas in the car, and the grocery store closed half the time, ten miles from home.

The good decisions she'd made had nothing to do with her *consciousness*, as it turned out. They'd been lucky guesses. She'd somehow known that flour would be important and so, before the shortages, had bought twelve pounds of it. And sugar. Baking powder. A can of Crisco, a thing she'd never even seen up close before she bought it. Now, late mornings, when the power was on and she could use the oven, Jiselle would make enough muffins to last a week. She'd gotten the recipe out of an old *Good Housekeeping* magazine she'd found in the garage.

She'd learned, too, how to take care of fresh food. Potatoes and onions lasted an amazingly long time in the cool dark. Bouillon cubes. Cabbage. Apples. She'd torn out an article from the same *Good Housekeeping* magazine on how to soak beans so long that they needed to be boiled for only an hour to make soup. After all those years of relying on frozen dinners and packaged bread, it amazed Jiselle that she could prepare a meal out of beans and water and a single carrot that was so delicious even Sara would ask for seconds.

224

She'd stocked the cupboards and filled boxes in the cellar with canned food and dried fruit after hearing a woman on the radio say one day, "I'm stocking up on food. I know we've been warned not to 'hoard,' but protecting your family is not the same as 'hoarding.'"

The woman's voice sounded like a sober and practical Martha Stewart's, but it couldn't have been. Martha Stewart had died of the Phoenix flu two weeks before. In any case, Jiselle had taken the woman's advice. She and Camilla had driven into town to the Safeco three times, loading the car each time with all the canned and dried goods they could buy. Ramen noodles. Crackers. Pop-Tarts. Broths. Powdered milk. The flour and sugar.

"Well, I have to go, but tell Bobby I stopped by and that I said I'd call in a couple of days, and I'll be home next week. By the way," Tara Temple said, stopping, turning to look at Jiselle, "how is Mark?"

225

"Well," Jiselle said. "Still in the quarantine, of course. He'll be in Germany still, for a little while, I'm afraid."

Tara Temple smiled, wistfully it seemed. She said, "Ah, Mark."

Jiselle said nothing. She waited for Tara Temple to go on.

"We've known him, you know, for a long time. Since long before the—" Here she paused and looked toward the road. "Since long before Joy, and all the years since. We were happy, I suppose, to hear he'd gotten married again. But not surprised. He was always such a—" She moved her hand through the air, as if trying to snatch the right phrase out of it. There was a look of unmistakable pleasure on her face as she said, "Mark was always such a fool for love." She shook her head. "Such a hopeless romantic. In and out of love, always rescuing some damsel in distress or being rescued by one." She let the hand dash back and forth in front of her for a few seconds before she went on, "And everyone put up with it because, as you must know better than anyone, he was so . . . *attractive*. It was a relief, and such a surprise, to imagine him settling down. There were *not a few of us* in this little town who were . . ." She looked, then, up to the sky and said, "Oh, never mind! I'm sure this isn't something you want to hear about, my dear!"

Tara Temple turned back around, and Jiselle watched her descend the steps.

Had she been trying to tell Jiselle what Jiselle thought she might? Had she and Mark . . . ?

Tara Temple was already opening her car door when Jiselle noticed that she was still holding on to the can of evaporated milk. (Absentmindedly? Or had she come to think of it as hers? Had she thought it was wasted on Jiselle, who would never take her advice about vitamin D or meditation, and so just die of the Phoenix flu anyway?) In any case, Tara Temple carried the can with her out the front door, and she still had it in her hand when she got behind the wheel of her car and called out her open window, "Goodbye!"

Jiselle said nothing about the milk. She had another can in the cupboard.

In the morning, Sara wandered into the family room where Jiselle and Camilla were reading together. She held up a pair of scissors in her hands. Jiselle instinctively sat up straighter, inhaling. The combination of Sara and a sharp instrument seemed full of dangerous potential.

But that morning Sara was wearing a white nightgown with yellow smiley faces on it—something Jiselle had never seen before and had not known that Sara owned. She said, handing the scissors to Jiselle, "Will you cut my hair? So it's all one color?"

"Of course," Jiselle said, taking the scissors from her, hoping she didn't sound as breathless to Sara as she did to herself, and stood to follow her into the bathroom.

Since school had been closed, Sara's hair had started to grow out of its ebony dye-job, and what had emerged were several inches of a sandy and reddish blond that reminded Jiselle of the color of fawns. The black fringe around her shoulders, contrasted with her natural color, made her look even more fearsome than when her hair was all one color, but Jiselle had assumed she liked it that way.

"This is so ugly," Sara said, flipping the ends of her hair with her fingers. "Get rid of it. Please."

"Sure," Jiselle said.

She got a towel out of the linen closet and spread it over the sink, and then put her hand between Sara's shoulder blades, pushed her forward gently. She rarely touched Sara on purpose—just accidentally when they reached for the salt shaker at the same time or when she found Sara's elbow pressed against her own as they tried to walk through a door at the

same time—and Jiselle was surprised how thin, almost fragile, Sara's back felt, and her neck. She could feel the knobs of
her vertebrae, and when Sara tilted her face to the side, Jiselle
could see the pulse beat in a fluttering vein at her temple.

"Okay," Jiselle said, taking a bit of the hair between her
fingers. "You're sure?"

"I'm sure," Sara said.

So Jiselle snipped at Sara's hair until the black fringe had
fallen either onto the towel in the sink or around their feet
on the bathroom floor. It took a long time. Jiselle wanted to
do a perfect job. "Okay," she finally said, and Sara straightened up.

Jiselle stared at Sara's reflection staring at herself in the
bathroom mirror, and it was as if she were seeing this girl for
the first time.

Sara, without the unnaturally black hair, seemed to have
skin the color of peaches. She wasn't, Jiselle realized, wearing her lip ring or her black makeup. Without these things
she looked like an awkward adolescent—a young girl with a
round face, wide eyes, soft hair, which Jiselle could not stop
herself from touching.

It felt like rabbit fur, she thought, running her hand over
the top of her stepdaughter's head.

It felt like infant hair.

❧

The next night they heard, in the distance, what sounded
like either fireworks or gunfire.

The sun had just set, and Sam, who was playing with

228

his action figures in the candlelight, looked up. He said, "Shouldn't we be celebrating?"

"Celebrating what?" Camilla asked.

"I don't know," he said. "Independence?"

It was the Fourth of July?

Sara was crocheting by candlelight, and Jiselle was trying to read *Far from the Madding Crowd* with a flashlight balanced on her shoulder. Next door, Diane Schmidt could be heard humming a vaguely familiar tune, something Jiselle thought she might recognize from a documentary about the Civil War she'd watched on PBS in what seemed like another lifetime, a century before.

Again, they heard what might have been fireworks or gunfire. When Sam said, "*See?*"—as if the sound were evidence of their call to celebrate—they all started to laugh, and Jiselle said, "Okay," and they headed outside, where they set the brush pile on fire, and Sara, Camilla, and Sam marched around it singing "The Star-Spangled Banner."

During the march, Jiselle suddenly remembered a trick from Girl Scout camp—how, if you boiled a closed can of evaporated milk long enough, somehow it turned to caramel. She went back into the kitchen for a can of milk and a pan of water.

When she came back out, Jiselle boiled the can over the fire, watching Sam and Camilla and Sara march around her. They looked beautiful and feral in their strange clothes—the girls in mismatched summer skirts and tops, their hair long and wild, like pagan princesses, forest creatures, flushed in the firelight, bare arms and legs glowing orange.

And laughing between his sisters in the circle, Sam, in

229

Laura Kasischke

his cutoffs, bare-chested, appeared to be half-human and half-elf.

They looked like children from a time before civilization, before television and computers, vaccinations and fast food and jets—or children *after* these things, singing a patriotic song written so long ago she was surprised they knew the words.

Later, when she opened the can of evaporated milk, and it was miraculously caramel, they went back into the kitchen and stood around, eating the dense sweetness with spoons.

CHAPTER EIGHTEEN

*Once there was a little boy who went out and got his feet
wet and caught cold. His mother undressed him, put him
to bed, and had the tea urn brought in to make him a good
cup of tea.*

It was two o'clock in the morning, but they had gotten
used to going to sleep later and later. They were wearing
their nightclothes—Jiselle, her long summer nightgown, and
Sam, his Star Wars T-shirt and checkered boxer shorts—but
it didn't seem past midnight to her, and Sam was wide awake,
although the girls had gone to bed after Bobby left, an hour
before, riding his bicycle off into the dark.

For eight days straight, the power had been out, so Jiselle
and the children waited each night until ten or eleven o'clock
to eat dinner by candlelight—a meal of bread, peanut butter,
raisins, and canned soup she could heat up outside on the

grill they'd bought at Wal-Mart the first week of March, before there were no more grills for sale anywhere, at any price. The charcoal was gone, and the lighter fluid, but Jiselle had the kindling that Bobby had broken up for her and left in a neat pile under an old plastic tarp on the deck.

If they ate earlier, the dark nights seemed to stretch on even longer.

Most days, until the sun set, they managed to keep busy reading, playing chess, Sara crocheting or writing in her journal, Sam throwing the Frisbee with Bobby, Jiselle trying to organize the pantry, dust the bookshelves. They had burned what trash had to be gotten rid of in the fire pit. Afterward, it was a perfect ashy black circle at the center of the brown lawn, but while it was burning, the fire there would glow in hundreds of shades of blue and orange. Watching it, you might have thought it was something magical, something biblical, if you didn't know it was burning trash.

Jiselle was still able to charge the battery in her cell phone off the battery in the Cherokee, but only occasionally could she pick up a signal. When she could, she called her mother, who answered the phone, "This is Anna Petersen," as if her office might be calling—but why would they? No one could be selling real estate now. When Jiselle asked how she was, and how she was going to be, and if she needed to come stay with them in St. Sophia, her mother would only chat about the weather, ending with a few last words about Jiselle's "impossible situation."

Mark hadn't called in two days—or if he'd tried, he hadn't been able to get through—and then it had been only to say hello and that he couldn't talk long. There were German officials coming to speak to the detainees that afternoon, and he had paperwork to fill out. He told her, "Don't get excited about a homecoming anytime soon. But I have a feeling we will, at least, be seeing a large monetary settlement from the German government when this is over."

"I just want you home," Jiselle said. "I don't care about the money."

"Of course you don't care," Mark said.

Jiselle was about to object—she felt a warmth spreading across her chest as though a hot soaked cloth had been placed there—but by the time she finally was able to open her mouth to speak, Mark said, "This is it. They're here. Gotta go," and hung up.

Jiselle did the laundry outside in the rain barrel and hung it on the line Paul had stretched for her between the deck and a tree at the end of the yard. That chore alone could sometimes take an entire afternoon before Jiselle even realized how long she'd been outside. The ravine seemed empty and completely quiet behind her as she twisted the shirts and socks until they were dry enough to hang. Occasionally, Beatrice might waddle up out of the ravine for a surprise midday visit.

The grass, which they'd had to let grow since the mower ran out of gas, had grown a foot in only a few weeks. Returned to what must have been an earlier, wilder state, there were long pale grasses mixed in with the green ones, and wildflowers Jiselle didn't know the names of—orange, ruffled cups swaying on thin stems, delicate white frills, purple beads and pearls on long straw-colored stalks—mixed in with those.

233

Now it was very unusual to see a plane, and when she did, it was almost always a military jet flying fast and high. The trees and sky seemed strangely empty even of birds. It was only the end of July. Could they have flown south early this year?

There had been news reports of dead birds, numbering into the hundreds, in yards and parks and in the streets of Chicago, but Jiselle had found, a few weeks before, only a single dead sparrow—a soft gray ball of feathers—in the backyard. One of its wings looked broken, spread out at a strange angle, and there was blood on its breast.

A cat?

She took a shovel out of the garage and buried the sparrow at the edge of the ravine.

234

The rodents, like the birds, seemed to have fled. Every morning, Sam's traps were empty, and he and Jiselle never saw mice or rats on their walks into the ravine any longer. Their absence was not reassuring. Jiselle felt more abandoned by their disappearance than relieved.

It was one of so many disconcerting things. Wave after wave of disastrous statistics on the news were being made human now by a few familiar faces:

Donald Trump's son. Brad Pitt's brother. The woman who'd founded Mrs. Fields cookies, and her entire family.

All of these cases proved what they'd already been telling people for months—that no amount of money, specialized medicine, private planes, or island hideaways could spare you.

The Fieldses, it was said, had retreated together to a house in Idaho, thinking it was an escape from the infected areas with higher populations—but they were found there by a UPS man delivering blankets, which they'd had shipped to them from Denmark because they were unwilling to use blankets that had spent any significant amount of time within U.S. borders.

"These people did everything 'right,'" a man who was identified by a caption on the television as "Health Expert" said, making elaborate quotation marks in the air, raising his bushy eyebrows knowingly, "which goes to show that you can't flee from a virus that's already circulating in your body. People need to keep themselves fit, mind their nutrition, and stay close to health experts who can help them at the first sign of illness."

But the story that completely eclipsed the others was "A Mother, a Saint, in Maine."

235

In Portland a mother of four had left a note on the kitchen table that read, "I know I have the Phoenix flu. I'm going away until it's passed, so I won't infect you."

Her husband and children and the local authorities had mounted a massive search. They'd posted flyers and bought a billboard on the interstate: MOMMY. WE NEED YOU TO COME HOME. WE LOVE YOU. PLEASE. But she was found dead and alone a few days later by a maid at a Holiday Inn in Concord, New Hampshire—her bed surrounded by photos of her family.

Now the family was suing the local authorities because they'd had her remains cremated before the family had a chance to identify her, to say goodbye.

That night, on the couch in the dark, Sam was a warm weight at her side, his head on her shoulder, and Jiselle could feel both the steadiness of his breath and the depth of his concentration. The flashlight was a bright zero on the page they were reading together. His hair was a little longer now, and it tickled the side of her face. Occasionally she'd rub her cheek against the top of his head. He snuggled closer to her when she did.

At the same time there came in the door the funny old man
who lived all alone on the top floor of the house—

236   As if on cue, there was a knock on the front door.

Sam and Jiselle both sat up fast, and Jiselle instinctively snapped the flashlight off and let the book fall closed on her lap. She was surprised to find her heart beating hard. She'd told everyone—Bobby and Paul Temple, Mark, her mother, the children, Annette, Brad Schmidt—that she wasn't scared in the house, in the dark, alone with the children, without a gun, and she'd believed it.

But now she couldn't move.

Sam whispered, "Who could it be?"

Jiselle shook her head. She put her finger to her lips. Another knock. Three times. More insistent. She felt every muscle in her body tense, as if her limbs were ready to take action, whether or not her mind agreed to it. A host of images flashed in front of her: Throwing herself over Sam to shield him. The ravine. Thrashing with his hand in hers through the brush and trees. The girls, in their nightgowns, running ahead of them. She wished that her feet weren't bare, that Sam was wearing long pants and sleeves, that the girls did not sleep so deeply. She'd just begun to form the terrible question of how loudly she would have to scream to wake them, and felt herself inhale, and sensed the instinctive, welcome rush of what could only have been called courage beginning at the base of her brain, readying her to stand, to make some kind of decision, although only her body knew yet what that decision would be, when a voice she recognized as Diane Schmidt's called through the crack in the door, which she had opened, because Jiselle hadn't even locked it, "I am a little old woman."

"Mrs. Schmidt!" Jiselle said, opening the door all the way. "What is it?"

"I am a little old woman," Mrs. Schmidt said again. She was wearing a white nightgown.

"Oh, dear," Jiselle said. "I'll go find your husband. You stay here with Sam."

As Jiselle ran across the yard to the Schmidts' house, she wrapped her arms around herself, shivering suddenly, although she wasn't cold. The moon lit up the backyard, and she hurried up the back steps, holding her flashlight in front of her. She knocked on the door. "Mr. Schmidt? Mr. Schmidt? *Brad?*"

There was no answer. Jiselle tried to look through the screen door and the kitchen window, but the shades were drawn, the curtains pulled. There were no lights on inside. Maybe he was asleep. She knocked harder on the door, and then stood waiting on the steps. She cupped her hands around her mouth and called to the window, "Mr. Schmidt?"

Certainly, if he were in there, he would have heard her by then. But still there was no answer.

She turned the knob on the back door.

It was unlocked.

She pushed it all the way open and stood in the threshold.

"Hello?" she called to the darkness, shining her flashlight into the tidy kitchen before stepping in.

Jiselle had never entered the Schmidts' house from the back door before. With her flashlight, she could make out checkerboard curtains on the windows. The cupboards were painted pastel green. There was a throw rug with a rooster embroidered on it beneath a Formica table. A little yellow rag was folded neatly over the edge of the sink. Jiselle walked through the kitchen toward the hallway that led to the living room, leaving the back door open behind her.

"Hello?" she called, but quietly.

The hallway was even darker, but when she shone her light on the walls, Jiselle could see photographs of Brad and Diane in younger days: Holding hands at the edge of a canyon. Standing with their backs to a waterfall. Diane Schmidt waving from a lounge chair at the side of a pool, wearing a two-piece bathing suit, her skin tanned and smooth, her hair still dark and pulled back, tied with a bright scarf.

238

"Brad?"

She peered into what must have been their bedroom.

The bed was carefully made, the white bedspread without a single crease.

He was not in the bed.

She walked past that room and what must have been the family room, and then the bathroom, which smelled of air freshener and floral soaps.

She stepped into the living room, which was darker than any of the other rooms had been. The television was off, of course, although Mr. Schmidt was sitting in front of it with his feet propped up on an ottoman, staring straight ahead with eyes that appeared to have melted deep into his skull, or fallen from it.

"Hello?" Jiselle said, although she knew he wouldn't answer.

CHAPTER NINETEEN

Very little had been said about what actually happened to victims of the Phoenix flu. The only person who'd spoken of the suffering—the Surgeon General—had been criticized for fear-mongering and replaced by a quieter Surgeon General. But his words—"I've seen people die of cancer and seen them die of AIDS, and had no idea God could come up with even worse ways to die"—had been quoted and repeated a hundred thousand times before they could be suppressed.

But after Brad Schmidt died, the paramedics wouldn't, or couldn't, answer Jiselle's question about what had happened to his eyes, so she was left to wonder. Had he scratched them out? Had they somehow swollen? Burst?

The paramedics said only that she shouldn't touch any of his things and that they were going to board up the house.

After they'd taken Brad Schmidt's body away, the officer in charge wanted to take Mrs. Schmidt to the Grove Home in the city, but Jiselle had heard such terrible things about the place—completely overcrowded, since so many nursing homes and halfway houses and mental institutions had been closed down, and also without staff. One of the Grove Homes had been investigated for euthanizing some of its patients when the generator failed and their oxygen was cut off.

"I suppose you think we should have just sat by and watched them strangle to death, flap around like fish for an hour until they suffocated in their beds?" the nurse in charge said as she was being handcuffed and taken away. "Well, I invite anyone who believes that a death like that would be more compassionate than a sedative and a lethal injection to come and volunteer at the nearest Grove Home."

Paul Temple had said, shaking his head, "During the Black Death, parents abandoned their children, children abandoned their parents."

241

Apparently, the Schmidts had never had children. If there were any living relatives, they could not be located.

"No," Jiselle told the police officer, who stood on the front porch in his biohazard suit looking like a visitor from space. "She can stay with us."

"It's irregular," he said, but objected no further. He seemed to make a note on a pad of paper, but when Jiselle glanced at the page, she saw nothing on it. There was, apparently, no ink in the officer's pen. Still, he'd wanted to give the appearance of being official, of following a procedure.

❧

Sara moved into Camilla's room so that Mrs. Schmidt could sleep in Sara's bed—but in the warm late weeks of the month, Mrs. Schmidt often fell asleep on the deck outside and could not be persuaded to come in.

Sometimes Jiselle would rise in the middle of the night, go to the windows, and see her standing in the backyard, grass almost to her hips, looking up at the moon. Sometimes she saw what must have been Beatrice at Diane Schmidt's feet, looking like a smaller moon, buried in grass, reflecting that reflection.

Once, when Jiselle rose and went to the windows, she found that Diane Schmidt had taken off all her clothes and was standing completely naked in the backyard, arms spread wide. The power had been out again for a week, and without light pollution, the whole sky above Mrs. Schmidt seemed to fizz with stars—some of them falling, arcing through the dark—and it looked as if Diane Schmidt might be trying to catch them in her arms, and as if she might be able to do so if she waited long enough.

Having her in the house was no more trouble than having a cat. She spent most of her time outdoors. She ate whatever was offered to her, politely. She took her medicine—which Jiselle found in the Schmidts' bathroom cabinet—without complaint. She was clean. She wiped the bathroom sink with a tissue after she used it and even went through the house once a day with the feather duster, whistling to herself as she dusted. When she slipped in and out at night, it was in complete silence, but she never left the yard. And some of the things she had to say struck Jiselle as deeply wise.

242

"'We are put on this earth but a little space,'" Diane Schmidt said one afternoon at lunch, "'that we might learn to bear the beams of love.'"

"That's lovely," Jiselle said.

"That's Blake," Diane Schmidt replied, and returned to eating her bowl of rice without dropping a single grain. "Once upon a time I was an English teacher."

∼⦵∽

Paul Temple said, "You know you're going to need wood. To burn. For heat. A lot of it. We all need to think about winter without electricity."

Jiselle nodded. She told him, however, that she supposed, really, he should be chopping and stacking wood for himself, and for Bobby, for the winter. Tara Temple had never returned from her week-long visit to her mother, and Jiselle had quit asking Paul if she had or would.

He said, "If you wouldn't object, it would be easier, if there's no power, for us to spend the worst of the cold spells here. Better to heat one house than two, and you have more people to move than we do."

"Of course," Jiselle said. She felt her pulse quicken and was hoping she hadn't blushed. They held each other's eyes for a few seconds before they both looked up at the emptiness of the sky.

"That is," Paul said, not meeting her eyes, "if . . ."

Jiselle held up a hand to keep him from saying anything else.

243

Paul Temple cleared his throat, ignoring—or not noticing—her hand. "That is, if Mark . . ."

"I haven't heard from Mark since . . ." She couldn't even say it. It had been a week. A woman answered the phone every day at the Gesundheitsschutzhaus and said, with a heavy German accent, "We have no phone service to the quarantine. You must stop calling here. Captain Dorn is perfectly well, and he will call you when he calls you."

The airline had said nothing, would say nothing.

"I'll get Bobby going on the wood. God knows the kid's got nothing to do."

Paul's face was tanned and lined in the sun. His beard had grown out through the summer, and it was full now, gray and sandy-blond. With the ax over his shoulder, in jeans and a flannel shirt, he looked like a woodsman: muscular, rustic. His eyes, however, were watery and tired. He'd had that toothache now for weeks—the dull throbbing of a molar, which kept him up at night, pacing around his house. Of course there were no dentists doing business in St. Sophia. No drugstores were open; nor would there have been any aspirin left on the shelves if they were. Paul had agreed to take the bottle of Advil Jiselle offered him only after she assured him that she had several bottles stored in the cellar. He'd refused it at first: "Who knows when you might need this, or when or where you'll be able to buy more?" But he took it when she insisted.

⸻

That week, Paul and Bobby repaired the chimney, too, and swept out the fireplace.

They shooed the swallows out and put a screen over the chimney so the birds couldn't come back.

The birds circled the roof for hours afterward, but finally they flew off for good, built their nest somewhere else, it seemed. Jiselle knew their departure was a good thing, although, after their eviction, she looked up, watched them circle in gray and feathered confusion, and felt sorry that they couldn't stay. "You don't think," she said to Paul, watching beside her, "that it could be . . . you know, bad luck, to send them away?"

Paul shook his head. He said, "No, Jiselle. Try not to think like that. When these superstitions start, and start being taken for truth, it's a kind of final bell tolling for civilization. We can't start believing in *luck*."

Jiselle was playing chess after midnight with Sam when Mrs. Schmidt came out of Sara's bedroom, held up a finger, and said, "Listen."

In the candlelight, she looked more than ever like a wraith. Her white nightgown was full of shadows, and her face was obscured by darkness. Jiselle assumed at first that she was in one of her sleepwalking states: Sometimes Mrs. Schmidt would wake from dreams and wander out of Sara's room with something important to say, unable to recall what it was.

But Sam and Jiselle stopped their game to listen anyway.

Sam heard them first, and his eyes widened, and then Jiselle heard them, too.

At first, a distant yelp.

A womanish moan, far away, singular.

But then came a whole chorus of bawling and ululating cries, whines, plaintive and angry at the same time—and as if she were the first person to hear such a sound, as if she were a woman in a cave, a woman born before language, listening, Jiselle felt the fine blond hairs on her limbs rising away from her flesh in a feathery wave of foreboding, traveling up her body, her neck, and she stood and reached out instinctively for Sam, pulling him to her.

"Who is that?" Sam asked.

"We don't know," Jiselle said.

When Paul and Bobby arrived in the morning, Paul told her they had heard them, too, from their own house.

"Were they coyotes?" Jiselle asked. "*Wolves?*"

246   Paul Temple said no, he didn't think so. He believed they might simply be the hungry pets of St. Sophia residents who'd died or fled without their dogs.

Jiselle thought then of the first day that Mark had driven her into St. Sophia—the brick façades of the buildings downtown, the little boy on his red bicycle, the shining fire engine outside the station.

St. Sophia—America's Hometown.

But like so many towns in America, St. Sophia was *no one's* hometown. Their families were elsewhere, as were their jobs. It *looked* like a town, but in the months Jiselle had lived there, even after the plague began, the Temples were the only people she'd gotten to know, and they were not from St. Sophia, either.

When trouble came here, people went somewhere else.

They went *back*.

They left their schools behind, their shining fire engine, their quaint downtown, their pets.

St. Sophia was just a town on a list given to people who needed a town, a town that could just as easily be crossed off the list and cease to exist.

After that, Jiselle heard them every night, and no matter how deeply asleep she was, the cries always woke her with her heart pounding and sent her hurrying to the doorway of Sam's room to check on him, and then past the girls' and Mrs. Schmidt's rooms, to see that they were in their beds, and then to the window, to stare into the darkness draped over the ravine, imagining those pets, lost and changed, calling out for the ones who had abandoned them.

247

∽≥

That week, Paul and Bobby stayed each night for dinner. Jiselle would make whatever she could from the cans and boxes she had. If the electricity was out, she would cook on the grill. Sometimes Diane Schmidt would sit with them, and sometimes Jiselle had to take a plate to her room or out to the yard, where she might be sitting beside Beatrice, watching the sun set. After dinner, Paul and Jiselle sat on the deck with their cups of tea. They said nothing about Mark, who had not called, but Paul confided in her that when Tara had not come back from Virginia, he'd felt mostly relieved. There had been trouble between them for years, but the Phoenix flu and the power outages had forced some things to the surface—like the fact that he and Tara had nothing in common, except for Bobby, who was getting older, getting on with his life.

He said that after Tara called to tell him she was going to stay longer, didn't know when she'd be back, he couldn't even find it in himself to feel surprised.

"She'd been ready to go for a long time."

Jiselle thought then of Tara Temple in the line at the bank that day but said nothing.

"And all this hocus-pocus stuff she got into. I couldn't stomach it. You know, during the Black Plague, these charlatans used to go door to door selling Abracadabras and charms and knots. People would give their last crust of bread for some worthless amulet. She wanted me to believe in her positive thinking and read her books, and I couldn't. I just couldn't."

248   Bobby was the one who was grief-stricken. "He misses his mother, and he's worried about her, of course. He's afraid she'll get sick in Virginia, and with no mail service and if the phone lines go completely—the way the electricity's been going—how will we ever know?"

Jiselle nodded and bit her lip.

"Shit happens," Paul said. "Look at Schmidt." He nodded in the direction of Brad and Diane's house, which had been covered by the county in yards and yards of yellow tape marked BIOHAZARD. Brad Schmidt had been gone only one week, and already the hedge between their houses had grown into a tangled thicket, a wild wall. Fat pink flowers bloomed on a few of the branches.

"Jesus Christ," Sara said. "It's a flowering hedge. Is that why he kept cutting it up? He was trying to keep the *flowers* from blooming?"

CHAPTER TWENTY

It seemed like a minor problem compared to the many other problems, but how could they simply watch her die? There was no more Fowl Feed Deluxe left in the can, and Beatrice would touch nothing else.

"Jiselle?" Sam said. "Can we go to the pet store? *Please?*"

He stood at the sliding glass doors shivering in the damp morning breeze, his arms wrapped around his stomach. He was wearing a long-sleeved shirt, but he'd grown so much in the last few months that the sleeves ended between his elbows and his wrists. Soon, if they couldn't go shopping, he would look like Huck Finn, a boy grown out of homespun clothes, barefoot.

"We have to get some goose food," he said. He looked at Jiselle. His eyes were wide and beseeching. "What if she starves?"

Already, at the end of May, when she and Sam had last made a special trip to the pet store and bought the last bag of Fowl Feed Deluxe off the shelf, there had not been any of the usual things. No gerbils. No fish. No rabbits snuffling around in their cages. Certainly no parakeets or parrots.

The pet shop owner had told them he thought he was going to close down until normal shipments could resume. That couldn't be too far off, he'd said hopefully. Truckers would have to be allowed to cross state lines before too long, and if the economy improved, it would sway the tide of world opinion in the direction of resumed trade.

Jiselle was trying to knock the last few ashes out of the can of goose feed. She stepped inside, shaking the rain off her hair. Her hair, which she'd always kept long, had grown several inches in the months without a trip to the salon. Now it nearly reached her waist.

"I don't know, Sam," Jiselle said. "Gas. If we waste it, and the store's not open . . ."

She had gone by herself into town three weeks earlier and found that even the stores that hadn't been closed before—the office supply store, the hardware store—had dark windows, padlocked doors. Certainly, she thought, none of these would have reopened.

"But we have to see," Sam said of the pet store. "We have to *try.*"

"No, Sam. We—"

But as Sam stood looking out at Beatrice, Jiselle could see the ravine reflected in his eyes and also the rain falling in staticky gray light over it all. In the dampness, everything shone. Slippery. Slick. She imagined Sam imagining Beatrice retreating into the ravine, never returning to them, disappearing.

What, Jiselle wondered, did farm geese eat if there wasn't any Fowl Feed Deluxe? She wished she'd asked the pet store owner the last time she and Sam had gone there. How wrong had it been to feed her from the beginning? She'd grown dependent on them, and now they had nothing for her.

Jiselle inhaled. She was having trouble looking into Sam's deep, tear-filled eyes.

"Please?"

"Oh Sam," she said.

There was, she knew, plenty of gas—for now. They'd siphoned the Cherokee's tank, but what they had in the Mazda would have to last, and she did not know for how long. She hesitated, but then she said, "All right. Well. I guess we could at least go see. And if the pet store's still closed, I'm sure we could find something at the grocery store. I'm sure Beatrice eats *something* besides"—she could find no words to describe the oil and ash of the food Beatrice ate—"and I have to go to the bank anyway."

251

It was true. She was out of cash, and although there was really nothing she needed to spend cash on anyway, it made her nervous to have none. The idea of an "emergency" was still alive in her, even now that she realized how few emergencies could be averted with cash. You could not eat cash. You couldn't use it to heat your house, reduce a fever. Still, Jiselle had stayed in the habit of going to the bank once a month to make sure Mark's check had been deposited. So far, it had.

"You have to stay here, though, okay?" she said to Sam.

In the last week, Jiselle had heard from Paul Temple and on the radio about carjackings and violence in cities—particularly on the West Coast—over gasoline and batteries. She'd begun to worry about her mother, living alone. Her mother had been fine through the power outages, making her own fires, cooking over them. ("I grew up in worse conditions than this," she'd said. "You have no clue, Jiselle, what life on a real farm is like.") But if there were violence, if there were thieves?

Her mother had said, as she had said before, "Don't worry about me, Jiselle. You're the one with the problems."

That things would deteriorate—slowly but certainly—seemed to be what most people believed. There would be more illness, more violence, before things got better—although most people also believed that the Midwest would fare better than the coasts. The last time Jiselle had been in town, the fountain was still bubbling at the center of the park and the flag was still flying (never again at half-mast) outside the post office, even after it had been closed down. Until mid-July they'd even kept the pool open. "We will not participate in Doomsday thinking!" a spokeswoman for the town was quoted in the newspaper as saying.

The newspaper, which had been a weekly, was now coming out only sporadically, but when Jiselle had bought it the month before, it was full of uplifting stories about canned food drives and Boy Scouts cleaning up the streets. There was no longer any obituary section at all.

When she went to the kitchen table to pick up her car keys, Jiselle found Sara standing there. She'd overheard Jiselle telling Sam she would go into town, and she said, "Well, you're not going by yourself. I'll go with you."

"No," Jiselle said. "I'll be fine. You stay, and—"

"I *want* to go," Sara said and turned into the bedroom, as if that were the end of the conversation.

"Will you be okay here alone?" Jiselle asked Sam. Camilla and Bobby were gone, helping Paul deliver firewood to some of his elderly neighbors.

"Sure," he said. "Besides, I'm not alone."

They were quiet for a minute and could hear, in Sara's old room, the light voice of Mrs. Schmidt singing some old, familiar song.

❧

The drive into St. Sophia was accompanied by the radio's static-filled starts and stops. Jiselle turned it first to the oldies station, but there was nothing there but a series of beeps. Morse code? The only other station they could find that wasn't religious sounded as if it were being transmitted from the moon—a few memorable bars of a song ("Miss American Pie," "Tea for the Tillerman") interrupted by fuzz.

Finally, they turned the radio off.

After the early morning rain, the sky had turned a dazzling white, and Jiselle took the Mazda's top down before they left. The air felt soft, and although there was less light, and the sun seemed to have crept farther away from the earth, a radiance was draped over everything. Summer cast its last, bright shadow on the ground. In the previous weeks, there had been a strange influx of hummingbirds, and also sandhill cranes. Paul thought that these species were stopping by from some more northern place, or that they were confused, detoured, blown off track, or had miscalculated and were headed south too soon.

For the hummingbirds, Sara had concocted her own recipe for nectar, melting down some stale cotton candy she'd found in the back of her closet, left over in a plastic bag from a carnival a million years before, and she left little saucers of it out on the railing around the deck. One night at dusk, there'd been masses of them swarming those saucers, glistening and iridescent and beating their wings in a supernatural blur. They zigzagged through the air around the house as if they were working together to sew an elaborate net, tying the house to the ground.

Sara managed to stand still long enough with a saucer of nectar held up in her palm that two of the hummingbirds— ruby-throated, soft, and motorized gems—landed on her fingers, dipping their long beaks into the dish, and stayed that way for several seconds before humming away, chasing one another off with angry stabs.

"Oh my god!" Sara said, turning to the doorway, where Sam and Jiselle and Camilla stood watching, holding their breaths.

Sara rested her elbow on the car door. Her fawn-colored hair flew around her face in a shining blur as they passed through the outskirts of town and into St. Sophia. It had been less than three weeks since Jiselle had been there, but the town looked strange to her. Had she simply not noted, then, the gradual changes that had resulted in this more *complete* change?

The lawns, which had been so neatly trimmed and bordered with petunias and impatiens, and the gardens dotted with pansies, seemed to have overgrown in crazed and unexpected ways. The grass and weeds in the lawns were hip high. The petunias in the gardens were tangled in poison ivy. The domesticated faces of those pansies were entwined with wildflowers—sweet pea, thistle. She slowed down to the twenty-five-mile-per-hour speed limit in town and saw a rocking chair on a front porch completely covered in vines that bore a kind of spiky purple flower she'd never seen. Windowboxes spilled their contents—long ropes of blossoms and leaves flowing out of them down the sides of houses. All the cars were parked, and no one was on the sidewalks or coming in or out of the houses. A thin black cat sat on the hood of a pickup truck parked next to the post office, licking its paw. It looked up when Jiselle and Sara drove by, seeming to watch them with distaste as they passed.

Farther into town, in the business district, no stores at all were open. The jewelry store where Jiselle had bought the bracelet for her mother, and outside of which she'd seen the reindeer, appeared to have been vandalized. The plate glass was shattered, and the shards and diamonds of the destruction glittered in the sunlight.

255

The bank was closed, too—the lobby windows dark— but Jiselle was happy to see that the drive-up appeared to be open. A little sign reading PULL FORWARD was illuminated over one of the lanes. She did. Behind the Plexiglas, a young woman was sitting very still, barely visible in the glare. Either the young woman was very deep in thought, or she was listening carefully to something. When she didn't move or look in their direction, Jiselle pressed the green button for service, and the bank teller jumped, snapped to attention. "Yes?" she said into her intercom.

"I just need some cash," Jiselle said. "And to check my balance."

"Okay," she said.

Jiselle could see the young woman more clearly now. Really, she was a girl. No older than Camilla. Maybe closer to Sara's age. Jiselle put her bank card and her driver's license into the metal tube, hit the Send button, and in seconds the tube had shot across the empty parking lot and into the darkened bank.

"I go to school with that girl," Sara said. "Or *went* to school with her. Her father manages this bank. I wonder where he is."

Jiselle looked toward the bank. It did not look like a place that needed a manager. It was impossible, really, even to think of it as the same place where she'd stood in a long line the day she'd seen Tara Temple. Or, before that, the professional-looking men and women in their glass offices, signing papers, fingers flashing over keyboards, the appearance of important transactions taking place, official forms needing to be filled out. After what seemed like a long time, the girl came back and said, over the intercom, "Mrs. Dorn?"

"Yes?" Jiselle said.

"This account has been closed. There's nothing in it."

"What?" Jiselle asked.

"The account's closed," the girl said. "Someone closed it."

Beside Jiselle, Sara shook her head. "*Asshole*," she said under her breath, and then to Jiselle, touching her shoulder gently, "Let's just go. We don't need money. There's nothing to spend it on anyway."

Jiselle said nothing. She was too stunned to speak. The girl raised her hand, as if in apology. She said, "Bye, you guys."

. . .

At the pet shop, Jiselle didn't even bother to slow down. The biohazard tape was draped across the front window and wound around the entrance.

❧

"He did this to my mom, too," Sara said. "He was always fucking around, of course. Captain Cliché. He cut her off completely just before she died. We were eating nothing but peanut butter. My dad was pretty much out of our lives until she died. I mean, he loved you, Jiselle, I'm sure. But. I'm sorry. My dad is—with women. My dad is a—"

"Fool for love," Jiselle whispered after a long silence between them. She was trembling, and tears fell in large drops from her eyes and onto her bare arms. She pulled over outside the smashed glass of the pharmacy and turned the car off to save gasoline. She got out, walked around to the passenger side, and asked Sara to drive. She'd turned sixteen the month before, and although, with the secretary of state's office closed down, Sara had been unable to get a license, she'd known how to drive for years.

Why, Jiselle thought, looking down at her empty hands in her lap, was she surprised? What kind of fuzzy logic had made her think that he would keep the money in the bank account for her, that he would not find some new love of his life, on a plane, in a foreign city, in the back of a taxi careening through narrow European streets, or quarantined at the Gesundheitsschutzhaus?

She heard her mother's voice:

Don't be even more of a fool than you've already been, Jiselle.

257

She remembered what she'd said in the car on the way to the wedding:

Look, your father was fucking Ellen since the two of you were fifteen years old.

Before starting up the Mazda, Sara said, "We understand. We understand if you want to go." She turned her face to the windshield and began to pull the car into the road. Jiselle reached over and grabbed Sara's hand so quickly she hadn't realized she'd done it. Sara didn't turn to look at her, but let Jiselle's hand rest on her own on the steering wheel, and Jiselle saw a tear slip down her perfect nose and drip from the end of it, disappear onto the upholstery.

In the oncoming lane, a figure on a red bicycle wobbled past them. He didn't look at their car as he pedaled past. He was bent over his handlebars, legs moving wildly, propelling himself forward, staring straight ahead, like someone on whom, recently, a terrible spell had been cast.

Jiselle thought of the little boy she'd seen so long ago, when Mark drove her through St. Sophia for the first time.

This was, she felt sure, the same boy.

258

~⟨⟩~

"Did you get something for Beatrice to eat?" Sam asked.

Jiselle swallowed before she said, "No." She had to look away when she saw the expression on his face. "But Sara has some ideas," she said, "about how to make food that Beatrice will like."

After the bank, on the way out of town, they had stopped at

the Safeco, surprised to find it open and with a few modest things still on the shelves—the kinds of things no one ate because they didn't know how to prepare them or didn't want to eat them. Lentils. Wheatberries. Bulgar. Dried seaweed. A few burlap bags full of raw chestnuts. From what was there, Sara had been able to gather up the three ingredients she thought might mimic those listed on the commercial bag of fowl feed: vegetable oil, corn meal, chestnuts.

"We'll crush up the chestnuts," she said, "and just mix the rest of it so it's about the same consistency as the other stuff. There's plenty of protein. If Beatrice doesn't mind the taste, she should be okay."

"How do you know so much about birds?"

Sara smiled, shrugged. "I've thought a lot about birds," she said.

As it happened, Beatrice loved what they came to call Sara's Fabulous Fowl Feed.

That night Jiselle stayed up long after the children and Diane Schmidt had gone to bed. She paced for a while, and then she simply sat in the family room looking out the window at the dark ravine, and then she made her way in the dark to Mark's room. Instinctively, she hit the light switch when she entered—an old habit that, it seemed, would never die—and was surprised when the overhead light came on. They'd made a new habit during the outages of being sure that all the appliances and light switches were off before they went to bed because it was so alarming to wake up in the pitch darkness to the sudden blazing of overhead lights, or the blare of the television, or the microwave beeping, or the stereo—or all of them at once—when the power came back on unexpectedly.

She rubbed her eyes in the bright, surprising light and saw, draped across the foot of the bed, an exquisite triangle of fawn-colored yarn spread on the bed: the shawl Sara had been working on.

Jiselle ran her hand over it.

It was fringed with silk thread.

She picked up the edge of it.

Soft and warm but also exquisitely light.

Finished.

She sat on the bed, still running her hands over it and then saw the note beside it:

> Finally, I got my act together to give something to
> you.
>   Happy Birthday.
>   xoxo Your Wicked Stepdaughter Sara

Her birthday. Jiselle herself had completely forgotten. How had Sara remembered?

She brought the shawl to her face and breathed it in for several seconds before she wrapped it around her shoulders.

It was light, like standing in summer air.

Then, on second thought, Jiselle slipped it off her shoulders and removed her wedding ring. She slid the narrowest corner of the shawl into the ring, and then, in a swift and elegant flourish, pulled the whole thing through.

Part
Six

CHAPTER TWENTY-ONE

The power returned mysteriously after two solid weeks without it, long enough for them to get dangerously used to the convenience of the furnace in the first cool days of autumn and to watching the news. The reporters were circling the story of the Princess Cruises liner that had disappeared in the Caribbean ten months earlier—a ship sailing from Fort Myers to Tierra del Fuego, with brief stops at all the small islands between them, before such cruises had been entirely proscribed.

This particular ship had never arrived in Tierra del Fuego, but, these many months later, had run aground on the shores of the Isla Mujeres, Mexico, instead.

PLAGUE SHIP: AN UPDATE!

Jiselle and Mark had been on a ship like it—perhaps even this very ship, she realized, the name of which was being withheld until the next of kin had been notified, although surely those kin must have noticed that their loved ones hadn't returned from the cruise they'd set out on nearly a year before.

Jiselle remembered the buffet table, every night—mounds of shrimp, oysters glistening in their half-shells, crystal bowls of cold crab and lobster meat, caviar on French bread, tropical fruit sliced into anchors and swans spread across yards and yards of crushed and sparkling ice. She remembered dancing with Mark, her head on his shoulder, the white silk shirt she'd bought for him against her cheek.

Now when she tried to call Mark, there was no answer at all.

By the time the cruise ship ran aground on the Isla Mujeres, all the passengers were long dead.

264

"A macabre scene greeted Red Cross workers on this small Mexican Island yesterday—"

Jiselle imagined the passengers in their lounge chairs on the deck, wrapped in their plush white velvet robes. Dancing on the parquet floor in their shiny shoes, the brass instruments of the band glittering under the slowly revolving disco ball suspended from the ceiling.

The volunteers had boarded the ship in their biohazard suits and returned from it with faraway looks on their faces, captured in photographs as they disembarked in the hours before the island was evacuated entirely of rescuers, of journalists, of residents, while decisions were made about what to do with the ship.

In the meantime, planes owned by American television networks flew over and around it, videotaping the great silence of that ship stalled on the coast of the Isla Mujeres, which Ji-selle remembered as a pale and nearly treeless expanse of white in the middle of the turquoise dream of the Caribbean.

꧁꧂

"Are you giving me this so I won't steal it again?"

Jiselle shook her head. She said, "No. I'm giving it to you because you love it."

"Thank you," Sara said as she slipped onto her finger the onyx ring Mark had bought for Jiselle on Isla Mujeres. "I do love it."

On Sara's finger, it sparkled darkly, absorbing their reflections as they looked into it. Jiselle took Sara's hand and kissed the ring goodbye.

265

꧁꧂

That night, Jiselle woke in the dark to a sound in the hallway and sat up in bed fast. She looked to the threshold of the door, which was open. "Camilla?"

There was no answer, but the shape of a woman in a white gown was there.

"Mrs. Schmidt?" Jiselle tried to focus her eyes, but the figure seemed to be made of shadows, waving rather than standing. She swung her legs off the edge of the bed and stood. Her heart was beating hard—in her chest, in her ears, all along her arms and neck. She was holding her breath. She stepped toward the door. "Sara?"

The figure seemed to float away from her then, and then float back, and then rise, and recede, and then flash in the threshold, and Jiselle gasped when she saw who it was.

"*Annette?*" she whispered to the doorway, before sinking to her knees.

There was a beam of light glowing on Annette's pale face, which was changed but familiar, and the light spilled down her chest to the place where she held a baby to her breast.

Jiselle looked from the baby and back up to Annette, and just before she vanished, Jiselle saw the look of pain and anguish on her face, and she reached toward her, touching nothing. She continued to reach toward the vanished figure long after she knew what she knew, and then she got back into bed.

266

~❧~

The power came on for four days again the next week, and although there was nothing on television or on the radio, they kept music playing all day on the stereo, as if they might never hear music again if they turned it off—Joni Mitchell, Bach, Britney Spears, Kool Moe Dee, the Muppets, whatever CDs they could find, one after another, without a pause between them beyond what it took to take one off and put another one on. Bob Dylan was crooning "Jokerman" when the power went out again.

~❧~

They went to bed early, and the sun came up bright, but the power was still out, so Jiselle went through the house resetting the electric clocks. It was a silly, optimistic gesture, she knew, but whenever the power was out, Jiselle reset the electric clocks every few hours. To see them frozen on the counters and on the walls disoriented her. *Could it still be two o'clock?* she'd think five times in a row before realizing it couldn't be.

"Why don't we just get rid of the clocks?" Sam asked. He pointed out that Jiselle's watch still worked—although the battery in his own was dead, and there was no way to replace it. "Anyway," he pointed out, "what difference does it make what time it is?"

Jiselle smiled a little apologetically and shrugged as she reset them.

267

After the clocks, she went to the refrigerator—the now-familiar routine of scouting through it for what had spoiled, what could be salvaged.

A few days earlier, a man in a white truck had pulled into the driveway. There had been no lettering on his truck, but Jiselle felt confident he was a farmer as soon as he stepped out. He was older, with a gray beard. He wore overalls and a straw hat, as if it were a farmer's costume or a uniform.

"Howdy!" he'd called to her when he saw Jiselle standing at the front door. "I've got dairy!" Jiselle walked around to the back of the truck with him.

The farmer smelled reassuringly of manure—pleasant, authentic: earth, and animals, and work. His cheeks were rosy, his smile warm, although one of his front teeth was missing. He opened the back of the truck, and Jiselle gasped when she saw it.

At least a hundred beautiful glass bottles of milk. Old-fashioned, dusty wheels of cheese. What must have been another hundred golden bricks of butter wrapped in waxed paper. "Where did you get all this?" she asked.

The farmer laughed, putting one hand on his round belly as he did. He looked at her, amused, and said, "Well, ma'am, I *made* it. From *cows*. That's where dairy products come from!"

Jiselle laughed, too, at herself. Farms. Animals. Had she forgotten? She said, "Well, I'm impressed."

"What would you like?"

Jiselle looked at the bottles, the waxed bricks, the wheels of cheese. She said, "I'm short on cash, will you take—?"

"I'll take gas, valuables, or cash, and that's my order of preference," the farmer said, counting them off on his fingers, which were dirty but plump. He'd been ready with the answer, as if he'd been asked it often. "I'll *consider* other things, such as canned goods, tools, and the like. But I sure as hell ain't takin' a check." Again, he put a hand to his belly as he laughed.

Jiselle went into the house and came back out with the jade earrings Mark had given her for Christmas. She held them up for the farmer.

In the sunlight, they looked paler than they did in the house. Green teardrops. Seadrops. The farmer held them in his hand, as if to weigh them. He held them up. He looked at her, and at the gold watch on her wrist. Mark had given that to her as well. "Those real diamonds?" he asked.

268

She looked at the watch face, the little sparkling aurora of jewels around it, and said, "Yes. Of course."

"I'd rather have that," he said, and handed the jade earrings back to her.

Jiselle took off the watch and gave it to him, and he carried four bottles of milk, two bricks of butter, and a wheel of cheese into the house for her.

She had paid, she realized, what might have been seven or eight hundred dollars for a few groceries, what might have cost twenty dollars in another time—but she didn't need the watch, and Sam looked thin to her, and she'd been thinking about Tara Temple's warning about vitamin D.

That night she made everyone—even Bobby and Paul, even Diane Schmidt—drink a large glass of milk and eat a huge piece of cheese with the bean soup she made for dinner.

She slathered the bread she'd baked for them with butter.

Now what was left of it, eight hours after the electricity had shut down, already smelled of bacteria, decay. She took the milk out of the dark refrigerator and set it aside. She took the butter and leftover cheese outside to the deck in a sack, which she tied to the highest branch of the oak tree she could reach, hoping the height would keep animals away and the cool air would keep it fresh a little longer.

Then she went back inside and gathered up the things to make tea—the kettle of water, the matches to make a fire in the grill—and wrapped her shawl around her.

. . .

269

It was a damp morning after the rain of the night before, but a clear morning—the sky a pale blue overlaid with thready clouds, as if spider webs had been carefully draped over a dome. The leaves of the trees in the ravine were wet and shining in the sunrise. The branches appeared to be wrapped in black velvet against the bright sky. She put the kettle down, opened the box of matches, and was about to strike one against the side of the box when something in the side yard caught her eye, and she turned.

"Bobby?"

He was standing over the woodpile with an ax. Not swinging it, just holding it.

Despite the chill, he had his shirt off, and he was naked to the waist. He appeared to be soaked with sweat.

270

"Bobby?" she asked again. "What are you doing here?"

He didn't answer. The ax dropped from his arms, and he made no sound when he fell into the long grass beside it.

CHAPTER TWENTY-TWO

After neither the Mazda nor the Cherokee would start, Camilla ran the two miles to the Temples' house and returned in the Saab with Paul—who, jumping out of it, loped in long strides around the house to the backyard and, without asking any questions at all, bent down and scooped up his son, cradling him in his arms as if he were a child instead of the large man he was and carrying him to the car. Jiselle ran behind them, and after Paul placed Bobby carefully in the backseat, she slid in with him, still in her nightgown, without asking if she should. Behind her, she saw Camilla, weeping, trying to break loose of her sister, who was holding her back.

✺

Over Paul's shoulder, Jiselle watched the speedometer inch past eighty, past ninety, and then to a hundred, while Bobby lay with his head in her lap. The boy breathed steadily, but there was an oddly hollow sound when he exhaled, as if the air, instead of coming out of his lungs, were rattling through a wooden box. A wooden box on fire. His head was damp and burning at the same time, and his breath, too, seemed strangely hot. His mouth stayed open, and although his eyes were closed, Jiselle saw, in the corner of one, a tiny teardrop of watery blood.

For as far as Jiselle could see, there was no one else on either side of the freeway—not another car, or cab, or truck—so when they pulled into the St. Sophia Mercy Hospital parking lot, she thought, at first, they must have accidentally pulled off at a stadium or a mall. Except that those places were no longer open, those sorts of gatherings no longer occurred. Paul squealed past the hundreds of parked cars, leaving the smell of his tires burning against the parking lot tar, pulling up at the Emergency Room entrance. He jumped from the car then and ran inside, without saying anything to Jiselle or closing the car door, and was back in only a few seconds, followed by a woman in a white lab jacket. She had a nametag that read DR. STARK on the pocket, and a stethoscope around her neck, but otherwise she was dressed as if she'd just been called in from a picnic—jeans, tennis shoes, a University of Illinois hockey team T-shirt. Her hair was wispy and blond. She looked no older than Camilla, Jiselle thought.

Paul opened the back door for her, and Dr. Stark leaned in.

Bobby's eyes were closed. His torso was naked but still sweat-soaked. Dr. Stark appeared curious but not alarmed. She took his arm and pressed his wrist with two fingers.

After a few other things—feeling the glands in his neck, asking Jiselle what his name was and then saying the name, slapping her hands in front of his face and then sighing as if he'd disappointed her when he didn't respond, Dr. Stark backed out of the car and stood in front of Paul in the parking lot.

"I'm sorry," she told him, not sounding sorry. "There's nothing we can do for him here except have him lie around in the hallway all day, until we send him away. I can't tell you what to do, sir, but if this were my son, I'd take him home and get some sleep in case he needed me in the night. He's probably in no immediate danger. No more so than any of us." She gestured around—to the parking lot, herself, Paul, the sky.

Paul just stared at her as if he were waiting for her to say something else, to go on. His tongue was working over the sore molar, as it did all the time now, and then he began to shake his head in little snaps, and reached out to touch the doctor's arm, but she stepped away and turned toward the hospital. When he said to her back, "But—" She turned once more and seemed to scan the parking lot behind him. Without emotion, she said, "If you're up for the drive into Chicago, you might hear a different story, but the word we're getting from there is that they won't even look at anyone with the Phoenix flu. Still," she said more softly, "you have to do what you have to do."

"Medicine?" Jiselle called out the car window to Dr. Stark's back.

Dr. Stark turned again, shrugged, and said, "Got any?"

273

Some people fell ill and recovered. Some lingered, it seemed. Some died quickly within a few terrible days.

Bobby Temple died quickly and terribly.

Weeping blood. Coughing blood. His sheets soaked with blood. His pillow.

The power was on, but Camilla went through the Temples' house and turned the lights off one by one. They watched Bobby die by candlelight, and when it was over, although the phones were working again, Paul said there was no point calling the funeral home, no point notifying anyone. Who could help them? They would stay with the body until the sun rose—no one could go anywhere until it was light out anyway—and then he wanted Jiselle and Camilla to leave. He wanted to burn the body of his son in his own backyard, and he wanted to be alone.

But Jiselle and Camilla washed Bobby's body before they left—carefully wiping the dried blood out of his eyes, swabbing the blood out of his mouth with a washcloth. Camilla clipped his fingernails, kissing each finger after she did. Jiselle went through his closet and found his best shirt and slacks. Paul knotted the tie around his neck, folded the collar of his shirt down over the tie. In the candlelight, Bobby's eyelids appeared to flicker as if he were dreaming, but there was a look of such relaxation on his face that Jiselle knew he wasn't.

They sat back in their places around the bed, Jiselle holding Paul's hand in one of hers and Camilla's in the other.

Paul and Camilla each held one of Bobby's hands. When the sun finally broke into the darkness, and the warm light of it seeped over the windowsills and cast the shadows of the bare tree branches against the shades, Paul said, "You need to go."

Jiselle looked up at him.

The swelling on the side of his face had gone down in the night, and he looked more like the man she remembered, making that brick path with Bobby and Sam in the backyard in the sun. He was not in physical pain. The afternoon before, after Bobby had finally fallen quiet—the screaming and the clawing having subsided into an awesome silence—Paul had left the room and returned with a pair of pliers.

"Please," he said to Jiselle. "I can't have this distraction while my boy dies."

Jiselle followed him into his bedroom, where he'd already spread a towel over the pillows. He'd brought two tennis rackets in from the back porch to hold on to. He said to Jiselle, handing her the pliers, "I sterilized them." He swallowed. "I passed them through a fire, and I just had a shot of whiskey. I'll try to be quiet."

When it was over, Jiselle wiped the blood from the side of Paul Temple's face with a towel, and the tears out of his eyes with her fingertips, and as she did, he reached up and pulled her down next to him on the bed.

She put her head on his shoulder.

For the first time in two days, for a few minutes there in Paul Temple's arms, Jiselle fell asleep.

275

CHAPTER TWENTY-THREE

She was reading to Sam the morning the National Guard came to the door. It was the end of November, and it had been snowing all night.

> *The walls of the palace were formed of drifted snow, and the windows and doors of cutting winds. There were more than a hundred rooms, all lighted up by the aurora, and so large and empty, so icy cold, so—*

Everyone else was still asleep.

Four men—boys, really, wearing army-green fatigues, stood outside the front door. Although they were taller and more muscular than Sam, they did not look much older. The same clear eyes, poreless skin.

They'd parked their Jeep in the driveway, and behind them, it looked strangely mechanical to Jiselle, out of place in the snow—primitive, like something cobbled together by a creative but unimaginative people. Prehistoric. They wanted to know if she had a vehicle, too, and, if so, did the vehicle have any fuel?

Jiselle pulled her shawl around her shoulders. A hard wind was blowing across the yard, bending the bare tree branches to the east. One of the boys was wearing gloves without fingers, and Jiselle saw that his fingernails were tipped with blue. There were matching blue circles under his eyes. Looking at that one, Jiselle invited them in, and then she stepped out of the way as they passed, one by one, through the door. She'd just added another log to the fire, and it was pouring warmth into the living room. The soldiers moved toward it as if magnetized.

The power had gone out the week before and hadn't come back on. Still, Bobby and Paul had stacked enough wood behind the house that Jiselle was hopeful that if she was conservative with it, she could keep the house heated until March, when the weather would surely get warmer, whether or not the power came back on.

She'd stopped assuming that it would.

The boys sat next to one another across from the fire, squeezing together to fit themselves on the couch, and apologized for their boots, which were wet but not dirty—huge black boots laced halfway up their calves, tightly, over olive-green pants. The snow on the soles was melting in clear and shallow puddles around them on the wood floors, but Jiselle said not to worry about it. She'd mop up when they left.

277

Along with the snow, a scent had been tracked in with them—the smell of burning oil, tarnished brass, old coins and canvas left in a trunk in an attic, taken out again. Industry, travel, commerce, the world. Nothing like the ordinary smells of the house—soap, candle wax, kindling, tea. It would take longer, Jiselle knew, to get that smell of the world out of the house than to mop up the melted snow on the floor around their boots.

"I'm Mrs. Dorn," she said.

The soldiers nodded to her but didn't introduce themselves. They seemed stunned into speechlessness by the warmth of the fire.

Sam stood beside Jiselle, staring in appreciative wonder at them. The soldiers nodded at him in unison, kindly—the understanding of soldiers for the great reverence they were held in by boys. Jiselle put her arm around Sam, pulled him closer to her, her shawl around his shoulders, too—although she wasn't afraid of these soldiers. In her house, in a row on her couch, these were just shivering boys in wet boots.

If they had rifles, they'd left them behind in the Jeep.

Answering their question, she said, "I have two vehicles. But no fuel," and then, "Would you like some tea?"

Three of the boys glanced for an answer to the one on the end of the couch, who looked no different from the others except that his green cap had two small black stripes glued to the brim. He shrugged at the others, and then at Jiselle. He said, "Sure."

So Jiselle went to the kitchen, poured water into the kettle, brought it back, hung it on a hook from the tripod over the fire. Back in September, Sam had rigged up the tripod, made from the legs of an old aluminum lawn chair. He'd gotten the idea from an illustration in the Hans Christian Andersen book, in which an old crone had been pictured stirring a pot hanging over a fire from just such a tripod.

"What are the vehicles, ma'am?" the boy with the black stripes on his cap asked.

"A Jeep Cherokee," Jiselle said, "and a Saab. And also a little Mazda. You're welcome to them—but, as I said, there's no gas."

The morning after Bobby's death, Paul had insisted that Jiselle take the Saab.

"I filled it up with the last can of gas I had in the garage. It can't get me to Virginia with one tank of gas," he said. "And you might need it, in an emergency. If you won't take it for yourself, think of your children."

"But we have the Mazda," Jiselle protested. "And the Cherokee."

Paul shook his head. "This has gas, and it runs," he said. He pressed the key into her hand. Its little teeth shone in the sunrise.

"What will you do?"

"I'm walking," he said, shifting the satchel he was carrying from one shoulder to the next. "I'd be walking before long one way or another."

"I could drive you as far as—"

He held up a hand, shaking his head. "You might never make it back, whether you had any gas or not." He didn't continue, and Jiselle didn't try to say anything else.

• • •

She took the car but had driven it only one time before it too was out of gas. That time had been the morning Diane Schmidt died.

Together, Jiselle and Sara had wound the sheet around her body and carried her to the car, placing her carefully in the backseat. Jiselle drove to the funeral parlor in town, where two ugly women—sisters, surely, with the same fierce jaws and close-set eyes, one of them with a wart on her nose from which a black hair sprouted—demanded two thousand dollars in cash. When Jiselle said she had no cash at all, they reluctantly took her wedding ring and pulled Mrs. Schmidt's body, without any grace or care at all, out of the back of the car.

From there, Jiselle had gone to find her mother. She had not been able to reach her by phone for a long time. Only once she'd gotten through and heard her mother answer, "This is Anna Petersen," before the connection was lost again.

What else could Jiselle do? Her mother might have been fiercely independent, but how independent could an older woman, alone while the world crumbled around her, be?

Jiselle had found herself having to drive straight through Chicago because there were roadblocks, looking unofficial, homemade, thrown together by mobs without machinery or organization, on the freeway—walls of cinderblock, and even a few places where old school buses had been parked to keep traffic from traveling from one state to another.

She'd had no choice but to wind her way through downtown, and so Jiselle had seen for herself the blocks of burned houses. The vandalism. The fountains clogged with garbage. The broken-down door of Duke's Palace Inn. The smoldering darkness inside it. The smoke pouring out of the highest floors of the Sears Tower. The debris littering Millennium Park. Windows of stores smashed all along the Magnificent Mile. Snowflakes falling peacefully and sparsely over all of it. On a few corners were boys like the ones in her living room now, wearing camouflage (why camouflage, she'd wondered, in the city?) with surgical masks, holding automatic rifles, and beyond them ashes everywhere.

It seemed possible to Jiselle that those boys had, themselves, set the fires—who else was there to do it?—but her mother had told her that it had been boys like those, with the National Guard, who'd stood outside B.C. Yu's dry cleaning business, weeks earlier, after the rumors began that a Korean scientist had created the bacteria that caused the Phoenix flu.

The rumors weren't quelled fast enough to keep the Korean-owned businesses in large cities and small towns alike from being destroyed. EVIL was spray-painted over the dry cleaner's sign, and the door was boarded over, and someone had thrown what must have been a bucket of red paint over that. But the windows weren't smashed, and the building had not been burned. The National Guard had prevented that. B.C. Yu himself had died of the Phoenix flu before the rumors even began.

Jiselle's mother had brought nothing with her but a large box from her sewing room filled with what looked like rags, her tea set, some clothes, and the Little Mermaid statuette from the mantel, which sat on Mark's mantel now, and they'd managed to drive back to the house in Paul's Saab, although the gas gauge was on *E* for the last forty miles.

Jiselle knew that the National Guard couldn't take the vehicles with them, that the possibility that they had some stash of gasoline with them was low. If they did, there were cars littered all over town—keys still in the ignition, thousands of dollars' worth of chrome and upholstery. Why would they have come all the way out here?

But she meant it, too. They could have the cars. They were welcome to the cars, which meant nothing to her now in their silence, in their huge weight and useless gravity.

Jiselle poured the water into her mother's teapot, over the dried mint, and the room was suffused with the scent of spring and fresh air, and the four boys seemed to lift their chins to it, as if to information they hadn't come in search of but were happy to receive.

After the tea had steeped, and Jiselle had poured it, they sipped gratefully from her mother's delicate cups.

"You're sure there's no gas left in either tank, ma'am?" the one with the stripes asked.

"None," Jiselle answered.

The soldiers finished their tea and handed the cups back to Jiselle carefully, one by one. They stood in a row in front of the couch. "Do you mind my asking, ma'am," the one with the stripes said, looking around the room, "do you have a plan? Do you have a weapon? Is your husband home?"

"Yes," Jiselle said, although none of these things was true.

"Good," the soldier said. "There's a lot of looting, you know. And illness. And rumors."

"I know," Jiselle said.

She did.

She had seen what had happened in the city.

"What are the latest rumors?" she asked anyway.

The boys looked at one another as if deciding among themselves, in silence, whether or not to tell her.

"Well," the boy with the stripes said after clearing his throat, "it's all over the world now, you know. One in three, they're saying. But this could just be the beginning. They're saying it's a bacteria. Biological warfare? It could be something as simple as a bit of some anthrax-like agent, sprinkled on the floor of a restroom, in an airport, maybe. Something entirely new. Someone could have stepped in it, worn the contaminated shoe all over the world. It could be potent enough that the spores—"

283

"Thank you," Jiselle said.

She held up a hand, glanced at Sam. She was sorry she'd asked. Somehow—how?—she'd hoped for something good.

The soldier nodded, understanding. He said, "But you need to understand, and so does your son. There are groups, gangs, on the roads. You're set back here in the trees, and without lights maybe they won't see you, for now. But we did. And there's a lot of desperation. And trust me, they'll figure a new way to travel without gasoline. They'll find a way, and they'll find you, too, eventually. There are—"

"The garage is open," Jiselle said, nodding toward the door, "and the keys are in the cars."

"Thank you, ma'am. And good luck."

They filed out then, back into the snow, turning once, in unison, to wave goodbye. They spent only a few minutes in the garage with the Cherokee, and then peering into the windows of the other two cars, before trudging back out to their Jeep and driving away, and Jiselle and Sam went back to the couch in front of the fire to finish the story they'd started.

It ended happily, with the witch vanquished. The spell broken. The children returned safely to their mother, whom they'd feared was dead.

❦

Only later did Jiselle go to the bedroom closet and pull out of the shadows the one shoe left from Madrid.

That lovely black shoe. Its mate had never been found.

The high, narrow heel. The way the arch fit her foot perfectly. The leather polished to a glossy shine.

She remembered again the salesman on his knees in front of her in that old-fashioned shoe store in Madrid. How he'd cradled her foot in his hands, as if it were a precious gift. How he'd slid the shoe on. "*Perfecto*," he'd said.

And it was. That shoe had fit her as if it had been made for her by elves, by fairies, by angels.

How many millions of places had she worn those beautiful shoes?

She'd walked through a thousand streets in a hundred countries. She had stood in lines, sat in theaters, strolled down cobbled paths, occasionally bending down to pet a cat, admire a baby in a bassinet. Years before, in Phoenix, Arizona, she'd stopped by a booth at a street fair and admired a silver bracelet, slipping it over her wrist, holding it up in the bright desert sun to look at it.

She'd handed it back to the jewelry maker, an old man with a windburned face, with an apologetic smile.

She could no longer remember why she hadn't bought it.

Now, she held up the one shoe, turned it over, ran her fingers over the sole, looked at her fingertips.

Nothing.

Not even dust.

She put the shoe back down in the shadows at the bottom of her closet, and when she turned around, she saw that Sam was standing in the doorway, smiling.

He said, "Jiselle," shaking his head, "it wasn't your shoe." Smiling. "It's nobody's *shoe*."

"But what if it was?" she asked him.

Still smiling, Sam shrugged. "What if it was?" he said.

CHAPTER TWENTY-FOUR

The beginning of December was warmer, although the sky, day after day, was a deep purple. The clouds scudding across it looked ink-stained, seeming perpetually to threaten snowstorms that never came. In the afternoons, Jiselle played chess with Sam, read with him in the evenings. Mornings, there were dried beans to sort and soak. There were a few novels left from Camilla's English Lit course to read. The fire had to be made and stoked. The ashes had to be swept up and thrown out the back door. They'd forgotten about Thanksgiving, so when Jiselle finally remembered, she gathered them all together and surprised them with a dinner of Swanson turkey and dressing from a can. She'd planned to save the turkey for Christmas, but by then, perhaps, she knew, there might be an entirely new plan.

The fire in the living room kept the house warm. There was still food in the cellar: soups, tuna fish, pasta in boxes, powdered milk. Fresh water still poured out of the faucets.

But Jiselle knew they needed fruits and vegetables. There were only a few boxes of raisins and cans of peaches left. There was enough toilet paper in the linen closet to last for months, and tampons—although Jiselle and Camilla had both stopped menstruating. (Sara said it was because they weren't drinking enough water. "You're not getting enough iron. You can get it in the water, you know.") They'd stopped using paper towels and napkins at the table, using rags instead, which could be rinsed out and hung up near the fire to dry with the underwear and socks.

How wasteful, Jiselle marveled now, they'd been, and for so long! She wished now she had just one of the large plastic bags she'd thrown away in the last year. So many things she could think of to do with that now. With only one notebook left in the house she realized that soon the only place they would have to write would be on the walls, in the margins of the books on the shelves.

She'd given that notebook to Sara, who had filled up all the pages of her black diary.

"You're the chronicler," Jiselle had said when Sara protested that there was no reason she should get the precious notebook. "Take it."

For the future, Jiselle took down a few books she knew they wouldn't be needing, in preparation. Some had wide margins, blank pages between chapters. *Aviation Through the Ages. Light Aircraft Navigation Essentials.*

The days passed so slowly they might have been lifetimes. Jiselle tried to impose a shape on each one:

The Day of the Spider in the Bathroom, The Day of Split

287

Pea Soup, The Day the Wood Seemed Wet and Would Not Light, The Day of Paging Through an Old Copy of The New Yorker *and Marveling at the Ordinariness and the Advertisements, The Day We Thought We Heard a Horse Whinny in the Distance, The Day the Lights Flickered, The Day We Might Have Heard Shots Fired in the Ravine, The Day Sam Invented Mint Toothpaste from Baking Soda and Tea* . . .

Because, if she failed to do this, she would go to bed at night and feel as if she were on a drifting ship with no idea where in the world, or in time and space, she might wake up.

Now, every night, the hounds in the ravine howled longer and louder, sounding closer, hungrier. Twice, Jiselle had glimpsed one wandering in the backyard through the snow. Some scrawny blond thing. Was it a dog, she wondered, as Paul had thought—someone's pet, altered by events? Or a coyote—something wild that no longer sensed danger from the human world it had once shunned?

It didn't matter. There was such a feral emaciation about the animal that there was no way to tell what else it might, at one time, have been. The creature itself might not have remembered whether it had once been something tame, someone's pet, or a dangerous predator. When Jiselle came to the glass doors to watch it, it would lift its muzzle to the air, seeming to smell her, and then slip back into the ravine.

After she was sure it was gone, she would go outside to see if Beatrice was still in the little wooden house Sam had built for her—carefully, ambitiously, nailing together some wood planks he'd found in the garage.

Each time, Jiselle was ready for the worst, but Beatrice

was always still there, sitting on a nest of Mark's old uniforms they'd piled up for her, ruffling her feathers.

But the next week the goose quit eating. Jiselle no longer had vegetable oil to mix into the feed, and it became a sticky mess, unconsumed, on the ground around the nest Beatrice never left.

Then, one morning, Jiselle saw a small rabbit in the snow, running like a vivid rag from one end of the backyard to the other. A few hours later, there were animal tracks in the snow, and blood, and the next afternoon, Jiselle saw another animal—something she didn't recognize, an animal with a long black body, pointed ears—low to the ground, sliding across the deck, disappearing under the Schmidts' hedge.

An enormous mink?

A wolverine?

Or an entirely new kind of animal?

Was it stalking Beatrice?

That night she woke to the sound of something like a fight between creatures in the dark—a yelping bark against a mewling scream, and she knew instantly that this was an animal, not human, scream, but still Jiselle jumped from the couch with her flashlight and checked the rooms where the children and her mother were soundly sleeping. Afterward, she went back into the family room and sat on the couch with her hands over her ears. The violence of those noises was terrible. There were teeth involved, she could tell, and claws, and blood, and when the silence came, swelling up around the house, she knew there had been a death.

289

In the morning, she found a dark path worn away around Beatrice's shack. Something had circled it in the night more than once looking for a way to get in. But when Jiselle pushed open the little makeshift door, Beatrice was still there, alive. Jiselle stepped in, knelt down, ran her fingers along the white feathers, and Beatrice shifted her wings beneath Jiselle's hand.

∼⊘∼

In the middle of December, Jiselle's mother decided that since they could not know if or when the schools would reopen, the children had to be home-schooled, and she would do it.

So, the long afternoons of chess with Sam were replaced by lessons carefully planned out by Jiselle's mother for the children. She'd sit up at the kitchen table in the flickering candlelight long after everyone else had gone to sleep, using the schoolbooks the children had at home, the encyclopedia, the dictionary, an atlas Mark had kept tucked into the glove compartment of the Cherokee, a medical handbook, and a book of baby names, which must have belonged to Joy.

The children were eager for the lessons, sitting down at the kitchen table in the mornings, thumbing through the books.

During "school," Jiselle would pick up one of Camilla's novels and read. She was halfway through *Anna Karenina*, but it was getting harder to concentrate. She'd find her mind returning again and again to Bobby. Those final hours.

Or Paul. Where was he now?

She'd try to imagine him, but the image that came to her was always the same: Paul walking down the center of a free-way littered with cars.

Since the day after Bobby died, and Paul left, none of them had spoken of it again. Every night, Jiselle could hear Camilla weeping in her bedroom, but in the morning she was dry-eyed. She studied at the kitchen table with Sam and Sara. She helped Jiselle around the house. In the evenings, she read while Jiselle and Sam played chess.

They kept busy.

Jiselle's mother and Sara were involved in a sewing project together that required hours of counting and concentration. Jiselle would overhear them bickering—"Did you *count* these?" "Yes!"—but they seemed on friendly terms. Sara had begun to call her "Anna," something Jiselle had known only her mother's best friends to do.

291

This forgetting, this continuing—how heartless was this, Jiselle sometimes wondered, and she would close her eyes and see Bobby, and Annette, and Dr. Smith, and Diane Schmidt—a dark line of familiar silhouette against the sky, each holding the other's hand, and instead of looking harder, Jiselle would open her eyes. She would read ten pages and comprehend not one word. She'd put the book down and find herself wandering through the rooms of the house— through the family room, and the bedroom, where Mark's slippers still waited under the bed. Like a ghost, she'd pass through the kitchen, overhear a few sentences: *He led the Mongols into China . . . Ferdinand and Isabella . . . Alfred hid from the Vikings . . .*

But these fragments meant nothing to Jiselle. They were like fuzz, radio static.

"Did you know," Sara asked one afternoon as Jiselle passed back through the kitchen, pointing to a place on a page in Joy's book of baby names, "that your name means—?"

"Hostage," Jiselle said.

"Princess," her mother corrected.

Sara looked up and smiled. "No," she said. "It means 'pledge.'" Reading aloud: "'Jiselle. Danish. Definition: She who keeps her promise. Pledge.'"

Jiselle went to the book and looked over Sara's shoulder. Her finger was on the name. Jiselle read the entry silently to herself. Sara was right.

Jiselle looked up at her mother, who shrugged and said, "Who knows? I always thought it meant 'princess.'"

Sara flipped the pages to her own name then, and looked up, laughing. She said, "Sorry to break the news to you ladies, but *my* name means 'princess.'"

292

One night, Sara insisted they play charades. The evenings were so long. The snow had been falling steadily for days, and it made a silencing moat around the house and the world. Even the hounds stayed away, or couldn't be heard over the insulating white.

Sam and Jiselle were playing chess by candlelight at the kitchen table, but they looked up from their game when Sara came in and announced charades. Jiselle shrugged. "Why not?"

They went into the living room, where Camilla and Jiselle's mother were listening to some distant station they'd found on Brad Schmidt's transistor radio. They'd had to put the radio on the windowsill, on its side, with the antenna pointed toward the fire, but behind the snowy crackle was the unmistakable sound of an orchestra playing something bright and rhythmic, full of exuberance, vibrant with possibility. The future, it seemed, was hinted at in every note. Even the static, which seemed to rise and fall with the wind through the dark night outside, couldn't drown that out.

When the radio finally died completely, they turned it off and started their game.

Camilla was first.

As soon as she waved her elegant hands around in the air, they all shouted, "Mozart!" at the same time.

293

&&&

"Jiselle," her mother said one morning while the children were still in bed, "Sam needs to get more to eat."

Jiselle nodded. She knew. It had been a growing sense of dread for weeks. She looked through the kitchen into the living room, where Sam and the girls were decorating the little tree they'd cut down at the edge of the yard. They'd found Joy's box of beautiful Christmas decorations in the basement—sugary angels, little gingerbread houses, gilded fruit—and they were hooking them onto the tree's bright branches.

In his T-shirt (one Mark had brought home for him: HARD ROCK CAFÉ TOKYO), which was at once too small and too large, he looked like a stick figure. The shirt rode up on his waist, and Jiselle could see his ribs, but it also hung too loosely off his shoulders, and she could see the blades of those jutting out of his back, too skeletal.

This was a boy who was starving.

It had been only a week since Jiselle had opened the cupboards and counted what she had left in them—the cans, the packages—and peered into the last box of powdered milk to assess how much was left, and then put a hand to her eyes to do the math. How long did she need to make what they had last?

Surely there would be enough food left for another month.

Or two, if she was careful.

But only if she was careful.

So she began to divide two cans of soup instead of three among them for dinner. She added an extra cupful of water. If they ate Ramen noodles for lunch, she saved the water she'd boiled them in and added it to that night's canned stew. There was always some flavor left in it. Surely there were some nutrients, too?

She started pushing her own bowl away before she finished her soup, asking Sam if he was hungry. Her mother did the same. But if Camilla or Sara tried to offer anyone else their food, Jiselle's mother snapped, "Finish your *own* food."

Although the girls quit offering Sam their food at the table, Jiselle had seen them taking their napkin rags away with them from their meals suspiciously heavy.

Once, she overheard Sam say to Sara in his bedroom, "Thanks, Sara, but I'm not *hungry*."

"Eat it *anyway*," Sara whispered back.

Now, in the bright winter light coming in through the family room windows, it was clear that Sam was a child who was not getting enough to eat. For how many decades had Jiselle looked at photographs of such children in newspapers and magazines, and how far away had those children seemed?

"I'm going to go look around the Schmidts' house," Jiselle said to her mother. "To look again. To see if there's anything stored we didn't find."

∽⌒

Jiselle hadn't been inside the Schmidts' house since a few days after Brad Schmidt died, when she'd gone over with Camilla and taken what appeared to be the only useful things—a few sharp knives, some cans of anchovies, the radio, Saltines, a sack of flour, and a canister of brown sugar—and had boxed up Diane Schmidt's clothes and medicines and brought them home.

But they hadn't been hungry then.

Had she looked in the basement? The attic? Brad Schmidt had spoken of being prepared. Why hadn't it occurred to Jiselle before now that he might have a cellar full of provisions?

The yellow biohazard tape had torn away from the doors and windows, and it fluttered like party streamers in the snowy wind. The hedge was white with snow, and the paving stones were buried under it, but Jiselle could feel them beneath her boots, and she followed the path to the back door, which was open. The threshold had warped and split. She stepped in.

"Hello?" she called.

Old habits. She couldn't help it. She even flipped the light switch next to the door, but of course the kitchen light did not come on, and there was no answer to her greeting.

Still—could she be imagining things? Jiselle sensed some movement somewhere deeper inside the house and instinctively stepped backward, and then stood quietly, letting her eyes adjust to the darkness, holding her arms protectively across her chest.

If it hadn't been that there had been no mice or rats around for so long, Jiselle would have expected the house to be full of them. Or squirrels. Swallows. A family of raccoons. They would be wild, unfamiliar with human beings.

What she hadn't expected to encounter—like a wild ghost, padding out of the bedroom and into the hallway, and then, barely bothering to glance in her direction before slipping into the hallway, and then into the living room—was this sleek and tawny cat, as long as a man, with enormous shoulder muscles, dark ears bristling with fur.

An enormous, magical cat.

Jiselle stood frozen in the doorway for several seconds, hand over her mouth, trying to breathe and not to scream, before backing out into the snowy light, running across the yard and around the hedge, home, heart pounding cou-gar, cou-gar.

Cougar.

How? In Wisconsin? In the Schmidts' house near the edges of St. Sophia, seventy miles from the heart of Chicago?

Jiselle knew, now, what had been making the tracks around Beatrice's shed. Now she recognized the paw prints in the snow for what they were. *Whose.* The pads and claws. She hurried in the front door of the house, as excited as she was alarmed. "Sam?" she called.

Where had it come from?

North?

West?

And how had it come to live in the Schmidts' house?

Was there so little of the usual human activity that the big cats had come back now after a century of hiding in remoter places?

Or was this someone's exotic pet, escaped? Abandoned?

Would there be more?

Were there more?

Sam would know. He would have a book, an idea.

"Sam?" Jiselle called out to the house, but the girls and her mother were no longer at the kitchen table. "Sam? You won't believe this. Sam? Where are you?"

297

Jiselle's mother stepped out from behind the curtain to Sam's bedroom then. "He's sick," she said.

❧

As soon as Jiselle stepped into Sam's room herself, she could smell it: The physical humidity of that sickness, the way it rose off him like a damp fire.

Outside the room, Camilla had collapsed at the kitchen table with her head bowed into her tightly folded hands. Sara paced in the family room, making circles around the half-decorated Christmas tree.

"Sam," Jiselle said, kneeling beside his bed, putting a hand on his cheek, and then on his forehead. "Sammy. Sweetheart. My baby."

❧

There was once a princess . . .
There was once a mermaid . . .
There was once a king . . .
There was once a kingdom . . .

They'd finished the book weeks before, so Jiselle started over again at the beginning.

❧

That first night, there were sounds all around the house.

Animals. And something else. Wind, but as if the wind were marching in circles.

"Jiselle, you need to sleep."

No.

The boy in the bed appeared to have been taken away and tossed back, bones beneath blankets. He did not open his eyes, and he'd eaten nothing—not a sip of water, not a cracker, not a spoonful of soup.

"Jiselle, what are we going to do?"

She closed the book.

In the morning she opened the door to the little shack, and the goose looked up.

299

Clearly, Beatrice had expected some animal other than Jiselle, bare-limbed, holding a long knife.

Did she understand that it was only a matter of time?

The path around the shack had been worn down to dirt, and now Jiselle knew what was making those tracks.

Had Beatrice also known? Was it why, before Jiselle cut the white throat, the goose let Jiselle gather her, stroke her pure and bristling neck, the gleaming wings, the elegant strangeness of the beak, and even closed her eyes as Jiselle drew the sharpened blade across the throat, and the blood poured over her bare arms and legs?

Afterward, Jiselle sat holding and rocking the beautiful goose in her arms.

Jiselle's mother brought the kettle full of scalding water into the kitchen. "We had to do it," she said, taking the bird out of Jiselle's arms, plunging it into the water, going to work right away, hands coming up full of feathers, pulled off the body, tossed out the kitchen window and into the snow, "if it could save our little boy."

It was clear to Jiselle, looking on, that this was something her mother had done a hundred times. Anna Petersen must have watched her own mother do it, and her father, and she had done it herself as a child on that farm, had done it in her dreams every night since then. She had, perhaps, been waiting her whole life, knowing that someday she would need to do it again.

Her mother boiled the goose soup in a pot that hung from the tripod Sam had made, and the whole house filled up with the warm smell of it, and then they brought a cup of the broth to Sam, who sat up long enough to take a sip of it, and then another.

Jiselle's mother had given the feet and the bones to Jiselle, sifting them out of the pot with a slotted spoon, and Jiselle took those along with a handful of feathers back to the shack, and put them in the nest of Mark's old uniforms, and left the door to Beatrice's shack open behind her.

That night, while her mother sat with Sam, Jiselle sat on the deck in the moonlight, watching, wearing an old coat of Mark's. She shivered as the snow fell around her, but she didn't feel cold, breathing as quietly as she could until the sun began to rise and she finally saw the cougar slip through the hedge—slow and low on its sinewy haunches, with nightmar-ish glamour, an elegance made of stealth—to the shack, and as soon as Jiselle saw that the cat was there, inside, busy with the feet and the feathers, which it must have believed to be the goose that it had been stalking for so long, she leaped to her feet and ran across the backyard and into the Schmidts' house, slamming and locking the door behind her.

❧

"Jiselle," her mother said, a hand to her chest, when she returned an hour later with the rifle. "You did it."

301

The girls and her mother stood around Jiselle, running their hands down the gloss and wood.

"Thank God," Sara said.

"Thank Jiselle!" Camilla said.

"It's all I could find," she said. "He didn't have any food. Not even any water. All he had were boxes of seeds and am-munition and this."

❧

There was once a king . . .
There was once a kingdom . . .
There was trouble in the kingdom . . . .
There was a little boy . . .

A little mother sat beside the boy . . . There was a knock at the door . . . A strange little man . . . An old woman in black rags . . . There was a woman in white, her arms full of white flowers . . . "Have you not seen Death go by with my little child? I have to fetch him back."

Another night passed, and then another.

"It's not the flu," her mother told Jiselle, standing in the threshold. "He's sick, but not with that," and Jiselle stood and went to her mother, put her arms around her, and sobbed into her shoulder for a little while, like a child.

~~~

302 On Christmas Eve, Sam drank a cup of mint tea in little sips on the couch beside the Christmas tree. Camilla sat at his feet, her hand on his knee. Sara fussed with the decorations.

Jiselle could do nothing but stand in a corner of the room and stare at the miracle of Sam. The December afternoon light shone through the window and over the snowy trees in the ravine, which seemed, also, to shine inward—breathing, botanical—with nearly unbearable brilliance. She went to the window and saw, for the first time, the potential beyond it. How little they might need that wasn't there waiting for them.

There was wood to cut down, and in the spring there would be berries in the ravine. Now that Jiselle knew she could kill an animal, and that her mother could clean it and cook it, the world could start all over again, full of possibilities. The whole house seemed radiant with these possibilities. With the seeds she'd found in the Schmidts' cellar, there would be vegetables, and with the rifle and the boxes of ammunition they would be able to hunt for small game and deer. Sara had found a handbook on the shelf, something of Mark's, that explained the gutting and tanning of antelope. Surely a deer would be no different from an antelope. Only that morning, Sara had come into the kitchen with the hunting book open like a hymnal in her hands, and said, "It says here that it's much less messy if you can string the antelope up, and bleed it before you clean it. See—"

She held up the book for Jiselle, open to an illustration of a man standing beside the carcass of an antelope hanging by its neck from the branch of a tree.

"Do we have any nylon rope, do you think, in the garage?" she asked.

Then Sara took Brad Schmidt's rifle off the mantel and held it in her hands, weighing it.

"You'll have to let me be in charge of this," Sara said, "since we don't have enough ammunition for target practice. I was the BB gun champion at Camp Newaygo three summers in a row. There isn't anyone else here who can claim that, is there?"

Jiselle pretended to consider it, and then shook her head. "No," she said.

The cougar had disappeared only two days before, and already the yard was full of rabbits again.

On Christmas Day, there was snow. A sparkling carpet of it over everything. The radio picked up some station—from where, they had no idea—that played carols all afternoon, until the signal finally faded away. For Christmas presents, Jiselle gave Sam the brass wings she used to wear above her heart. Camilla and Sara got the bracelets Mark had bought and hidden for her for Valentine's Day. She gave her mother the jade earrings, which looked beautiful on her—exotic and lost in her hair, which had grown wild and white in the last few weeks.

"I want to give you your present now," her mother told her. "It's been a long time in the making. I don't want to wait."

Jiselle turned from the fireplace, where she'd been stirring the stew for dinner, and said, "Okay."

"Sara helped me," her mother said. "I could never have finished it without her."

Her mother and Sara dragged out the box Jiselle recognized from her mother's sewing room—the one full of rags—into the kitchen and hoisted it up onto the table. Sam and Camilla pulled up chairs and waited for Jiselle to open the box. Sam's cheeks were flushed with health. Both he and Camilla looked radiant. Camilla had been gaining weight since the gauntness of the fall, and her hair had grown down to her waist. It hung heavy and loose tonight around her bright, rounded face.

Jiselle hesitated, without knowing why.

"Well, aren't you going to open it?" Sam asked, nodding at the box.

Jiselle pulled open the cardboard flaps and pushed them away, peering in. Then she looked up. "What is it?" she asked, looking around the table.

"A quilt!" Sam said. They were all nodding.

"But not *just* a quilt," Sara said.

Jiselle began to pull it out then: an enormous patchwork of multicolored flowers. Little hand-stitches held the hundreds of pieces of it together.

"Your mother saved everything. *Everything*," Sara said.

They all stood around Jiselle, watching. She ran her hand over the quilted flowers as they watched, until, slowly, the bits and pieces came into focus.

"Do you see?" Sara asked.

A scrap of bright green satin: Prom dress?

A polka-dotted flower: a blouse she had worn almost every day the summer between fifth and sixth grade?

"This," her mother said, "is from your costume, remember? *The Nutcracker?*"

Jiselle nodded.

"And this you couldn't remember. This is a piece of your baptismal gown. And this"—she pointed out a soft pink scrap—"is what I was able to snip from your baby blanket, the one part you never managed to drag through the mud or throw up on. And here: your high school graduation gown. This is a bit of your first flight attendant's uniform. This—"

Her mother went on and on.

Jiselle couldn't speak. She ran her fingers over familiar lace and then a bit of suede. A purse, high school, which came back to her with a whole year of sights and sounds: Ellen tossing a French fry at her across the cafeteria. A carnival at the edge of town. A huge wheel of lights spinning slowly in the sky. Jiselle closed her eyes and saw that wheel again, and this time, spinning there, she was one of the lights.

They laughed at her when she opened her eyes again, still unable to speak, until finally she managed to say, "Thank you."

It was the only thing she could say.

∿

The rest of the day was like any other, taken up with chores. The stoking of the fire. The boiling of water. The sweeping of the floors. The hunting and skinning of the rabbit.

306   For Christmas dinner they ate a stew of that rabbit and a can of potatoes. It was delicious. Jiselle's mother had spiced it with things she found in the cellar and things she found growing under melted snow in the backyard.

"Believe me," she said, "when you grow up the daughter of a poor farmer, you learn how to cook a rabbit."

∿

After dark, they gathered in the living room to play charades by candlelight. Because Sam was too happy to sleep and the color was back in his cheeks, when he begged Jiselle to let him stay up ("It's Christmas!"), she couldn't refuse.

So Sam started the game, marching around the room staring straight ahead as a candle flickered on the coffee table and the others shouted wrong guesses at him, sidetracked by the idea that he was a chess piece, and then a knight, and then a sandhill crane.

"A *soldier*," he told them when they finally gave up, and then it was obvious to all of them: the stiffness of his limbs, that weapon he'd had resting on his shoulders, the grim expression on his face.

"I'm the king of charades!" Sam shouted, and Sara threw a pillow at his head. Over them, Joy wore her beautiful gown. No one had said a word about the portrait, which Jiselle had taken out of Sara's closet after Sam was well again and hung in its proper place from the nail over the mantel, above Brad Schmidt's rifle and her mother's Little Mermaid statuette. Now Joy smiled down at them, offering that bright piece of cake to the future, as if it were her life.

Jiselle was a coffee mug, which they all shouted out at once as soon as she put her hand on her hip.

When it was her turn, Camilla rowed a boat down a river. "That's not fair!" she said when they guessed it after only a second of rowing. "Let me go again." This time she put her arms together and rocked them back and forth.

"A mother?" Sam asked.

"A baby?" Sara asked.

"Both!" Jiselle's mother called out. She looked around the room. "Am I the only one who can see that Camilla's going to have a baby?"

Jiselle put a hand to her throat.

How had she not seen it? Camilla's growing waist. Her breasts. Her face. Of *course*.

307

"Camilla—" she said, but Camilla waved her words away. She said, "We can talk about that later. It's Anna's turn."

There was a quiet moment while Jiselle's mother stood before them, seeming to be trying either to decide what she was or how to express it. She wore a silk kimono Jiselle hadn't known her mother owned. Her shins and feet were bare. The candlelight on her legs made the sparse downy hair on them shimmer, and the flame made the sound of little insistent wings.

But there was another sound, too, in the distance. Something familiar, Jiselle thought, and also completely new, was out there in the dark. She looked around at the others, but they didn't seem to hear it. She turned her face to the front door. When she held her breath, she could hear it more clearly.

A purring. A propulsion. She lifted her chin and listened. *Yes.*

Whatever it was, it was moving steadily, inexorably, in their direction. The hum of an enormous cat or a gathering of winds—accumulating, approaching. A vast population, migrating. An army shuffling, shoeless, toward them, marching through high grass or over gravel.

Or a parade of children. In robes. Holding lanterns. Silk banners slapping at the darkness.

Or—could it be?

Was it some forgotten piece of machinery crawling toward them: its motor grinding closer, its small oiled teeth and gears, its wheels rolling over the earth, or its wings sailing over their heads?

Jiselle stood up.

She was holding a hand to her ear, trying to hear it when Sam and Camilla and her mother shouted at the same time, "A plane!"

Jiselle turned around quickly to see Sara before them now with her arms outstretched, soaring, and then shaking her head of shining, tangled, tawny hair with an exasperated, victorious expression on her face.

Jiselle sat back down.

Outside, there was silence again.

She'd imagined it, hadn't she?

Or was it still far enough in the distance—just something picked up by the wind? Something that might never arrive. Or something that had already come and gone. Or something that was there, now, waiting for them outside as Sara stood with one arm held over her head in a graceful white arc—so clearly and beautifully the neck of a swan that Jiselle chose not to say a word as the others called out, "Question mark! Fishing rod! Coat rack!" so that she might prolong the mystery of that bird, the passing of that night, and the end of a perfect world.

309

~⊃⊂~

The End

ACKNOWLEDGMENTS

I am deeply indebted to Katherine Nintzel for her help with this novel. I also owe thanks to Laura Thomas and Carrie Wilson for stories and insights that found their places here.

Insights,
Interviews
& More ...

Meet Laura Kasischke

LAURA KASISCHKE was born in Lake Charles, Louisiana, but raised in Grand Rapids, Michigan. Her mother was a teacher, and her father was in the Air Force and later worked as a mailman. She was an only child. Of her early interest in writing, she says: "I was bored. Reading, writing, and watching television were good time-killers in Grand Rapids, where other distractions were hard to come by. By the time I was in high school, I was hooked on reading and writing, probably because we didn't have cable television."

After high school, Kasischke went to the University of Michigan for her BA and MFA in creative writing. She is now an associate professor there, in the Residential College and the MFA program. She has published seven collections of poetry and seven novels, two of which have been made into feature films, and has received fellowships from the National Endowment for the Arts, the Guggenheim Foundation, and the United States Artists, as well as several Pushcart Prizes and numerous poetry awards. Her writing has appeared in *Best American Poetry, The Kenyon Review, Harper's,* and *The New Republic.* She has a twenty-two-year-old stepdaughter (Lucy), a thirteen-year-old son (Jack), a cat (Geoffrey), and a husband (Bill), and lives with them in Chelsea, Michigan. ∼

Bill Abernathy

An Interview with Laura Kasischke

What was the inspiration for In a Perfect World? *Was it a scene that first came to mind or a character?*

In general, I begin a novel with not much more than a sense of my main characters, some conflict, a setting/season, a few scraps of imagery. After half a draft of this or so, I get nervous and make an outline, but often I veer far from the outline as I continue drafting.

I had my first inkling that I was about to write a novel, which would become *In a Perfect World,* when the image of a parched backyard, a new stepmother, and a small plot of violets hidden under some dead leaves came together with a vision of a tense dinner with two adolescent girls on the night their favorite pop star has died. I knew then that there was something wrong in the natural world, and that it would influence and mirror the lives of the little family at the center of it.

When you write a novel, do you know exactly what is going to happen in each chapter, or is it an organic process?

At a certain point in the revision process, I have a sense of an ending, but during the first draft, I'm generally as ▶

3

surprised as anyone else by what happens to my characters and what they do and say. With this novel, I was able to cheat a bit because of the historical record, the many myths and anecdotes and facts surrounding plague, crises, great conflagrations of the past. I was able to read about the beautiful and terrible ways people dealt with the kinds of things happening in my novel, and to transform and incorporate some of that material for my own purposes.

Did you do a lot of research on plagues in writing this novel?

I've been interested in the Black Death for many years—the art, the stories, the history of the period. At the same time that, to me, the fear and devastation of the period is almost impossible to imagine, imagining it, in its mysterious distance, seems compelling and important.

Although on a grander and more horrific scale, the opportunities the Black Death presented for those who lived through it, in terms of betrayals, self-sacrifices, madness, hysteria, and denial, seem to me not that different from the opportunities encountered in the course of one's life. At points in every life, one's values and priorities—our truest loves, our deepest devotions— can be seen in high relief. In the case of my novel, one of the questions I wanted to answer was, as the world begins to crumble, and the isolation of the small family at the center of the story becomes more complete, and the eeriness of their situation grows, and death becomes more and more a part of life—who, I wondered, does one become?

As I've said, as well, many of the specific details in *In a Perfect World* were inspired by events from the Black Death of 1347–1349, and also the Great Plague of London, 1665–1666. Birds were reported to be flying in strange patterns. Animals were found in death mounds. Suspicion and superstition became ever more a part of daily life. Cults were formed. People fled to the countryside. Economic and social structures were torn apart. Xenophobia was rampant. Miracle "cures" were sold. Ships full of the dead washed ashore. Wild theories were formed. Ghosts and religious visitations were commonly reported. People danced, and people hid, and people continued to live their lives. All of these details prove what we already know: that the scariest horror stories are the true ones.

There are many accounts of the complete devotion of some people to their loved ones, and also the opposite: extraordinary abandonment, shocking betrayals, cruel quarantines. I've visited, myself, the closes of Edinburgh, Scotland, that were walled up when the plague was discovered among the residents, leaving hundreds of people to die in their rooms. (A haunted place if there ever was one!)

There also was said to be a tremendous celebratory element to the years as the old mores began to seem unequal to the brevity of life. Some suggested that the "indecent clothing" of the period was causing the plague to spread.

And—a story especially moving to writers—in Ireland during the terrible year of 1349, the monk John Clynn wrote, after watching his fellow-brothers die one by one: "I . . . waiting among the dead for death to come . . . have committed to writing what I have truly heard and examined and . . . leave parchment for continuing the work, in case anyone should still be alive in the future and any son of Adam can escape this pestilence and continue the work thus begun." Beneath his words, another monk has written, "Here, it seems, the author died."

Another important facet of the novel seems to be motherhood, or in this case stepmotherhood. Can you comment on that?

Certainly another concern of the novel for me was the passage—which I have experienced myself, as a mother and a stepmother—in a woman's life from daughterhood to motherhood. I wanted to trace the journey I think women take into the realms of self-sacrifice that come so strangely and naturally and dramatically at a point in their lives, whether they are biological mothers or not. The crisis of plague in the novel to me presented a chance to explore that journey. ▸

And I also wanted to write a fairy tale of my times, a romance of motherhood. Despite the love affair with Mark, the true romance of the novel, I feel, becomes the love of Jiselle for the children whose lives were put in her care—as I've said, the romance of motherhood, which, for me, has been the most mysteriously transformative experience of my life.

Are you also speaking in the novel about the threat of global warming?

Much has been documented about the climate changes that preceded the years of the Black Death, and there's been speculation about whether or not the unusually fair weather of the Medieval Warming Period contributed to the spread of the disease, particularly because it was followed by the Little Ice Age, which began with three years of torrential rain. We know that there were volcanic eruptions, major floods, tidal waves, swarms of locusts, unusual new patterns of bird and animal behavior. There were also reports of blood-colored rain and of a dimming of the sun. Cassiodorus wrote, "We marvel to see no shadow on our bodies at noon, to feel the mighty vigor of the sun's heat wasted into feebleness."

And, as is our own time, it was a period of tremendous political upheaval, and change. Many things around me fueled a sense of urgency as I wrote *In a Perfect World:* the ever-growing worry of global warming, the terrorist attacks both of 9/11 and throughout the world, the spread of new viruses and the reemergence of diseases previously believed to have been eradicated, the continuing wars, the energy crises, the general economic slide in the U.S. and other countries, and the sense that a way of life was beginning necessarily to change, and that this will continue to change, and with what ramifications we don't know—the sense that the kind of consumer lives we've lived, the easy traveling we've done, the sense of security we've had, is coming to an end, or at least entering a phase of violent change.

I tried to put this atmosphere of a world in transition into every detail of the novel. I have always liked Jorge Luis Borges's words that "every detail is an omen and a cause" in fiction, but I have never felt as compelled to follow those words as advice as completely as I did during the writing of this novel.

Is the Phoenix flu actually avian influenza, or bird flu?

I did research on bird flu, and I used much of what I learned as raw material. However, I quickly began to realize how much I could not know, and could not hope to learn, about bird flu, the bubonic plague, hemorrhagic plague, multidrug-resistant plague bacillus, pneumonic plague, and the mechanisms of pandemics. My niece, Julia Gargano, is an epidemiologist at the Centers for Disease Control in Atlanta, and having even the briefest of conversations with her about plague brought home the complexity of the subject of infectious diseases. The Phoenix flu is my fiction, though informed by the layman's research I did on plague, and bird flu in particular.

Jiselle has a book of Hans Christian Andersen fairy tales from which she reads to Sam. Do you have a favorite fairy tale?

Andersen's "The Story of a Mother" was an influence on the novel, I would say. Like Jiselle, I've had a gilt-edged edition of the complete Hans Christian Andersen stories since childhood. This particular tale is one of his more sinister and lovely ones. In it, Death steals away a mother's child, and in her search for her son she comes upon an old woman, who is Night, who will only tell the mother where Death has taken the child if she agrees to "sing to me all the songs that you have sung to your child; I love these songs, I have heard them before . . ."

As with so many of Andersen's stories, the journey is long, with many miracles and terrors, and full of displays of devotion and self-sacrifice, and although the end isn't a happy one, it is an inevitable one. ▶

An Interview with Laura Kasischke *(continued)*

In addition to seven novels, you have written seven books of poetry and have won a number of awards for your poetry. Which do you prefer writing: poetry or novels?

If I were told I could only write one, it would be poetry. I love the sort of athletic mysticism of it. But writing novels is important to me. I like having something to chisel away at every day, rather than the worrisome undertaking of starting something new.

I find the writing of poetry and of novels to be quite different, but my first interest is always in language, and particularly in figurative language. I like discovering new ways to describe things. In both the poetry and the prose, I compose mostly via association. I begin with a sensory image—something like a river, or a snowstorm—and move through the details until I find an event or an emotion correlative to that imagery. My novel *Be Mine* began with the idea of blood in the snow—a grim valentine—and February in the Midwest. *Boy Heaven* started with the National Forest, and summer there, and the cicadas I remember from my own experience in northern Michigan, and spun out from that.

Are your characters based on real people?

No. For one thing, I am not the most character-driven of writers, and I suppose this is because I am primarily a poet. I'm a lot more interested in the things around a character—her time, her place, her physical experiences—than I am in thinking about whether she's a noble person, or an evil person, or even a believable person. I've always been more attracted to allegory, to myth, than to contemporary fiction that works too hard to make human behavior explicable or sympathetic. Even in real life, I often don't find human behavior to be either of those things.

Where and how do you write? Do you show your work to anyone during the drafting phase?

I have a study in my house. It's a mess but very comfortable for writing. My family is quite lovely about leaving me alone when the door is shut. My husband is my first reader and, if I do say so myself, quite brilliant!

As for how I write: I used to have many superstitions and rituals. I had to write at a certain time of day, in a certain place, with a certain kind of pen, et cetera. I had so many superstitions I can't even remember what they were. Then, I had a baby. After that, I learned to write when I could, where I could, with whatever was handy. Now, my only consistency is that I try to write every day. I don't write every day. But I try to write every day.

What was the first book you remember falling in love with? What do you read now?

The whole Laura Ingalls Wilder set, which I received one Christmas. I can still remember the smell of the gray, pulpy pages, and the welcoming illustrations on the covers.

Now, I am primarily in love with reading poetry, and writing it; therefore, I suppose, many of my fiction influences have been experimental writers: Woolf, Joyce, Borges. My favorite novel is *Ethan Frome;* my favorite poem is "The Love Song of J. Alfred Prufrock." What I like about poetry, I look for in fiction: a "felt change of consciousness," as Owen Barfield puts it. That's a harder experience to find in fiction than in poetry, I think, because it has nothing to do with character development or plot but is a kind of ineffable quality of language, music, arrangement, atmosphere, all working at once.

What book do you wish you had written and why? What do you think a novel should do?

Well, it's a stretch to imagine having the genius to have written *Mrs. Dalloway,* but if I truly had such a choice, that would be my novel.

I like to think a novel offers a shaped experience of the world. ▶

It should resonate at many levels—language, atmosphere, imagery, music. It should be formed out of a half-conscious and half-subconscious effort made by a writer, and it should become that experience for a reader.

You teach creative writing. What advice do you give to fiction writers?

My advice to students is always to write through the trouble spots, not stopping to reconsider until a whole draft of something is on the table. I find a lot of writers to be perfectionists, and that is generally unhelpful. Also, I tell anyone who'll listen that I think writing is one of the most exciting and worthwhile uses of one's time—the focus it encourages and the surprises and revelations it brings. The only thing better is reading!

Another piece of advice I give (whether I'm asked for it or not) is to find the subject matter and writing style and form you can stay passionate about for a lifetime, and then do whatever you must to maintain that passion. Most of a writer's time is spent alone, with the page, so it's impossible to sustain a life in writing if you don't find incredible pleasure in that.

Reality in your novels is always so different from appearances. When reading them, we always discover some hidden threats. What gave you the wish to consider that things are always darker and more dangerous than what they seem?

I wrote about this elsewhere, but in writing it I felt as if I'd figured that out a little for myself. Now, of course, I'm not sure if it's the answer to your question, or just a story I tell myself, but I had a wonderful high school creative writing teacher with whom I was secretly, madly in love and who had once dated my mother.

I was only subconsciously aware of his past relationship with my mother until my devotion to him must have alarmed her, and she revealed it one day, many years into my tutelage, just before dinner. I still remember standing at the refrigerator when she told me, and the way the layers of secrecy, the hidden lives of the people around me and their agendas, the subtexts and shadows and incestuous estuaries, the awesome significance of little gestures and half-spoken truths, became immediately fused with the act of writing for me.

It's never left. When I write now, I'm still sort of standing at the fridge suddenly realizing how complex everything is if you can just figure out the whole story. ᑐ

Have You Read?
More by Laura Kasischke

FEATHERED

This provocative and eerie tale flies readers from safe, predictable suburbia to the sun-kissed beaches of Cancún, Mexico, and into mysterious Mayan ruins, where ancient myths flirt dangerously with present realities.

"Kasischke spreads her poetic wings, using lyrical language and lucid imagery to create a transcendent novel. Readers will be enchanted."

—*Kirkus Reviews*

BE MINE

On Valentine's Day, Sherry finds an anonymous note in her mailbox: Be Mine.

"What makes this erotic thriller disturbing and, therefore, successful is how convincingly Kasischke renders Sherry's life and feelings so eerily normal and familiar, ensuring the unsettling portents are all but unnoticed until it is too late."

—*Booklist*

"Kasischke has proven herself again to be a bold chronicler of dark obsession."

—*Publishers Weekly*

BOY HEAVEN

They were seventeen, with perfect tans and perfect bodies. They planned on a joyride in a convertible on a hot summer day. They planned on making it back to camp before anyone noticed they were gone.

"*Boy Heaven* is a wild ride into the unknown—with a genuine shock of an ending."

—Joyce Carol Oates

"Kasischke's writing imbues the book with such an eerie sense of apprehension that the pages keep turning."

—*SLJ*

THE LIFE BEFORE HER EYES

Now a major motion picture starring Uma Thurman and Evan Rachel Wood, the novel opens with a shocking scene from a Columbine-like school massacre and becomes an imaginative exploration of a teenage girl's world and the profound transformation of that world in midlife.

"It is not enough to call Kasischke's language 'poetic,' a word that has come to mean 'pretty.' Rather, her writing does what good poetry does—it shows us an alternate world and lulls us into living in it."

—*New York Times Book Review*

WHITE BIRD IN A BLIZZARD

A real-life crime is transformed into a meditation on cruelty, beauty, and love.

"The soft, almost ethereal language makes the horrifying reality at the core of the book shockingly powerful, the hidden underside of a quintessentially normal domestic tableau."
— *Library Journal*

SUSPICIOUS RIVER

Young married Leila Murray is working as a motel receptionist and a prostitute on the side.

"Reading the second half of this novel is like driving too fast. . . . The claustrophobic horrors of American small-town life are evoked with austere precision."
— *New York Times Book Review*

"Kasischke has woven a tale of amazing subtlety and depth. . . . *Suspicious River* is years beyond any first novel published in the last decade. . . . Kasischke is an amazing new voice."
— *Minneapolis Star Tribune*

Don't miss the next book by your favorite author. Sign up now for AuthorTracker by visiting www.AuthorTracker.com.